"I suppose this is the part where I fall into your arms, flutter my eyelashes and tell you that you're my hero."

Quint grinned. "I wouldn't mind one bit, Natalie."

"Don't hold your breath, cowboy. You lied to me. You're a bodyguard, aren't you?"

"Sometimes."

Quint leaned forward, rested his elbows on his knees and rotated his shoulders to relieve the tension in his back. Rescuing Natalie like that had been a crazy stunt, and he was damned lucky that he'd succeeded. If he'd failed, they might both be dead.

He felt N_____uint? Are you okay?

"Fine," he s_____

"You're shak_____

From fear, the fear of losing her. He swallowed hard. "I'm glad you're all right."

"And you?" she asked. "Are you hurt?"

Looking at Natalie, knowing that she was alive and well, he felt the soul-deep pain beginning to heal. "I'm just fine."

"Good." She straightened her shoulders. "Because I'm going to kill you."

Dear Harlequin Intrigue Reader,

We've got another month of sinister summer sizzlers lined up for you starting with the one and only Familiar—your favorite crime-solving black cat! Travel with the feisty feline on a magic carpet to the enchanting land of sheiks in Caroline Burnes's *Familiar Mirage*, the first part of FEAR FAMILIAR: DESERT MYSTERIES. You can look for the companion book, *Familiar Oasis*, next month.

Then it's back to the heart of the U.S.A. for another outstanding CONFIDENTIAL installment. This time, the sexiest undercover operatives around take on Chicago in this bestselling continuity series. Cassie Miles launches the whole shebang with *Not on His Watch*.

Debra Webb continues her COLBY AGENCY series with one more high-action, heart-pounding romantic suspense story in *Physical Evidence*. What these Colby agents won't do to solve a case—they'll even become prime suspects to take care of business…and fall in love.

Finally, esteemed Harlequin Intrigue author Leona Karr brings you a classic mystery about a woman who washes up on the shore sans memory. Good thing she's saved by a man determined to find her *Lost Identity*.

A great lineup to be sure. So make sure you pick up all four titles for the full Harlequin Intrigue reading experience.

Sincerely,

Denise O'Sullivan
Associate Senior Editor
Harlequin Intrigue

NOT ON HIS WATCH
CASSIE MILES

HARLEQUIN®

TORONTO • NEW YORK • LONDON
AMSTERDAM • PARIS • SYDNEY • HAMBURG
STOCKHOLM • ATHENS • TOKYO • MILAN • MADRID
PRAGUE • WARSAW • BUDAPEST • AUCKLAND

Special thanks and acknowledgment are given to Cassie Miles for her contribution to the CHICAGO CONFIDENTIAL series.

To my old friends, critique groups, the guys at Merrick and Rocky Mountain Fiction Writers. Thank you for your caring support, for your laughter and your love. And, as always, to Rick.

RECYCLED PAPER · RECYCLED PAPER

ISBN 0-373-22670-5

NOT ON HIS WATCH

ABOUT THE AUTHOR

Cassie Miles was born in Chicago, and now lives in Denver, one of the fastest-growing cities in the country, with the traffic jams to prove it. She belongs to the film society and enjoys artsy subtitled cinema almost as much as movies in which stuff blows up. Her favorite entertainment is urban, ranging from sports to museum exhibits to coffeehouse espresso. Yet she never loses sight of the Rocky Mountains through the kitchen window.

Books by Cassie Miles

HARLEQUIN INTRIGUE

HARLEQUIN AMERICAN ROMANCE

†Colorado Search and Rescue

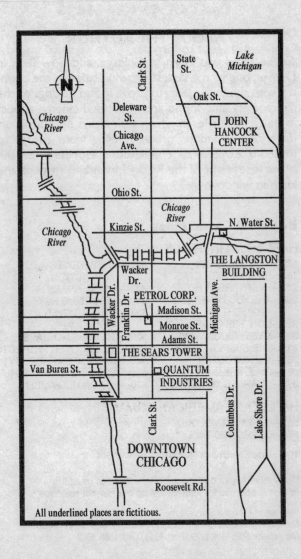

N

Chicago River

Clark St.

State St.

Lake Michigan

Deleware St.

Oak St.

Chicago Ave.

☐ JOHN HANCOCK CENTER

Ohio St.

Chicago River

Kinzie St.

Chicago River

N. Water St.

Wacker Dr.

THE LANGSTON BUILDING

Wacker Dr.

Franklin Dr.

PETROL CORP.

Madison St.

Michigan Ave.

Monroe St.

Adams St.

☐ THE SEARS TOWER

Van Buren St.

☐ QUANTUM INDUSTRIES

Clark St.

Columbus Dr.

Lake Shore Dr.

DOWNTOWN CHICAGO

Roosevelt Rd.

All underlined places are fictitious.

CAST OF CHARACTERS

Quintin Crawford—The long, tall Texan became a Confidential agent to forget his dark personal tragedy. He never expected to find sunshine in Chicago.

Natalie Van Buren—Daughter of the CEO of Quantum Industries, she struggled to earn her vice president title and learned never to settle for second best.

Henry Van Buren—The CEO of Quantum Industries, a megapowerful international oil distributor based in Chicago.

Nicco, alias Nick Beaumont—The mysterious expert in timed explosives. Who was he working for?

Gordon Doeller—The Quantum vice president in charge of marketing had his fingers in too many pies.

Eugene "Hutch" Greely—The leader of the eco-cult Solar Sons held a dangerous grudge against Quantum.

Zahir Haji Haleem—A force to be reckoned with in oil-based Middle Eastern economies. Was he a hero or a snake?

Maria Luisa Moreno and Jerome Harris—Loyal Quantum employees. Or were they?

Vincent Romeo, Whitney MacNair Romeo, Lawson Davies and Andy Dexter—Agents with the newly formed Chicago Confidential.

Daniel Austin—Founder of Montana Confidential and close friend to Quintin Crawford.

Javid Haji Haleem—A Middle Eastern ruler and twin to Zahir. He came to Chicago to aid the Confidential investigation.

Kathy Renk—The receptionist in the Confidential offices.

The Confidential Agent's Pledge

I hereby swear to uphold the law
to the best of my ability; to maintain the
level of integrity of this agency by my
compassion for victims, loyalty to my
brothers and courage under fire.

And above all, to hold all information and
identities in the strictest confidence....

★★★★

Chapter One

Outside the square granite entryway to the office building, dirty snow marked the curb where a white Fiat sedan and a blue Toyota were parked. The sidewalks appeared to be deserted. No lights shone from the office windows. The stealthy gray of dawn thinned the night shadows into faded streaks.

If Quintin Crawford had to guess, he'd place the time in the snowy scene to be somewhere between six and six-fifteen in the morning. Quint and four other agents stared at the high-resolution video on the large flat monitor in the special-ops room. They were watching, waiting for something to happen.

On the screen, a bearded old man came onto the street. His lips moved. His hands, in ragged mittens, pounded the air and twitched as he mumbled incomprehensibly. He could've been anyone—any tired soul who got fed up with the daily struggle and opted out. Not too long ago, Quint silently acknowledged, that guy could've been him.

Trudging aimlessly, the bearded man pulled his brown knit cap low on his forehead. His filthy, rumpled jacket and grease-stained trousers were also brown. The only hint of color showed in the dark red woolen scarf wrapped around his neck. Beside him, a three-legged black-and-white Border collie bobbled along in syncopated gait. When the dog hopped ahead, the man hurried for three paces, then slowed again as he rounded the corner and disappeared.

It was quiet on the street, windless. Nothing moved.

For one fleeting instant, the building shuddered and shimmered with an eerie glow. More light than color, this brief flash signaled the onset of danger.

Quint's muscles tensed. His senses alert, he watched the screen.

The gray dawn shattered in flames.

With a deafening roar, a fierce explosion erupted from inside the stone walls. Glass splintered. Metal door frames crumpled. A ball of fire pitched the Fiat and the Toyota like empty tin cans, sending them crashing and rolling on the concrete street. The Fiat landed on its roof with tires spinning in the air. Black smoke gushed across the sidewalk. The granite entrance gaped like the ragged jaws of hell, spewing flame and soot.

In the wake of this man-made thunderhead, a remembered pain—more intense and fearsome than any physical hurt—sliced through Quint's gut. The knife twisted. He closed his eyes and catapulted backward in time. Two years, three months and nine days ago, he had faced another senseless explosion. In those fire-streaked skies over Texas, he had lost everything.

In his mind, he saw the single-engine Cessna. His wife, Paula, on her first solo flight. The white winter skies over the prairie. Another plane. A blast of gunfire.

On the ground, Quint was helpless. He could do nothing to stop the attack.

The Cessna was caught—trapped in the cross fire between earth and air. Lethal flares. Tracer bullets. There was a flash. A shimmer. An explosion. The underbelly of the clouds glowed blood-red.

Pieces of the Cessna, debris, fell to the earth.

Quint's heart dropped. His world stopped rotating on its axis. He was numb, yet aching in every fiber of his being.

Without Paula, he had no reason to live. In the months

that followed, he prayed for death—a dark, silent embrace to fill the inconsolable emptiness. He rode into the plains alone and stayed for days, waiting, begging for the end to come. But death was a stubborn bastard.

Eventually, Quint's bitter tears ran dry. The remnant of his life was nothing better than a sick joke. He had his health, his oil business, his ranch…and no reason to enjoy any of it.

Somehow, he forced himself to go on, learned how to laugh to keep from crying, told himself that he'd be able to accept Paula's death. Someday. He'd pull himself together and become a whole man again. Someday.

Someday wasn't here. Not yet.

His eyelids pried open as the last echoes from the office building explosion on the high-resolution screen faded and the picture went black. It would've been nice to pretend this bombing was a DVD from Hollywood where the macho hero would stride through the flames with a smudge on his forehead and a beautiful starlet tucked under his arm—but real life was seldom so neat and tidy. All too often, people died. Real people.

It was the job of Quint Crawford and the other members of Chicago Confidential, a special division of the Federal Department of Public Safety, to confront the violence and end it. They pursued their investigations undercover— deeply undercover. All agents had other lives. When not on assignment, they worked at successful careers that weren't necessarily related to law enforcement.

The Confidential program had started in Texas under the direction of Mitchell Forbes, and there was another branch in Montana. Here in Chicago, the front for their operations was Solutions, Inc., a fictitious corporation located on the penthouse floor of the Langston Building, a skyscraper in the heart of the city.

With a quick glance, Quint surveyed the faces of the other four agents who sat at the round table in the high-tech confines of the special-operations room. Everybody but the boss seemed shocked by the explosion, a little off balance. Quint was the new guy in town, on loan from Texas Confidential, but he wasn't sure he liked the way this assignment had been introduced with a bang. It might be good to lighten the mood.

"I have a couple of questions," he drawled. "First off, what happened to the dog?"

Three of the other four agents chuckled, but Vincent Romeo, the head of operations, did *not* crack a smile. This dark, brawny man, a former National Security Agency operative, was responsible for setting up this new Confidential branch. Though Vincent had the reputation of being a good man and an effective agent, his attitude seemed aloof—somber as his black turtleneck and trousers.

In Quint's estimation, Vincent was a serious tight ass. The only time he brightened was when he looked at his redheaded wife, Whitney MacNair Romeo, who had to be the prettiest agent in any Confidential branch.

Coolly, Vincent responded, "By the time the authorities responded to the explosion, the dog and his owner were long gone. No one—not even the security guards in the building—were injured in this explosion."

"So, they never saw the dog again," Quint clarified. It seemed odd that the authorities on the scene wouldn't make a point of finding a witness.

"The dog isn't our problem," Vincent said. His tone was near sarcastic. "If there are no more questions, we'll continue with our briefing."

Quint stretched out his long legs and leaned back in the surprisingly comfortable ultramodern chair that hugged his behind like a handcrafted leather saddle. If Vincent wanted to play it cool, Quint would oblige. "Cause of the explosion?"

"The mechanics of the bomb will be explained in a moment."

"When was this video taken?"

"Two days ago."

"Where?" Since it was March, Quint assumed the snow on the curb indicated a colder climate. Something about the shadows and light made him think of northern latitudes.

"Reykjavik, Iceland."

"Why?" Quint asked. This was the hard question—the one that would surely drive their undercover investigation.

Vincent's jaw tightened. The corner of his mouth pulled into an expression that could've been a frown or a sneer. "You don't waste words, cowboy."

"Y'all have to excuse my impatience." Quint purposely exaggerated his Texan drawl. "I didn't know we were chitchatting at an afternoon tea party. You just take your time…city boy."

Vincent's coal-black eyes flared. Apparently, he didn't like to have his leadership challenged.

Beside him, Whitney groaned. "This is what I hate about working with men. Everything turns into a contest."

She was much too ladylike to call this altercation a spitting match, but that's what it was. Neither man would quit until they knew whose spit flew the farthest.

Ever since Quint arrived in Chicago two days ago, Vincent Romeo had been treating him like a brainless hick from the sticks. That attitude was going to stop. Right now.

"Let's get one thing straight," Quint said. "I hail from Midland, Texas. My business is oil, but I run a few head of cattle on my ranch so it's true I'm a cowboy. Damn proud to be one. And I surely don't mind if you call me 'cowboy' or 'Tex' or 'good old boy,' but you'd better learn to say it with a smile."

"You might not have noticed," Whitney said, "but my husband isn't big on unnecessary grins. I think it's a brooding Italian thing."

"I think his shorts are too tight." Andy Dexter gave a snorting laugh and shot a loopy grin in Quint's direction. Like most guys who spent a lot of time with computers, Andy was lacking in social skills. He was, however, a genius in telecommunications and computer forensics. His specialized computer equipment made the special-ops room look like the cockpit of a 747, with wall-to-wall blinking lights, switches, screens and dials. In an instant, Andy could analyze and match voiceprints or fingerprints, pull up Interpol data or reproduce satellite photos of troop movements in Zaire. It had been his idea to install built-in laptops in front of each chair at the round table for briefings.

"Could we get back to business?" Lawson Davies glanced at his Rolex. "It's already nine-fifteen, and I have a deposition in forty-five minutes."

"Really, Law?" Whitney arched a delicate eyebrow. "I wouldn't think the vice president in charge of a big corporation's legal department needed to bother with such mundane legal tasks."

"I'm observing and training a new attorney." He turned toward Vincent. "That bombing in Iceland. It was the building where Quantum Industries has its offices. Correct?"

"Yes," Vincent said.

"The story they put out to the media claimed the explosion was an accident caused by a gas leak," Law said thoughtfully. He was well acquainted with the ins and outs of the oil business. When not on undercover assignment, he worked for Petrol Corporation, an oil distributor whose competition was the multinational giant, Quantum Industries, the largest buyer and seller of oil worldwide. "Why was the bombing covered up?"

"There was a need for an undercover investigation." Though Vincent directed his reply toward Law, he trained his gaze on Quint. "Within Quantum, nobody but the CEO knows the truth."

Staring back at Vincent, Quint asked, "Do we know who set the bomb?"

"Not yet."

"Any of the usual terrorist suspects?"

"Not as far as we can tell." Vincent nodded to his pretty redheaded wife. "Please proceed with the briefing information."

"Right." Whitney tapped a few computer keys on the laptop in front of her. The built-in screens all around the table came to life. "First, you have detailed information about Quantum Industries, which you can read later. Second, we have an analysis of the bomb—a high-tech mechanism on an override timer which appeared to be deactivated long enough for the old man and his dog to pass safely. We're assuming the terrorists didn't want to attract unnecessary attention with fatalities. The third point is most important for our investigation. Although nobody took credit for the bombing, there was a message. It said: 'Next time, home base.'"

"Are we sure they meant Quantum?" Law asked. "There are other offices in that building."

"We're sure," Vincent said.

"Then, home base is Chicago." Law looked away from the screen and removed the wire-rimmed glasses he wore for reading. "If we had windows in this special-ops room, I could point out the Quantum Building over toward the Sears Tower."

"Right here in our own backyard," Whitney said. "That's why we're involved. Several other agencies are working on security and surveillance. We'll be undercover, as always, trying to prevent another strike."

Law asked, "Where did we get this video?"

"There was a routine surveillance camera across the street."

"Digitally enhanced," Andy said, calling on his expertise. "I'm sure the original wasn't in color and wasn't so sharp. If you want, I can run a downgrade to give us the actual picture."

"Not necessary," Vincent said. "But I would like your digital analysis on the incendiary and the trigger mechanism. Your assignment, in addition to the usual telecommunications, is to study the Quantum Building blueprints and pinpoint probable locations for explosives.''

Andy beamed. Excitedly, he dragged his skinny fingers through the wild mop of blond hair that perched like a bird's nest atop his narrow forehead. "Oh, man! I love a challenge.''

The younger man's enthusiasm brought a smile to Quint's lips. It had been a very long time since he'd been so eager about anything. "I'm assuming,'' he said, "that since both Law and I are in the oil business, we're going to investigate Quantum.''

"Correct,'' Vincent said. "There's the possibility that this is an inside job. However, it's much more likely that we're looking toward the Middle East.''

"We'll start with the nation of Imad.'' Whitney tapped another key on her computer. A map displayed on their individual screens. "Imad is on the Arabian Peninsula, bordered by Oman, Anbar and Arabia. This oil-rich emirate is under the thumb of Sheik Khalaf Al-Sayed. Though it's not general knowledge, the sheik is suspected of human rights violations. Imad is on the verge of being sanctioned by the United States.''

Quint exchanged a glance with Law. Both men nodded. Whitney's information wasn't news to them.

Law said, "Several distributors are already refusing to buy oil from Imad. Quantum is among them.''

"Correct,'' Whitney said. "Quantum was the first distributor to back off from Imad.''

"Sounds like a motive for terrorism,'' Quint said. "Maybe the sheik blew up the Quantum Building in Iceland for revenge.''

"Revenge doesn't make sense,'' Whitney said. "The sheik wants to be friendly with Quantum, to have them buy his oil reserves. In any case, we have reason to believe Sheik Khalaf Al-Sayed has plans to come to Chicago. He has a daughter, Miah, who lives here.''

"In Chicago?'' Quint asked.

"Yes, and I'll have more information about her later," Whitney said. "This is our most recent photograph of Khalaf."

Their screens displayed a sharp picture of a trim, older man, dressed in a tailored military uniform. Though his expression was stiff, his dark eyes burned with a sinister inner flame.

Whitney continued her briefing. "This trip is highly unusual. Sheik Khalaf seldom leaves Imad, especially now when he appears to be building up his military."

"What's the reason for the buildup?" Quint asked.

"Money," Whitney answered. "The bottom line is always money. Unless Quantum starts buying oil from him again, the sheik's regime will go broke. He might attempt to gain leverage by taking over the country to the north of him—Anbar."

"We're friendly with Anbar," Law said.

"Yes," Whitney said. The photograph on the screen changed. "This is Prince Javid Haji Haleem of Anbar. He's next in the line of succession for the throne of Anbar."

With curling black hair and dark piercing eyes, he was a good-looking man. Even Quint would call him handsome, and Quint didn't generally notice such things about other men. "I'll bet the ladies are standing in line to join this guy's harem."

"Not funny," Whitney chastised as she displayed a series of photos of Javid. "The future ruler of Anbar believes in treating women as human beings and not chattel. In many ways, he's an enlightened leader, promoting literacy and education among his people. He travels all over the world as a goodwill ambassador for Anbar, and he investigates."

"Investigates what?" Quint asked.

"Javid is an expert on terrorism. With his assistance, a lot of tragedy has been averted."

The last in the series of pictures showed a subtle difference. Javid's features were honed by a sharper edge. "Whoa," Quint said. "Was this picture taken on a bad day?"

"Very observant." Whitney sounded impressed. "That photograph is not, in fact, Javid. It's his identical twin brother, Prince Zahir Haji Haleem. Notorious international playboy."

Her information came as a surprise to Quint, who generally kept up on events in oil-rich countries around the world. He knew there were brothers in Anbar, but he didn't know they were twins.

"Both Zahir and Javid are half-American and were raised here. Now, they both live in the Middle East. It's important to keep in mind that Zahir is more than a jet-setter," Whitney said. "He's been involved with supposed freedom fighters in the Middle East, most recently with Khalaf when he deposed the government in Nurul. Which brings up another issue."

Quint leaned forward, listening carefully to this complex explanation. "Does this have something to do with Khalaf's daughter?"

"Good guess. Miah Mohairbi's lineage links her to the throne of Nurul. If Zahir marries her, his claim is solidified." Whitney brought up the map again. "Nurul is on the Red Sea by Yemen."

Law frowned at the screen. "I'm familiar with Nurul. Quantum isn't buying oil from them until the political situation settles down. Other distributors, Petrol included, are following their lead."

"How does Zahir fit into the picture?" Quint asked.

"If he's allied with Imad," Law said, "his tactics are questionable."

"As in terrorism?"

Law shrugged. "There's no stated U.S. position as yet."

Whitney spoke into the intercom that connected with the front desk. "Kathy, would you please escort our guest into the special-ops room?"

While waiting for the electronic door to open, Quint scrolled through the data on his screen to a section with information on Quantum Industries. In his dealings with the megapowerful oil distribution giant, he'd met many of the principals, including the CEO, Henry Van Buren. He noticed an unfamiliar face in their briefing notes, a very lovely face. He paused on her photograph. Natalie Van Buren, vice president in charge of public relations. Her soft brown hair fell neatly to her shoulders. Her green-eyed gaze was cool and direct and somehow mysterious, as if she had a secret. Why was the photograph of a public relations vice president included in a briefing about terrorists?

As soon as the electronic door whooshed open, their screens went blank.

Whitney stood. "Gentlemen, I'm pleased to introduce Prince Javid Haji Haleem, future ruler of Anbar."

In person, Javid was impressive. Though he was probably only in his early thirties, he carried himself gracefully. As he shook Quint's hand, he said, "I know you."

"No, sir, I don't believe I've had the honor."

"We have not met. I know your reputation." His slight accent made his speech seem formal. "You have led wildcat oil crews."

"Not for a long time." In his twenties, Quint built the resources of Crawford Oil by wildcat exploration around the world, usually in Central and South America. He quit traveling when he settled down with Paula, five years ago on his thirtieth birthday.

"You discovered oil in many nations," Javid said. "Yet, you never exploited the local population. Instead, you created employment. In some cases, you won freedom for oppressed peoples. I admire you, Quintin Crawford."

"Thank you, sir." Embarrassed by the tribute, Quint got back to the topic at hand. "How can Chicago Confidential be of service to you?"

Javid strode around the table and sat beside Vincent. "I

believe my brother, Zahir, helped in the overthrow of Nurul by Sheik Khalaf. It is no secret that Khalaf would like to put Zahir on the throne in Nurul. The alliance between these two is perilous for my nation. If Imad and Nurul combine their military resources, they could conquer Anbar."

"If they conquer Anbar," Law said, "they might become the most powerful force in the Middle East."

"Unfortunately, yes." Javid frowned. "I have come to you because I am also convinced that Zahir was involved in the Reykjavik bombing."

"Do you have proof?" Quint asked.

"Not direct evidence." A pained look crossed his face. "It saddens me to think my own brother is linked with terrorists, but I am not naive. Zahir is capable of…anything."

Quint said, "We just heard that Sheik Khalaf is coming to Chicago. How about Zahir?"

"He will be here soon," Javid said. "There are rumors he is betrothed with the estranged daughter of Khalaf, but his stated purpose in coming to Chicago is to meet with Quantum and to discuss the future sale of oil from Nurul. And possibly to convince them to buy from Imad."

"But he supposedly bombed Quantum in Reykjavik," Andy said.

"My brother negotiates with one hand," Javid said. "He plots with the other."

Andy nodded, seemingly unconcerned about human treachery. "What can you tell us about the incendiary?"

"If you'd like," Whitney said, "we can review the specs right now."

Vincent nodded his assent, and the large high-resolution screen lit up with a three-dimensional blueprint for an incendiary.

Once again, the door from the outer office opened, and Kathy the receptionist stepped inside. "Excuse me," she said. "I have an urgent phone call for Quint."

"I'll take it out front." He rose from his seat, glad to be leaving a technical discussion of bombs and bombing.

In the outer office, he winked at Kathy Renk. "Thank you, ma'am. All those switches and coils are way too much information for me."

"Me, too. When Andy explains mechanical stuff, it's hard for me to stay awake." A pleasantly plump woman in her late thirties, Kathy couldn't be considered beautiful. But when she smiled, the world was a friendlier place. She pointed toward Whitney's office. "You can take the call in there. It's Daniel Austin."

Quint closed the office door behind himself, picked up the phone and said, "If it isn't Daniel Austin, the head hound dawg at Montana Confidential."

"Surprised you can remember with that peanut-size buzzard brain of yours. How the hell are you?"

"Can't complain," Quint said. "I'm in the middle of a briefing, so I got to keep it short. What's up?"

"What's your take on Javid?"

"He's not afraid to look me straight in the eye. He seems a mite quick to turn on his brother, but I don't know the family history. And, I'd have to say, Javid's a real handsome fellow."

"You got that right." Austin chuckled. "And don't we sound like a couple of prancin' Nancy boys?"

"Don't know about you," Quint said. "I happen to be confident enough in my masculinity to notice when another guy is good-looking."

"Boy, you're beginning to sound like Oprah."

"Well, perhaps that's why I was sent to Chicago," Quint said. "Now, was there a reason for this urgent call?"

"The CEO at Quantum, Henry Van Buren, is an old friend of mine, and I'm worried about him." All the joking left Austin's voice. "I want you to take real good care of him and his family."

"Yes, sir."

"Most especially," Daniel said, "I want you to look

out for Henry's daughter, Natalie. From what I understand, she's a single woman."

"You're matchmaking," Quint said. "Now who sounds like Oprah?"

Austin gave a hoot of laughter. "Seriously, how are things going with the set-up of Chicago Confidential? What do you think of Vincent Romeo?"

"A good man." Quint didn't choose to mention his personal spitting match with Vincent which was a man-to-man private matter. "This is a real high-tech operation, and they're doing just fine."

"Take care of yourself," Austin said. "Don't do anything I wouldn't do."

"That leaves me a lot of room, sir."

After saying goodbye, Quint disconnected the call and returned to the outer office where Kathy Renk was scowling at a half-eaten candy bar.

"Something wrong?" Quint asked.

"It's that new maintenance man, Liam Wallace, who thinks he's God's gift. The ego on that man!" She fluttered her hands. "Oh, listen to me. He's got my feathers all ruffled. It's not important. You go back to your meeting."

Quint smiled at Kathy as he returned to the special-ops room. The discussion with Javid continued, outlining the arcane politics of Imad, Nurul and Anbar. Why had Austin alerted him? What did he suspect about Javid? Quint wondered if the twin brothers really were estranged.

As Vincent wrapped up the briefing, Lawson Davies was given the assignment of researching other terrorist groups and ferreting out possible traitors inside Quantum Industries. Quint wondered how he was going to be used in this investigation. Infiltrating Quantum was out of the question. Even if he buried his Texan accent, he couldn't disguise his identity; too many people at the company already knew him. Nor was it likely he could go undercover with the terrorists.

As the others left the office, Vincent caught his gaze. "Stay behind. We need to talk."

Quint returned to his chair. Idly scrolling through the information on his laptop, he paused again on the photograph of Natalie Van Buren, a lady who should be safe at her desk, escorting visiting dignitaries and sending out press releases. What was her connection?

Vincent returned and took the seat beside Quint. For a moment, they sat quietly, allowing the energy in the room to settle.

"When I started out," Vincent said, "I never planned to be the guy behind the desk. The administrator. The boss. It's harder than I expected."

"'Uneasy is the head that wears the crown,'" Quint quoted.

"And the butt that sits on the throne."

A joke from Vincent Romeo? Quint could hardly believe it.

"Except," Vincent said, "I'm not a king. We all work together, and I want you on my team, Quint."

"I'm ready to play." Quint figured this was as close to an apology as he'd get. And it was enough.

"I'd like to hear your opinion on the briefing information."

Quint glanced toward the woman's face on the screen. It would be her job with Quantum to make sure these Middle Eastern dignitaries were entertained while in Chicago. "From what Javid said, I'm worried about his brother, Zahir. He's convinced the world that he's just a playboy, but his plan might be to take over the whole Middle East."

"Wish we had solid proof against him." Vincent sighed. "It's easier to go after known criminals. We know how they think, how they operate."

"Not always." Paula's death had been caused by a drug cartel, a viperous nest of professional criminals who had ultimately been stopped by Texas Confidential. Unconsciously, Quint's gaze wandered toward a mounted set of cow horns over the door in the special-ops room. The horns—an anachronism in this high-tech arena—were a good-luck gift from Daniel Austin. "The only thing to count on is the unexpected. Mitchell Forbes gave me that bit of advice."

"Mitchell's a good man. He told me a lot about you. Information that wasn't included in your dossier." Vincent's voice lowered. "I'm sorry for your loss. Deeply sorry."

Quint acknowledged his sentiment with a shrug. Neither of them were men who spent much time expressing their emotions. "What's my assignment?"

Vincent pointed toward the computer screen. "You're looking at her."

"Natalie Van Buren?"

"She and my wife went to boarding school together, and Whitney is worried about her. It seems that Natalie has been receiving threatening notes."

"For how long?" Quint asked.

"A couple of weeks. They started before the bombing in Reykjavik and might be unconnected threats from a crank, but we need to keep an eye on Natalie."

"Shouldn't be a problem," Quint said. "She's not hard to look at."

"Here's the complicated part," Vincent said. "We don't want to alert the terrorists to our presence. You can't tell anyone you're her bodyguard. Not even Natalie herself."

"Wait a minute," Quint said. "Are you saying that she won't be told that I'm there to protect her?"

"Exactly."

"How am I supposed to shadow her every movement, without letting her know why I'm there?"

"Turn on that famous Southern charm." Vincent grinned broadly. "Okay, cowboy?"

STANDING ALONE at the floor-to-ceiling window in her father's office on the thirty-first floor of the Quantum Building, Natalie Van Buren stared at the familiar Chicago skyscape. Tall, solid buildings thrust into the cloudy March day, defying the blistering winds from Lake Michigan with their muscular presence. She loved the character of her big-shouldered city. Chicago had been built from the honest sweat of plain, hard-working Midwesterners. Chicago was a city that got things done.

Usually, this view comforted and inspired her, but not today. Natalie knew, in her heart, that someone was lying to her. Behind the bland reassurances from the other corporate vice presidents that everything was business as usual, she sensed a thin veil of deception.

When it came to Quantum business, Natalie trusted her instincts more than she did data, meetings or memorandums. This was her home; she'd grown up here. These corporate offices had been her childhood playground. As the eldest daughter, she'd always aspired to taking over the family business. Her life had been dedicated to proving herself worthy of running the largest oil distributor in the world.

Impatiently, she turned away from the window. Where was her father? Why was he taking so long? The minute he stepped through the door to his office, she'd pounce and demand to know the truth. As if that would make him tell her. Nobody ever forced Henry Van Buren to play his hand.

Her father entered his office and closed the door. Though he strode with his usual athletic vigor, his green eyes—exactly the same color as Natalie's—seemed tired. "Good morning," he barked.

"I need to know what's going on," she said.

"Read the *Tribune*." He sank into the black leather chair behind his desk. "I have a job for you, and I don't want you palming it off on an assistant."

She never shirked her responsibilities. Why would he

even insinuate that she wasn't a hard worker? "Before we talk about anything else, I want some answers. In five days, I'll be speaking to that energy consortium in Washington, D.C., and I must be sure of what I need to say."

He tilted his head to one side, studying her as if he didn't see her every Monday through Friday. "You look nice today, Natalie. That's a pretty color."

"Loden green." Her tailored, silk-blend blazer with matching knee-length skirt ought to look more than simply "nice." This suit had cost a small fortune. "Back to business, Henry. I have a few questions."

"Shoot."

"The security in this building has been increased. New fish-eye cameras have been installed on the floors. There's a new machine in the mail room for x-raying packages. Why?"

"It was time for an upgrade."

He had on his poker face. Natalie recognized the expression because she often wore it herself. She and her father were very much alike—hardworking, skilled businesspeople who were absolutely dedicated to Quantum. Yet, they weren't close. They never hugged. And they weren't confidants.

Natalie strolled across the carpet to his desk and casually picked up a clumsy-looking ceramic paperweight that she'd made for him when she was in fourth grade. "I hope we're not going to the expense of upgrading security because of those stupid threatening notes I've received."

His poker face slipped. "I'd do anything to protect you, Natalie. You know that."

His sincere concern worried her. Though Natalie had been a bit disconcerted by the first couple of notes, she was more angry than anything else. She refused to be intimidated. But if her father was taking the threats seriously…

"Next question," he said.

"Does this extra security have anything to do with the explosion in Reykjavik?"

"You have the PR information on the explosion. An accident. What else?"

"I've heard that someone is buying oil from Imad."

"There's no law against it," he said. "What does that have to do with Quantum?"

"We're not dealing with Imad?"

"Hell, no. Sheik Khalaf Al-Sayed can take a flying leap, as far as I'm concerned. In my opinion, the man is a murderous terrorist."

"I'm glad." The moral center at Quantum always made her proud. Though they were a megacorporation in a sometimes dirty business, her father kept them on the high road. The suspected human rights abuses in Imad truly disgusted him. "What's our position on Nurul?"

"I've agreed to meet with Prince Zahir next week. Though he's not officially part of their new government, he's acting as emissary. But I don't intend to buy from Nurul until their politics have stabilized."

"What's the story with Zahir?"

"Even though he's supposedly engaged, he has the reputation of being a ladies' man. Which makes me glad that you're going to be out of town meeting with the energy consortium while he's here."

Though her sense of being deceived lingered, she had to smile. Her father didn't want her getting involved with a renegade prince from the Middle East. "Do you really think I'd fall for Zahir?"

"You never know." He scooted a stack of papers to the center of his desk and eyed the top sheet, apparently anxious to start work. "Are we finished with your questions and ready to start your new assignment?"

"I'm not quite finished," she said. "About my speech to the consortium, the legal department has compiled proof against the allegation that Quantum is a monopoly. Our contracts are clearly nonexclusive. According to—"

"Hold it! This job assignment will give you a new perspective on contracts. I want you to spend the next couple of days with one of our oldest suppliers, the owner of Crawford Oil. His name is Quintin Crawford. He's up here from Texas and would like to be shown around the town."

"You're joking!" She had tons of work to do before she left town. "You want me to waste my time baby-sitting some minor-league supplier?"

"Watch your attitude, Natalie. The loyalty of men like Quint is what keeps us in business." He pressed a button on his intercom and spoke to his secretary. "Please show Mr. Crawford in here."

"No, Henry, my schedule is full. I can't... I don't want to..."

Her objections faded to helpless sputtering when the door to her father's office swung wide and an extremely tall man swaggered into the office. From the top of his black Stetson that almost scraped the upper edge of the door frame to the toes of his brushed-leather cowboy boots, he was every inch a Texan. He was not—definitely not—the type of sophisticated escort Natalie preferred.

Though his denim jeans and suede jacket might pass for an eccentric fashion statement, the rest of his outfit was over the top. At the throat of his white cotton shirt was a bolo tie with a silver concha that matched the blindingly polished silver in his gigantic belt buckle.

"Howdy, Miss Natalie," he drawled. "Your daddy tells me you're going to show me the town. I am much obliged."

"Hello, Mr. Crawford." Her brain raced, trying to figure out ways she could dump this assignment. "Pleased to meet you."

"Call me Quint." He removed his ridiculous cowboy hat, strode toward her and stuck out his hand. "And the pleasure is all mine."

When she accepted his handshake, Natalie looked up at him. His brown hair was a little too long and untamed. A dark tan bronzed his features. His startling blue eyes, surrounded by crinkles from the sun, held her gaze. Strangely mesmerized, she saw wide-open skies, unlimited vistas and wildflowers—a breath of fresh air through her sterile corporate existence. His handshake was firm. His large hand engulfed her soft palm, but his touch was gentle and controlled.

She swallowed hard. No way would she allow herself to be interested in a shaggy-haired cowboy.

Her father came out from behind the desk and rested his hand on each of their shoulders. His gesture startled her. It felt as if he was giving them his blessing.

"You two have fun today. All day. That's an order, Natalie."

She didn't mistake his meaning. Natalie would not be allowed to assign the task of sightseeing with Quint to an assistant. According to her father—the CEO of Quantum—this Texan was *her* problem.

Chapter Two

Before leaving Confidential headquarters, Quint had checked out the blueprints Andy had for the Quantum Building, a post-World War II skyscraper that had been upgraded and renovated several times, creating a security man's nightmare. If a terrorist planned to hide a bomb within these walls, the options were endless. Thousands of square feet of cubicles, offices, boardrooms, bathrooms, cafeterias, mail rooms, exercise facilities and a parking garage made this structure into a thirty-two-story labyrinth of danger.

Therefore, Quint had decided before he got here that he'd feel safer protecting Natalie on the streets of Chicago—far away from potential threats at Quantum. The way he figured, randomly selected destinations would lessen the opportunity for a planned assault, if, in fact, she was a target for these unnamed terrorists.

After he and Natalie left her father's office, he trailed her into the elevator. His gaze flicked to the ceiling. The center panel could be easily removed to gain access to the elevator shaft. In spite of security cameras, any of the eight elevators could be considered a possible bomb location.

Disembarking on the twenty-fourth floor where her office was located, she asked, "Is there something special you'd like to see while you're in Chicago? The stockyards, perhaps?"

"We got steer in Texas, Miss Natalie. While I'm here, I got a hankering to see the sights of your fine city. If you don't mind."

"The Art Institute?" she suggested.

Her smooth alto voice held a challenge, as if she wouldn't expect a cowboy to be interested in an outstanding art collection, but he didn't take offense. He was undercover. His exaggerated "good old boy" routine was meant to be disarming; nobody would suspect him of being a bodyguard.

Reinforcing her impression that his idea of culture was the local hoedown, he asked, "At the Art Institute, do you suppose they've got any of the cows?"

"Cows?" Her eyebrows lifted.

"Y'all had painted cows on the streets for a while. Isn't that right?"

"Oh yes, the Chicago Cows. Dozens of life-size cow statues with designs by contemporary artists. It was a very successful public display." She strode down the hall toward her corner office. "But I'm afraid the herd has gone back to the barn."

Though her tone was professionally cordial, Quint had the impression that she'd be thrilled if he, too, would retire to the hayloft and leave her alone. "Too bad," he said.

"After I check in with my secretary," she said, "I have a lunch date with an old friend from boarding school. I should make other arrangements for you. I'm sure you'd be bored to death with our girl talk."

"Don't inconvenience yourself." Quint already knew about the lunch date. Natalie's school friend was none other than Whitney MacNair Romeo. "I'll tag along with you ladies."

When she hesitated, probably trying to come up with another excuse to dump him, Quint added, "Your daddy told me you got real good steak in Chicago."

Her father was the only person at Quantum who knew the nature of Quint's assignment, and Henry Van Buren was relieved to have a bodyguard for his headstrong daughter. The mention of his name had the desired effect on Natalie; she wouldn't disobey direct orders from the Quantum CEO.

With an icy smile, she said, "Of course, you're welcome to lunch with us."

Entering the outer office, Natalie tossed off a casual introduction of Quint and her executive secretary, Maria Luisa Moreno.

But he wasn't so cavalier. He'd been raised by his grandma from Alabama, who insisted on good manners and Southern hospitality. He shook the secretary's hand and looked straight into her dark pretty eyes. "Pleased to meet you, Miss Maria Luisa. I'm a supplier for Quantum, visiting for a few days from Texas."

The slender black-haired woman sized him up in a glance, then she smiled, slow and sultry. "I would've guessed Texas."

"I reckon the Stetson is a dead giveaway." He sensed her approval and felt gratified by her warmth. It didn't hurt to have Natalie's secretary on his side. "I used to have a girlfriend named Mary Lou. Mind if I call you that?"

Her sooty eyelashes lowered seductively. "For you, I'll be Mary Lou. And you can call me anytime—"

"Maria Luisa." Natalie interrupted their flirtation. "Was there anything important in the mail?"

"Not really." She released Quint's hand and resumed a professional pose. "When I came in, there was another of those hand-addressed envelopes marked Personal. I left it unopened on your desk."

Quint was immediately alert. Where there were threats and a bombing, mysterious envelopes raised a red flag. He strode into the office behind Natalie, but he beat her to the desk and snatched the padded brown envelope before she had a chance to touch it.

"Looks like you've got a secret admirer."

Obviously irritated, she reached for the package. "If you don't mind, I can handle my own mail."

Not if it's a letter bomb. "I don't see a postmark. Your secret boyfriend must be somebody in the building."

"I doubt that."

She made another grab, and he changed hands, keeping the package beyond her grasp. "How come you're so sure?"

"If you must know, I've been receiving similar packages for the past couple of weeks. The contents are definitely not love notes."

"Then, what are they?" He pretended ignorance, wishing like hell that he could simply tell her his job. This game of keep-away was getting silly. "Gosh, Miss Natalie, this package isn't a threat, is it?"

"What if it is?"

Her hands balled into fists, which she planted on her hips. A red flush of anger climbed her slender throat, coloring her smooth, delicate skin a bright pink. Though she wasn't aware of the change, she looked vivacious and pretty as a rose petal. By contrast, her voice was like steel.

"That's *my* mail, Quint. I'll thank you to set the package on my desk."

He shook his head. "Your daddy wouldn't like that, especially after he went to all the trouble of installing an X-ray machine in the mail room."

"How did you know about the security upgrade?"

Quint was impressed that she'd already caught him off guard. Within minutes after meeting him, Natalie was poking holes in his cover. "I'm just naturally nosy, I guess. Let's just run this package down to the mail room and check it out."

"I'll take care of it," she said.

Quint knew that with the other packages, she had followed procedure and turned them over to security. They had found no traceable evidence. No fingerprints. A generic brand of paper. The messages were printed using a common brand of computer printer.

He wondered why she was reluctant with this package. Did she have a reason for downplaying the threat? Her father had warned him that Natalie liked to do things *her* way. Quint's game of keep-away had probably ticked her off.

Turning away from him, she stepped around her desk and began shuffling through the phone messages. "I prefer not to waste time with this package. Just toss it in the trash."

He did as she asked. Later, he'd find a way to retrieve the package and give it to Andy at Chicago Confidential for more detailed analysis. It would've been a whole lot simpler to just take it with him, but being undercover created a lot of complications, especially on a bodyguard assignment. Since Quint couldn't carry a side arm without causing questions, he counted on a modified .22-caliber Derringer hidden in his belt buckle. The hollowed-out heel of his left boot concealed a switchblade. The silver band on his black Stetson could be used as a garrote. All things considered, he felt well armed.

It wasn't so simple to get around the fact that Natalie didn't know he was guarding her and, therefore, had no particular reason to pay attention to what he advised. Still, he urged her to be prudent. "Seems to me, Miss Natalie, that if you're getting threats, you ought to be more careful."

"Thanks for your opinion."

"Maybe," he suggested, "you should have a bodyguard."

"I can take care of myself." Standing behind her desk, she signed a few standardized forms and made a couple of notes that she tossed into the out basket. "I've traveled extensively for Quantum, sometimes in hostile regions where the possibility of kidnapping was imminent. I'm fully trained in hand-to-hand combat, the use of firearms and evasive techniques.''

Quint had a hard time imagining how this slim, sophisticated woman would deal with an actual assault. She was too tightly wrapped to scream, too manicured to risk breaking a nail. Though her green eyes sometimes sparked with energy, she seemed to be the perfect corporate vice president—predictable in every way.

Her L-shaped office, though pleasantly furnished, was nothing spectacular, except for the well-lit painting on the wall opposite her desk in a conversation area. It was the only piece of artwork in the room. Quint strolled over to take a closer look at a misshapen square of yellow. When he got nearer, there seemed to be other colors trapped inside the yellow. The big canvas seemed alive, teeming with secret color.

''It's an original,'' she said. ''The artist studied with Rothko.''

''Valuable?''

''Very,'' she said. ''I spent almost the entire budget for furnishing my office on that one painting.''

Her choice said a lot about her character. She liked nice things and didn't settle for second best.

An interesting woman, Quint thought as he watched her clean up the accumulated work details on her desk. It'd be a damn shame if anything bad happened to her. Even if she'd had decent self-defense training, he doubted her amateur karate chops would stop a terrorist. ''These—what did you call them—evasive techniques? What are they?''

''Mostly common sense. Avoid danger. Stay within the boundaries of safety. If you see someone coming after you, run away.'' She pantomimed jogging as she came around the desk. ''Don't be a hero. If you have a chance to escape, grab it!''

In the blink of an eye, she thrust her arm into the trash can and retrieved the padded envelope. Her fingers poised at the edge, prepared to rip the seal.

Quint reacted on pure instinct. His hand caught hold of her wrist, preventing her from opening the package. He yanked her toward him. Furious, he glared down at her. "You might have a death wish, Natalie. But don't take me with you."

"I had no intention of opening this envelope," she said defiantly. "I'm not an idiot."

Her wrist trembled in his grasp. Her body was inches from his. He could feel her heat, could hear the soft exhale of her breath. Her expensive perfume tickled his nostrils.

Quint felt a prickling of his own, a twitch at his nerve endings as if something paralyzed inside him had begun to waken. By grabbing her wrist, he'd chosen survival over death. Was living another day so important to him? Or did his reaction spring from an innate urge to protect?

Natalie wrenched away from him, leaving the package in his hands. She straightened the lapels of her blazer. "On our way out, we'll take this possible letter bomb down to the X-ray machine in the mail room. Will that make you feel safer?"

"It will."

Her unexpected action had thrown him off-kilter. He had underestimated her—a mistake he wouldn't make again. Natalie Van Buren was a woman who needed to be in charge and liked to have the last word.

IN THE EMPLOYEE'S PARKING LOT outside the private plane hangars at Midway Airport, Nicco waited patiently in his rented van. Ten miles from downtown Chicago, he watched the corporate jets take off, soaring like sleek javelins hurled by the gods. The spectacle of flight never ceased to amaze him, even with his practical experience as a pilot.

The cell phone in the pocket of his ground crew jumpsuit trilled and he answered, "Speak."

"Daughter has left home base. A man in a cowboy hat is with her."

"Follow them."

He disconnected with a scowl. Who was this cowboy accompanying Daughter? Not a lover. According to their research, Natalie Van Buren had no special male companions. Perhaps the cowboy was a client of Quantum Industries. Perhaps a media representative.

Thoughtfully, Nicco stroked his clean-shaven chin, glad to be rid of his beard. He was tempted to call the communications man who had bugged Natalie's office, but he generally avoided using the unsecured cell phone. Anyone might be listening.

On the passenger seat beside him, a black-and-white dog thumped his tail against the door and stared up at his master. The canine expression seemed expectant and wise— far more intelligent than many of Nicco's companions. At least Scout knew how to obey simple commands.

Nicco scratched the soft fur between the dog's ears and checked his wristwatch. His contact was eight minutes late. Such carelessness was to be expected from a low-level baggage handler. Americans had no work ethic. In Nicco's experience, most Americans tried to do the least effort for the most reward. Their only ethic was greed as they stormed through the world leaving devastation in their wake.

Through the windshield, Nicco saw the contact approaching the van. He was a square-shouldered man wearing a jumpsuit. An unfiltered cigarette dangled from his thick lips. In his right hand, he carried a black metal lunch pail.

Nicco nodded to Scout, and the three-legged Border collie maneuvered agilely into the rear of the van.

The contact opened the passenger-side door and climbed inside. "How you doing?"

There was no need to exchange pleasantries. Nicco acknowledged the contact with a nod, started the engine and drove toward the exit from the parking lot. They never conducted business at the airport where too many security men might notice. On South Cicero, Nicco headed toward a tavern beside a vacant lot.

After he parked, he asked, "Have you placed the parcels?"

"All three in the Quantum hangar beyond Security. Just like you told me." The contact lit another cigarette. The offensive stink poisoned the air in the van. "But there's a change in plans. I want more money."

Nicco said nothing. He was amused that this pitiful underling would attempt to dictate terms, especially since he had already served his usefulness.

"Five thousand," the contact said. "Or else I give my boss those packages and you're out of luck."

"Do you enjoy smoking?" Nicco asked.

"Yeah." The man took a long drag on his cigarette. It would be his last earthly breath.

WITH A RIGID GRIN pasted on her face, Natalie listened to Quint finish placing his luncheon order at the Hamilton House on Wacker Drive.

"…and I want my filet cooked so rare that I can hear it say moo…"

Could he be any more cornball? Every other word he drawled was some kind of down-home expression. She twisted the napkin on her lap into a knot. In public relations, she frequently socialized with oddballs, and she was able to cope with them. But Quint had gotten under her skin. More than once, she'd had the distinct impression that he was being annoying on purpose, playing up his cowboy act to irritate her.

As the waitress departed, he asked, "Something wrong, Miss Natalie? You look like you got a burr under your saddle."

"I'm fine." She peered across the table at her old friend, Whitney MacNair Romeo, and said, "I should visit the ladies' room."

"I'll come with you," Whitney said.

Politely, Quint stood while the two women left their seats and moved through a maze of rose-colored linen tablecloths in the elegant dining room. Inside the rest room, Natalie rolled her eyes and exhaled a loud groan.

"Whitney, I'm so sorry I had to drag him along."

"No problem." Whitney looked in the mirror and pushed her thick red-gold hair into place. "As I said before, he's a client of Solutions, Inc., and I like Quint. He's kind of cute."

"Or not!" she said, more loudly than she intended.

Even more exasperating than his hee-haw commentary was the effect he seemed to have on women. Maria Luisa, her secretary who was usually utterly aloof when it came to men, allowed Quint to call her Mary Lou. She'd practically propositioned him. *Mary Lou?*

"Really," Whitney said. "It's endearing the way his hair falls across his forehead. Incredible blue eyes. And he's got a great body."

"Hadn't noticed. I was blinded by the dinner platter he wears for a belt buckle."

"If you really didn't notice, Natalie, you ought to start taking hormones. There's no harm in spending a couple of days with a handsome cowboy."

"Quint? Hah!"

"Why not? You're an eligible thirty-year-old woman."

"So what?" Natalie said. "Quint is obviously *not* eligible. His gold-and-silver wedding band is almost as big as the buckle."

An odd little frown turned down the corners of Whitney's mouth. "I happen to know he's not married. His wife died over two years ago in an accident."

"Then, why is he wearing a ring?"

"Possibly, he hasn't gotten over her death."

Natalie confronted her reflection in the mirror. Her cheeks were more flushed than usual. The green in her eyes seemed murky and confused. She didn't want to think of Quint as a tragically wounded figure—a man who was sensitive and caring. How could he be? He'd grabbed her in the office, manhandled her.

She touched her wrist where his masterful grip had closed like a vise. He was rude and crude. But he'd thought he was protecting her, which made his quick action seem somehow gallant. Stupid, but gallant.

She sighed. "He's not my type."

WHEN THEY RETURNED to the table, Quint was staring at the note that had been inside the "Personal" package. After it had been x-rayed in the mail room, he insisted on taking the note and padded envelope with them.

Natalie eased into her chair. "Put that away. Please."

"Your fan mail is interesting," he said as he passed the paper to Whitney. "Natalie got this delivered to her office by messenger."

All the notes contained stick-figure pictures and typed messages. This one showed a person being hanged—a drawing that was chilling in its simplicity. It read, "Here's how we shut your big mouth."

Natalie felt embarrassed to be worried by a threat that seemed as childish as that of a bully on a grade-school playground. Yet, there was something primal about the purposeful lack of sophistication. The threat was direct, uncluttered by logic or reasoning.

Yet, the message didn't make sense. She wasn't supposed to talk. To whom? About what?

Whitney's brow furrowed as she gazed down at the sheet. "Do you have any idea who might be sending these notes?"

"Since almost all of them refer to my big mouth, I assume the reference is to something I've said in a press release or a media interview." Natalie reached for the single glass of white wine she allowed herself at lunch. "Let's talk about something else, shall we?"

"No," Whitney said firmly. "I want to know who's threatening my friend."

She'd always been bossy. When they were in boarding school together, Whitney generally led the charge, and Natalie organized the necessary elements to implement their projects, ranging from later curfews to a vegetarian menu in the school cafeteria. Early in their relationship, the two women decided never to compete against each other because neither one of them could stand losing.

Natalie sipped her wine and glanced toward Quint. "Surely you don't want to hear more about this nonsense."

"Surely, I do." His gaze was calm, steady and reassuring.

For a moment, she thought he might reach across the table and pat her hand. "All right," Natalie said. "I'll tell you what I've been thinking about these notes. Then, we change the subject. Agreed?"

They both nodded.

"Because Quantum Industries is the largest distributor of oil in the world, we're a target for all kinds of hate groups. First, there are the environmentalists."

"I don't much care for the tree huggers," Quint said. "But I thought they were peaceable."

"Not all of them. There's one group in particular. An eco-cult based somewhere in southern Illinois. Their leader is a guy named Hutch Greely, and they call themselves the Solar Sons." She looked toward Whitney. "My sister thinks they're heroes. You remember my sister, Caroline?"

"The research genius? Isn't she inventing alternative fuel or something?"

"She's close to a breakthrough on a hydrogen-combustion engine," Natalie said. "Last week, she e-mailed me that she's taking some time off, which isn't like her at all. I'm afraid she might have joined this Solar Sons cult."

"Then, they can't be threatening you," Whitney said. "Caroline wouldn't let them."

"Probably not." But she wasn't sure. She and her younger sister had gone through some stormy times.

"How dangerous are the Solar Sons?" Whitney asked.

"They do protests. And they've been linked to acts of civil disobedience like spiking trees." She and Caroline had argued about their tactics. No matter how pure the motivation, the Solar Sons had no right to physically interfere with legitimate businesses. "Of course, they hate Quantum, the big bad oil distributor."

"Anybody else who hates Quantum?" Whitney asked.

"Several nations in the Middle East who we're not buying from. And then, there are the U.S. politicians. We're not real popular with them."

"But I thought you were flying to Washington on Monday," Quint said.

"It's not a friendly visit," Natalie said. "My trip to D.C. is to address an energy consortium and to dispute some unfounded concerns about Quantum's operating as a monopoly. Which reminds me, I wanted to talk to you about your contracts."

"Maybe later," Quint said. "When did you start getting these notes? Before or after your trip to D.C. was scheduled?"

She thought for a moment. "After. Possibly, somebody doesn't want me to meet with the politicians."

"Why not?"

She said the first word that popped into her head. "Imad."

"Ruled by Sheik Khalaf Al-Sayed," Quint said. "You think he's behind these threats?"

Quint's quick grasp of the international situation surprised her. Few people had even heard of Imad. "How do you know about Khalaf?"

"I generally try to keep current with world events in the oil business. Have you met this sheik?"

"No."

"What made you think of him?" Quint asked.

"Quantum refuses to buy from him. I've done several press releases stating that fact." If half of the suspected corruption in Imad was true, Sheik Khalaf was a monster. "But I've always been careful to avoid accusations about his government."

"Could it be," Whitney suggested, "that the sheik doesn't want you talking to someone in Washington?"

"It's kind of obscure. A direct threat would be more effective. You know the kind of thing—'Don't go to D.C. or else!'" She nearly laughed out loud. What a melodrama! Nasty notes with stick figures and obscure threats. "How can I possibly meet a demand when I don't know what's being asked of me? The whole thing is ridiculous."

"I wouldn't laugh it off," Quint said. "Most people are frightened by anonymous threats."

"Not me. I don't get scared. I get mad."

"Amen to that," Whitney said. Turning to Quint, she added, "I've never seen Natalie back away from a fight."

"There's always a first time," he said.

He caught Natalie's gaze. His breathtaking blue eyes held her attention. There was nothing hokey about his manner when he said, "The first rule of self-defense is avoid danger."

Their salads were served, and Natalie took the opportunity to slide into a different topic. "So, Whitney. How's married life? Are you learning how to cook?"

"Vincent didn't marry me for my culinary skills," she replied with a grin and a wink. "And I don't have a single complaint about him."

"I can't believe you married a man named Romeo. I'm so sorry I couldn't make it to the wedding. Tell me about it."

While Whitney described her gown and the flowers and the ornate service, Natalie picked at her romaine lettuce and croutons. She didn't have much of an appetite. Her thoughts kept drifting back to the stick-figure notes. Should she be more concerned? The vague malaise she'd felt about deception at Quantum returned tenfold. Was there real danger? The explosion in Reykjavik worried her. What if it had been a bomb? Why was her father beefing up security?

Earlier, Quint had mentioned hiring a bodyguard. Should she consider that precaution before going to Washington? In some of the South American countries where she traveled for Quantum, she had been assigned a full-time guard. In the Middle East, she had an interpreter *and* a bodyguard, which meant she had absolutely no privacy. She hated being shadowed every waking hour. *No bodyguard!* Not in the United States. Unless there was obvious cause, she refused to believe she needed such extreme caution.

When the entrées arrived, Quint took one bite of the slab of beef on his plate and proclaimed it the "second-best steak he'd ever had." He informed them that number one was beef slaughtered on his own ranch and cooked up by his grandma from Alabama. "But Grandma's true specialty is barbecue. Melts in your mouth and sets your tongue on fire at the same time."

"Of course," Natalie said. Her own lemon-grass chicken seemed dry and unappealing.

"Are you a good cook, Miss Natalie?"

"I'm not half bad."

"She's brilliant," Whitney said. "When we were in boarding school, she used to make pizza from scratch with fresh mozzarella. Any project that Natalie undertakes, she does well."

"Cooking is no big deal. It's just following a recipe." She sliced her buttered asparagus. "I was wondering about Sheik Khalaf. If he has a bone to pick with Quantum, why wouldn't he send the nasty little notes to my father?"

"Because," Whitney said, "your father is an incredibly principled man who would walk into fire rather than back down to a threat."

"An incredibly stubborn man," Natalie agreed.

"On the other hand, your father would do anything to protect his family. A threat to you would make him sit up and take notice."

Though Natalie hated to think of her presence at Quantum causing a weak link in the company's moral armor, she had to admit that Whitney had a point. "Why would Sheik Khalaf warn me to keep my mouth shut in Washington? What could I say that would damage him?"

"You're the spokesperson for Quantum," Whitney said. "Which makes it look like you're advocating sanctions against Imad."

"Also Nurul," Natalie said. Nurul was where Prince Zahir Haji Haleem might become powerful. Should she worry about him?

She laid her fork across the plate, lacking the desire to eat or to discuss the threats. She turned to Quint and said, "The best steak I ever had was in Cartagena, Colombia. I still don't know all the seasonings, but they were delicious."

"There's some fine cooking in South America," he said.

"My father mentioned that you had done a lot of wildcatting. Have you been to Colombia?"

He blinked. A shadow darkened his eyes. "That's where I met my late wife, Paula."

"I'm sorry," Natalie said. "I didn't mean to—"

"It's okay. I like thinking about when we met. Those are good memories."

His thumb rubbed against the braided surface of the ring he wore on his left hand. After Paula died, he had taken the remains of her wedding band to a jeweler, where he had the gold of her ring entwined with the silver of his own. Together forever.

After their lunch, Whitney talked Natalie into letting her take the threatening note to Solutions, Inc. for computer analysis. When Whitney described the software and telecommunication services provided by Solutions, Quint almost believed it was a real business instead of a front for Chicago Confidential.

They bid her farewell, then he and Natalie caught a taxi to the Art Institute. Though the mention of Paula had tossed him into a more introspective mood, he remained alert to his assignment, scanning the faces of bystanders on the street. In the taxi, he played the sightseer, giving him an excuse to twist his head around to see if they were being followed. With all the identical yellow cabs, that was a near-impossible effort.

When they disembarked on Michigan Avenue outside the Art Institute, he noticed another vehicle, half a block away, that came to a sudden stop. Only one man got out. Average height. Longish brown hair and a Vandyke beard. Probably in his early thirties. He wore a shiny black windbreaker. Though he took out a cell phone and started talking, Quint had the sense that he was waiting for them to make the first move. Had they picked up a tail?

When Quint started up the wide marble stairs leading to the fluted columns of the Art Institute's entryway, he lightly touched Natalie's elbow, politely escorting her, trying to protect her from unseen, unnamed threats.

She glanced up at him. "Is something wrong?"

It was hard to sneak anything past her. "I'm just looking around, enjoying your city."

The man in the windbreaker stayed a good distance away, a few stairs behind them, doing a fairly good job of hiding among the visitors to the Art Institute.

"Miss Natalie, do you mind if I take a gander at those shops across the street?"

"Not at all. And, by the way, I prefer when you call me Natalie. 'Miss Natalie' doesn't suit me."

"I'll try to remember that." As they backtracked down the stairs, Quint watched the black windbreaker. Would he follow them?

The man with the Vandyke continued up the stairs and

disappeared into the shadows of the columns. He must be just an innocent tourist, here to appreciate fine art.

When they reached the curb, Quint said, "Changed my mind. I'll shop for souvenirs later. Let's go see some art."

"Fine."

A slight edge of irritation crept through her professional politeness, and Quint figured he was driving this lady crazy.

Inside the Art Institute, Quint felt relatively safe. There were plenty of guards on every floor. Nobody was going to grab Natalie in here.

He allowed himself to relax.

"What sort of art do you like?" Natalie asked. "Old masters? Asian? Photography?"

"I like Remington."

"Pictures of cowboys," she said. "Of course."

In his wildcatting years, Quint had blown through life like a Texan tumbleweed. He'd viewed art collections around the world from the Louvre in Paris to the Georgia O'Keefe Gallery in Santa Fe. In fact, he'd visited the Art Institute of Chicago once before.

As they toured the postmodernists, he stopped in front of a painting by Edward Hopper depicting a night scene of a near-deserted cafeteria on a city street corner. "Must be lonely living in the city," he said. "After the crowds go home, there's nothing but you and the concrete walls."

"Sometimes, it's lonelier in a crowd," she said.

He stepped back, supposedly to get a better perspective on the painting. His gaze rested on the back of Natalie's head. Her smooth, thick, brown hair fell in a delicate swoosh to her shoulders. Highlights of gold shimmered in the light. Her hair looked soft, touchable. He hated to think she might be lonely.

In another part of the gallery, he paused in front of the famous portrait by Grant Wood of a bald farmer with a pitchfork and his plain wife, *American Gothic*. "They look bored."

"Not much action on the old homestead," she said.

"Depends on your viewpoint. I've spent a whole afternoon on horseback, watching the prairie grass grow and the clouds roll by. But I wasn't bored."

"No?"

"Sameness is a comfort, knowing that every morning the sun is going to rise in the east. Whether or not I'm there to watch, the clouds will build and the rain will fall. I don't need a lot of excitement to be content."

For once, she didn't sneer or smirk. "I understand."

"Do you?"

"I can appreciate the stillness in nature. The touch of the wind on your face. The amazing beauty of a pink sunset." She nodded toward the old couple in the painting. "Maybe they're the smart ones. Knowing what to expect. Being together no matter what."

"I like that," he said. He liked her, too. He wanted to take her to his ranch and show her the vistas that went on forever until you could see the curve of the earth. Natalie would enjoy ranch life. From the way she handled those threatening notes, he knew she was tough and brave—not a sissy.

She was a city gal with a highly competitive nature. She didn't like to be second best, and she wasn't shy about stating her opinions. If she came to his ranch, she'd likely be running the damn place within a week.

When Quint turned away from the painting, he glimpsed a face—shaggy hair and a Vandyke beard. It was the guy from the street, but he wasn't wearing his black windbreaker. Was he following? Was his presence a coincidence?

The cell phone inside Natalie's purse rang out, and she quickly grabbed it. "Sorry," she whispered. "I hate to interrupt anyone's appreciation of these paintings."

"Don't worry on my account."

She stepped into the foyer and conferred in hushed tones. After she disconnected the call, she returned to him. "We have to leave. Prince Zahir arrived a week early. He's at Quantum."

Chapter Three

The unexpected arrival of Zahir Haji Haleem sparked a warning inside Quint's head, and he tried to recall the details from this morning's Confidential briefing when they discussed Middle Eastern politics. He remembered that Zahir—identical twin brother of Javid—was estranged from his family in Anbar but was still referred to by his hereditary title of Prince of Anbar. He had a reputation as a playboy. Zahir expected to be named leader of Nurul. What else? There was a connection between Prince Zahir and Sheik Khalaf of Imad. In fact, Zahir was planning to marry Khalaf's daughter so he could be sure of taking over the throne of Nurul.

As their taxi neared the Quantum Building, Quint thought it might be useful to have a backup expert at this meeting with Zahir. "Say, Natalie, don't you think Whitney would get a kick out of meeting a real prince? Maybe we should call her."

"Absolutely not." Natalie was all business. She'd spent the whole time in the cab on her cell phone, making arrangements with her staff. "The fewer people at this meeting, the better. It's important to avoid any publicity. Until the Quantum board of directors decides our position regarding oil purchases from Nurul, we can't be placed in a position where reporters would ask those questions."

"Why not tell the media the truth?"

"Protocol." She dug into her purse and pulled out a tiny gold mirror and lipstick. "Zahir is, in title, a prince. As such, we should treat him with a certain deference. At the same time, we need to avoid any substantive discussion of policy."

"You're the expert," he said. "Why do you think Prince Zahir showed up early?"

"My guess? He wants to force our hand, to make Quantum commit to using Nurul as a supplier before he's even on the throne. His early arrival throws us off guard."

"An ambush," Quint said.

"Exactly."

As she outlined her lips with a soft cranberry color, he watched the purely feminine procedure with fascination. Her pretty mouth pouted then smiled, showing pearly white teeth. Damn, she was a lovely little thing. He wanted to kiss that war paint off her lips, to taste her womanly sweetness. His pulse speeded up. He felt the stirring of desire, numbing all logical thought, and he told himself to look away from her. But his eyes refused to obey. It was going to be a struggle to keep his brain above his belt buckle.

When the taxi pulled up at the curb, she suggested, "I'm going to be awfully busy for the next few hours. Maybe you should return to your hotel, and we can make plans for tomorrow."

No way. "If it's all the same to you, I'll just tag along. You think the prince is going to wear his native costume? Long flowing robes and a scimitar?"

"Doubtful. From research, I know he prefers western dress." She hopped out of the cab. "Not western like you, of course."

Quint adjusted the bolo tie at his throat. "Of course not."

Inside the Quantum Building, they took the elevator to the thirty-first floor and went down the hall to her father's office. Though this was nearly the end of a long day, Natalie's attitude was crisp and alert. She'd been given a public relations challenge and had risen to it. By contrast, Quint felt ill-prepared. Still thinking about her cranberry lips, he could barely remember his own name, much less recall the pertinent data about Zahir…until he shook hands with the handsome prince in his classy-looking tailored suit and silk necktie.

When Quint looked into the dark opaque eyes of Zahir, he remembered. Zahir was dangerous. He'd been trained as a freedom fighter in a regime where cruelty was sometimes prized as much as courage.

Quint's instincts warned him to shoot this rattlesnake before it had a chance to strike, but he kept himself in control. "Pleased to meet you."

Zahir waited a few seconds before responding, a subtle tactic to make the other person uncomfortable. But Quint didn't fidget or rush to break their handshake. He wasn't intimidated by Zahir.

"I know you," Zahir said, echoing the words of his brother when he first met Quint. Déjà sheik. This was getting a little spooky.

Quint played his part by saying, "I don't believe we've met."

"I know your reputation as a wildcat oil surveyor. You are, I suppose, my competition."

In more ways than one. Quint was up-front, honest and direct. He would always try to do the right thing. Zahir, he reckoned, was out for Zahir.

If Quint hadn't been undercover, he would've pushed for more information about links to Imad and a true definition of "freedom fighter." Did Zahir's secret occupation include the slaughter of helpless women and children? Was he also a secret terrorist? And, by the way, what did he know about a bomb in Reykjavik?

But this wasn't the time to pick a fight. Quint's job meant blending inoffensively into the woodwork. He released Zahir's hand and slapped a friendly grin on his face.

"Heck, I'm not much competition for anybody in the oil business. Right now, I concentrate on ranching. I like to keep my butt in the saddle from dawn till dusk."

"What brings you to Chicago?"

Same thing that brought you. "Just a little vacation. I've been imposing on the public relations lady here at Quantum to show me around."

"Natalie," Zahir said.

Quint didn't like the way the syllables of her name rolled around in Zahir's mouth. "That's right. Natalie Van Buren."

"Daughter of the CEO." Zahir's glance slithered across the room toward Natalie, who was chatting with her father and another Quantum employee. "A very pretty woman."

Quint's muscles tensed. "Looks to me like you've got your own entourage."

Zahir was accompanied by three attractive ladies and a bland guy who looked like a classic hanger-on.

"It's the title," Zahir confided proudly. "All women dream of being with a prince, and I hate to disappoint them."

"You married?" Quint asked.

"Not yet. Soon however I will be—a bride is necessary before I ascend to the throne of Nurul. It will be merely a political marriage."

Again, his gaze strayed toward Natalie, and Quint had the urge to smack him upside his handsome face. His impulse was stifled by the arrival of the man Natalie and her father had been talking to.

He introduced himself. "Gordon Doeller, vice president in charge of marketing. I've had the pleasure of meeting you before, Prince Zahir."

"Indeed," Zahir said.

Though Zahir presented a decidedly cool face to Gordon Doeller, Quint noticed a nervous spark between them. He reckoned these two men were more than nodding acquaintances, and made a mental note to have Gordon Doeller checked out through the computers back at Solutions, Inc.

Gordon didn't look like a bad guy. He was all angles, from his flattop haircut to his square-toed shoes. His shoulders and torso formed a perfect rectangle. A straightforward guy. But looks could be deceiving.

Natalie clapped her hands, drawing their attention. "Prince Zahir," she said, "we are honored by your visit to Quantum and have prepared a simple reception upstairs in the penthouse. Would you all please come with me."

Quint made a point of being on the same elevator as Zahir and Natalie. He watched with satisfaction as the prince made smoldering advances toward her, and Natalie politely kept him in his place. Every woman wants a prince? Obviously, not Natalie! She was a professional public relations person, able to put everyone at ease and make them feel accepted. And to rebuff unwanted attention.

In the penthouse lounge where several windows offered an impressive view of the city, Natalie had arranged via cell phone for canapés, snacks and an open bar for beverages. Several Quantum employees milled around, waiting to meet the prince, who was escorted toward a comfortable sofa by Natalie's father.

"Nice job putting this together," Quint complimented her.

"It wasn't hard," she said. "We have a chef on payroll, and he's accustomed to quick receptions. Getting the employees to hang out was probably more difficult, but Maria Luisa can be incredibly persuasive."

"I'm still impressed," he said.

She whispered, "I had to act quickly. To head off the ambush."

He liked that she was confiding in him. Maybe she was only being nice to him because of her job, but he still appreciated her talent. He appreciated her...a lot.

She made a flicking motion with her hand. "Go mingle."

"Yes, ma'am." If she'd asked him to jump out of the penthouse window, he might have given her suggestion serious consideration.

NATALIE STOOD at the edge of a conversation, not really listening as she sipped her Perrier with a lime twist and considered the possibility of eating something. The crab cakes, miniquiches and assorted hors d'oeuvres looked appetizing, and she needed caloric sustenance. But when she reached for a thin cracked-wheat cracker brushed with Asiago cheese, she pulled back her fingers. The inside of her stomach felt like a pinball machine—an unfortunate reaction to the stress of Zahir's surprise visit.

She couldn't fault her staff for the way they'd responded—they'd created a simple reception for the prince without alerting the press and thereby pressuring Quantum to take a position on future dealings with Nurul or questions about Imad. Their work had been satisfactory and things had gone smoothly. All lines of protocol remained intact. Why, then, was she feeling so edgy? Was it her forced association with Quint?

Glancing around the room, she spotted him easily. In his cowboy boots, he towered above everyone else. Though he interacted with perfect manners, he seemed to stand apart. A stillness surrounded him. Yet, she sensed, he was not at peace. His body language bespoke a certain tension. Even when he grinned, his jawline was taut. Occasionally, his gaze drifted, and he squinted as if searching a distant horizon.

Natalie found herself wondering about this habit. Though he made his money in oil, he was also a rancher. She imagined him on horseback, tall in the saddle as he surveyed his lands and tended the little lost calves gone astray. He was a natural protector—solid and reliable, staring into the distance, anticipating the arrival of wolves and

predators. But now, he was in the city. What was he looking for?

When her father touched her elbow, Natalie startled,
spilling a lithe cascade of Perrier on his sleeve. "Sorry,
Henry. I didn't see you coming."

Brushing off his sleeve, he said, "Tomorrow morning,
first thing, I'm going to have cameras installed in your
office."

Her reverie of Quint and his ranch vanished as she
snapped back to reality. Natalie didn't like the idea of being under constant surveillance. Most especially, she didn't
want protection dictated by her father. It felt like he was
asking for a baby monitor.

"Why in *my* office?"

"The package you received today—the one you handed
over to your friend, Whitney—didn't come through the
mail room. It was hand delivered."

"The hall cameras must have—"

"Our security men reviewed the tapes. A couple of
times, the door to Maria Luisa's office opened and closed,
but they couldn't identify anyone going in or coming out."

"Not even after they paused and enhanced the image?"
Natalie asked.

"Nothing definite. And, of course, there were people
who had legitimate reasons to enter your office. The guy
from the mail room. One of your assistants. Gordon
Doeller." He exhaled a slightly ragged sigh. "I'm worried
about you."

Which was exactly why she didn't want special security
measures. All her life, Natalie had struggled with accusations of nepotism. Of course, she'd ascended through the
ranks at Quantum more quickly than someone not named
Van Buren. She was the youngest vice president and the
only female one at corporate headquarters. Still, her job
performance justified her position. She worked hard and
was more than competent.

She asked, "If someone else—Gordon Doeller, for example—had received these threats, would you insist on a camera in his office?''

Her father's hesitation provided an answer.

"I thought not,'' Natalie said. "Please understand, Henry. I don't want an office camera. It's an unnecessary expense, and I need privacy.''

Henry scowled. "What for?''

"Sensitive aspects of public relations. I might leak information to one reporter and not another. My staff meetings need to be confidential. I don't want a record of everything I do.''

She thought of her confrontation with Quint this morning. Their game of grab-the-package would have made embarrassing viewing for a bored security guard. "Please, Henry. Respect my wishes.''

"We'll see.''

She and her father moved forward to say their goodbyes to Prince Zahir and his entourage, who were preparing to take their leave. As if she'd needed further confirmation that her position at Quantum was unique, the prince singled her out for his attention.

He clasped her hand, then lifted her fingertips to his lips. His dark eyes devoured her with an embarrassing, lip-smacking lasciviousness.

Though she had to admit that he was impeccably handsome, she wasn't swept away. The exotic fragrance of his cologne, reminiscent of sandalwood and sage, was too strong for her taste. His features were too perfect. His voice oozed like rancid oil. Also, as Zahir admitted himself, he was engaged. She snatched her hand from his grasp. What a creep!

"Until we meet again, Natalie.''

Crisply, she lied, "I look forward to it.''

As the prince and his companions departed with their uniformed chauffeur, the Quantum employees left behind heaved a collective sigh of relief. This impromptu reception had not been on their agendas.

"Thank you, everyone," Natalie said. "We'll have more information on the prince's visit tomorrow. Be prepared for some extra meetings."

Jerome Harris, head of Accounting, popped up beside her. He was a rabbity little man who would've been irritating if his fussy attention to detail had not saved Quantum hundreds of thousands of dollars.

"Pencil me in for tomorrow, Natalie. I have details you'll need for the Washington trip."

"New information?" His prior briefings had seemed utterly complete.

Jerome nodded three times in rapid succession. "I've been talking with Quint Crawford. He pointed out a contract clause I might have overlooked in my accounting review."

Not only was it hard to believe that fidgety little Jerome had allowed any detail to escape his scrutiny, but she was surprised to hear that Quint had been so cleverly precise. "Really?"

"Tomorrow," he repeated. "Gotta go. I'm late."

As Jerome bustled toward the exit, Natalie was reminded of the white rabbit from *Alice in Wonderland,* running off with his pocket watch and mumbling about being late for a very important date. No such image occurred when she saw Quint sauntering toward her.

"Miss Natalie," he said, ignoring her instruction to call her only Natalie, "I hate to trouble you, but I have one more request for today."

Now what? "Yes?"

"I'd like to stretch my legs a bit," he drawled. "May I walk you home?"

Suspiciously, she asked, "How do you know I live close enough to walk?"

"Your daddy might have mentioned your address."

She glanced across the room toward Henry, a man she hadn't called "daddy" since she was a very little girl. It seemed he was pushing her toward Quint who was—apparently—an eligible bachelor. Never mind that he was definitely not her type. Never mind that he was still grieving the loss of his wife. Her "daddy" wanted them to spend time together. "Dear daddy" was doing a lot of pushing lately.

Natalie dug in her heels. She'd spent most of her day with Quint. An after-work assignment was too much. "Sorry, but I planned to stop off at the gym."

"That's fine by me," he said. "I'd enjoy a workout myself."

An amused grin tugged at the corner of her mouth as she visualized Quint wearing his Stetson, cowboy boots…and jogging shorts. "You work out?"

He flexed his biceps and leaned toward her. "Feel that."

Oh, good grief! Did he have to be so consistently embarrassing? "I'd rather not."

"Go ahead," he urged. "I'm in shape."

"Well, I'm sure you are."

Maria Luisa sidled up to him. "I'll feel it."

Her long slender fingers reached up to curl around his upper arm, and she exhaled a soft moan. "Very hard."

"Thank you, Mary Lou," Quint said.

She purred, "Any other muscles you want me to touch? Maybe your glutes?"

Quint peeked over his shoulder at his buttocks. "Sorry to say, I've never had a whole lot of muscle mass back there. My rump gets worn down from too much time in the saddle."

"Looks fine to me," Maria Luisa said.

On the verge of a snarl, Natalie looked down her nose at this blatant display of innuendo. Coolly, she suggested, "Perhaps, Quint, you could make sure Maria Luisa gets home safely."

"Though I'd be much obliged to spend more time with Mary Lou, I'm real interested in taking a gander at your condominium." He slapped his Stetson on his head. "Let's head out, Miss Natalie."

"Yee-haw," she muttered, as he herded her toward the elevator.

AFTER DECIDING it was really too late for the gym, she insisted they stop at her office so she could change into comfortable sneakers for the mile-and-a-half walk home. As she sank into the chair behind her desk and changed shoes, Natalie eyed the new stack of memos, clippings and invoices in her in box. Losing an afternoon of work meant she needed to come in early tomorrow, especially since she'd be out of town next week with the Washington trip. Her stomach twanged again, and she winced.

"Are you okay?" Quint asked. "Maybe we should catch a cab."

"A walk sounds good," she said. A stroll through the night air might clear her head and settle her persistent ache of uneasiness.

Though she hit the sidewalk at a brisk pace, she found herself slowing down to match Quint's ambling stride, easygoing as a tumbleweed. Only his eyes were busy, constantly scanning the steady traffic along Michigan Avenue, darting upward toward the soaring outlines of buildings and glittering lights.

At Lake Shore Drive, he stared out across Lake Michigan, a rippling reflection of the skyline. Then he peered straight up. "You never see many real stars in a city," he said. "It's like the skyscrapers swallowed them up."

The wind across the water ruffled her hair and cooled her cheeks as she stared at the familiar outline of her hometown. "I love city nights. There's an excitement you don't find anywhere else. An energy. A buzz. It's invigorating."

"Do you like the nightlife?"

"Not really. I'm not a very social person."

"Too busy with work," he stated, as if it were a fact.

She frowned at the implied criticism. All too often her family and friends urged her to take more vacations and spend more time enjoying herself, as though it were fun to stagger through pointless conversations with strangers. She resumed her pace.

"I like my work."

"Hell, Natalie, I understand. Back home, I'm a kind of workaholic myself. There're always a million chores to do on a ranch. I like to keep moving."

She gave a perfunctory nod, unable to accept that she and Quint had anything in common. "I'll bet you're a real dynamo."

"The way I figure, you got to keep dodging back and forth. Up and down." He came to an abrupt halt in the middle of the sidewalk, causing the few other pedestrians to detour around him. "When you stand still, all the things you've been holding back catch up with you."

Natalie came back toward him. "Like what? What kind of things catch up?"

"The doubts about jobs you could have done better. Regrets about bad decisions. Angry thoughts and petty frustrations. I think you know what I mean."

She knew exactly. In quiet moments, emotions spilled around her in an unassuaged flood. Regret. Frustration. Loneliness. "It's not easy to be alone."

Gently, he clasped her hand and gave a light squeeze. "If you need a friend, I'm here."

As if she'd confide in someone she'd only met a few hours ago.

She tried to pull back her hand, but he held fast until she looked up at him. The reflected glow of the city emphasized the chiseled line of his features. "I mean it," he said. "You can talk to me."

A knot of tension inside her belly loosened. His simple sincerity touched her. Her guard dropped, and she said, "You actually want to be my friend."

"Is that so hard to believe?"

Most men would've taken this opportunity to tell her she was special and they wanted to get her into bed. Quint had no discernible ulterior motive.

For a moment, she rested in his gaze, enjoying an unusual feeling of safety. With Quint, there was nothing to prove, no need to play a role or to compete. He was, unapologetically, himself.

"Okay," she said, "we're pals."

When they resumed their stroll, a pleasurable silence descended over them. She felt free to indulge her thoughts. "About these threatening notes I've been getting," she said. "Should I really be worried?"

"I take any threat seriously."

"Henry wants to put a security camera in my office. I told him no." She pointed across the street. "That's my building."

Quint looked up at the eighteen-story apartment building—an impressive postmodern structure with sleek black marble facade and gold-tinted windows. He gave a low, appreciative whistle. "Mighty nice."

She thought so, too. "Thank you."

He took her elbow to escort her across the street. "You know, Natalie, a camera in your office might be a healthy precaution, at least until the person who's threatening you is caught."

"Possibly. I truly resent the need for extra security, but I don't want to be foolish." She paused outside the entryway. "Would you like to come up?"

"You bet."

By the time she had unlocked the glass front door, the doorman was already holding the second door for her. As always, there were two men on duty in the front lobby: a doorman and an armed security guard, who sat behind a bank of monitors that displayed minute-to-minute video from each floor and the parking garage.

She introduced both of them to Quint, and waited while he asked about their jobs. What kind of handgun did the guard carry? How many other entrances were there to this building? Did they have a panic button to alert police to any disturbance? Quint seemed honestly impressed to hear that there had been only two robberies in the sixty-year history of these Gold Coast condominiums. His conversation with the doorman and the guard was longer than a month's worth of Natalie's interaction with them.

On the elevator ride up to the eleventh floor, she said, "You're one of those people who's never met a stranger."

"Sure have, but they don't stay strange for long." He glanced down at her. "It's a Texas thing. Partly, I'm being friendly. And partly, I'm curious. I guess life's different in the city."

Of course, it was. From the time she was young, Natalie had learned to walk fast, avoid eye contact and be wary of people who struck up unnecessary conversations. Despite Quint's ingenuous attitude, she was certain he knew the difference between city and country. In the Art Institute, he'd betrayed a level of sophistication. She knew from his background that he'd traveled the world and wasn't a simple, rustic cowboy.

It occurred to her that he was playing a role, exaggerating his Texan background. At the same time, he showed flashes of sterling honesty. She had no doubt that his conversation with the doorman and the security guard were motivated by sincere interest in their jobs. But why? Why should Quint care what kind of gun the security guard carried?

While Natalie unlocked her apartment door and dead bolt, he spotted the security camera down the hall and gave a wave to the guys downstairs. Quint was down-home and friendly. But he was also more complex than she'd previously thought. Did he have something to hide? Why did he insist on being with her all day long?

Entering her apartment, she flicked on the track lighting. The full-length windows displayed a panoramic view of Lake Michigan and a partial glimpse of the city lights, including the towering Hancock Building. She seldom bothered to close the curtains. At this altitude, no one could peek inside.

Quint walked directly to the windows and stood utterly still. Only his eyes moved as he scanned from north to south and back again. Against the night sky, his outline defined masculinity with broad shoulders, lean torso and long legs. There was absolutely nothing wrong with his gluteus maximus.

"What are you looking for?" she asked.

"Answers."

"What are the questions?"

"Here's one question, Natalie. How does a pretty, smart, courageous woman like you end up living alone?"

"None of your business," she snapped.

"I'm serious." He came toward her, one slow step at a time. "This isn't a line or a come-on. I'm curious. Have you ever been in love?"

"A couple of times." Defiantly, she stood her ground. "But this really isn't any of your—"

"Never been married?"

"No."

He was so close that she could see the startling blue of his deep-set eyes, a sharp contrast to the sun-burnished tan of his complexion. She could feel the warmth of his body, the energy radiating from him. And she was pulled toward him against her will, drawn magnetically. For a moment, she thought he was going to kiss her.

She ought to object. She ought to break away before she did something she would surely regret. But Natalie was paralyzed.

"Here's my opinion," Quint said. "You've never really been in love, Miss Natalie. If you had been, you'd have gone after that man with every resource you possess until he was yours forever. And—in my opinion—he'd be one lucky son of a gun."

She had no idea how to react to his blunt assessment,

but she knew that she wanted this moment to continue. She wanted Quint to stay here until she could figure him out. "Would you care for a nightcap?"

"No, thanks. I should get home to bed." He turned on his heel and strode toward the door. "I'd advise you to keep those curtains closed until the security men at Quantum figure out who's sending you those threats. Good night, Natalie."

As he closed the door behind himself, she exhaled a breath she hadn't been aware of holding. A riptide of confused emotions swirled around her. Damn him for leaving. But she wanted him gone. All day long he'd been an anchor around her neck.

She sank into a chair, glad that he'd left and praying that he'd come back. As if life weren't already complicated enough, she had to accept the inescapable fact that she was attracted to a Texas cowboy.

AFTER WALKING TWO BLOCKS on the street outside her apartment, Quint sensed that he was being tailed by experts who knew better than to have someone merely slog along in his footsteps. He suspected more than one person was involved in this surveillance. There were relatively few people on the street. Some kept walking past him when he slowed. Others paused at the curb and waited when he glanced back over his shoulder. But he could feel their eyes on his back as he made his way to the Loop hotel, where he had been staying since his arrival in Chicago.

He took the cell phone from his pocket and contacted the Confidential offices to inform them that he had left Natalie at her condo. He was assured that there would be other surveillance outside her building for the night.

Now that Quint had his assignment to bodyguard Natalie, he would have to find a location closer to her—possibly in her building, preferably in her condo. He wasn't sure how he'd manage that move. She wasn't the kind of woman who indulged in casual affairs. And he wasn't the kind of man who took advantage of his work to stage a seduction.

He smiled to himself. Seducing Natalie was a very pleasant idea.

Walking home with her and checking out the security in her apartment building had put his mind somewhat at ease. All things considered, she was safe in her high-rise condo. A beautiful place with a spectacular view. Though he didn't know much about interior decorating, Quint guessed that somebody professional had arranged the glass-topped dining room table and conversation area in front of the fireplace. All the colors harmonized except for a stuffed parrot on a fake perch in the corner and a colorful painting that looked like a real Chagall. The classy modern decor reminded him of Natalie herself—perfectly polished with hints of humor and passion beneath the surface. He liked this woman. Her ambition and directness made her edgy and interesting. Plus, she was damn fine to look at. Those haunting green eyes…

He turned abruptly and doubled back, passing a man in a suit who stood at the curb and a scruffy-looking teenager who reminded him of the same guy who'd been at the Art Institute this afternoon.

Surreptitiously, Quint tried to memorize their features. If he was going to find out who was following him, he'd have to stop somewhere and wait for them to catch up. He couldn't approach them, couldn't make a grab and start asking questions. For now, it was better to back off and maintain his cover as a lonely cowpoke who didn't suspect a thing.

At the hotel, he paused in the lobby, hoping to keep an eye on people coming through the revolving door. He wanted to see who had been following him. He needed to recognize the face of impending danger.

His attention was immediately distracted by the approach of Gordon Doeller, who waved too energetically as he came across the lobby with the unsteady gait of a man who'd had one drink too many. The angles of his body seemed all disjointed.

"Quint Crawford!" Gordon hailed him. "What a co-incidence!"

"Sure enough is," Quint drawled. He didn't believe in coincidence; Gordon had set up this meeting. "What are you doing here, Gordon?"

"I came over here to check on Prince Zahir. He's staying at this hotel, you know. In the penthouse suite. Man, these guys know how to live."

"Have you worked with Zahir before?"

"Nope, but I've spent my fair share of time in the Middle East. We got to keep our relations good, you know. Keep the oil supply flowing."

Though it was hard to believe that Gordon was any sort of terrorist mastermind, Quint recalled Javid's allegations that someone at Quantum had been secretly buying oil from Imad. Such transactions could have been arranged through Gordon Doeller's marketing office.

In any case, it was worth Quint's time to probe Gordon's alcohol-soaked brain. "How about a drink? Are you in any rush to get home?"

"No rush." His laughter was bitter. "The wife divorced me six months ago."

"Sorry," Quint said.

"Don't be. She's a bloodsucker. Took the house. Took the good car and left me with the SUV. And she wants more."

Gordon was a man in need of ready cash, someone who might be seduced by the promise of easy money. Quint guided Gordon to a table in the bar where he ordered a martini. Quint asked for a beer.

"Tell me about your time in the Middle East," Quint said.

"Come off it, cowboy. I know you've been all over the world."

"Sure have," Quint said. "But I'm mostly just a tourist. Not a businessman like you."

"Or Natalie?" Gordon's eyebrows lifted. "You've been sticking pretty close to her."

"She's been kind enough to act as my tour guide." Quint said. He suspected that Gordon's real reason for this supposedly coincidental meeting was to ask a few questions of his own.

"You haven't given her much choice. It's almost like you're her bodyguard or something."

Gordon's deduction was worrisome. How would Gordon know about a bodyguard? Quint couldn't imagine a leak in the Chicago Confidential operations. More likely, Gordon was just fishing, trying to figure out Quint's motives in sticking like glue to Natalie.

"To tell you the truth, Gordon, there is a special reason I'm keeping so close to Natalie."

Gordon leaned across the table with an avidness that belied his apparently drunken state. "What's that?"

"I saw her photograph in some Quantum literature," Quint said, sticking as close to the truth as possible. "And I couldn't get her out of my head. I guess I've got a little crush on Miss Natalie Van Buren."

As soon as the words left his lips, Quint realized that he was being more honest than he'd intended. He really did like Natalie. More than he'd thought possible.

Chapter Four

The time had come for Nicco to escalate his campaign of terror against Quantum. Conveniently, the CEO had provided an excellent opportunity when he ordered the installation of a security camera in his daughter's office.

Wearing a uniform from Apex Electronics, the company that installed Quantum security equipment, Nicco approached the front desk at ten minutes to six in the morning and handed the guards an official work order, stolen from Apex stock. For weeks, one of Nicco's men had been working for Apex, placing bugging devices in key offices.

Nicco laid on a thick Southern accent. "I'm supposed to get this job done afore the lady comes to work."

"Better hurry," the guard at the front desk said. "That's Natalie Van Buren's office. Sometimes, she gets in real early."

"Yeah? I thought she must be some high muckety-muck to rate her very own security camera in her very own office."

"Boss's daughter."

The guard focused on Nicco, memorizing his face. This was no problem. Nicco had expertly altered his features using actors' makeup and prosthetics to widen his nose and chin. Contact lenses turned his blue eyes to a muddy gray. The shape of his body was changed with the addition of padding to form a potbelly and heavy shoulders. Nicco removed his Chicago Cubs cap to show off his light brown wig for the guard and the security cameras in the lobby.

The guard said, "I'll have to look in your workbox."

"Sure thing." Nicco handed over his satchel, which had also been stolen from Apex and filled with their brand of equipment. While the guards inspected the many parts and pieces, he strolled through the metal detector.

Later, he knew, these films would be studied, enhanced and replayed. To no avail. There were no accurate photographs of Nicco on file anywhere. Not with the FBI or CIA. Not with Interpol. Not with British M6 or the Israeli Mossad. He was the ultimate professional, able to strike in a moment and then vanish like smoke in the wind.

On the other side of the metal detector, Nicco picked up his workbox, allowing the guard to see the fake tattoo on the back of his hand. Then, he stuck the cap back on his head and sauntered to the elevators, accompanied by another armed guard who would unlock the office doors for him.

His arrival at Quantum was timed to coincide with the six o'clock changing of shifts. And he was glad to see the guard checking his wristwatch as he opened the doors and followed Nicco inside Daughter's office.

Working at an extremely slow pace, Nicco blabbed about yesterday's basketball game and how Michael Jordan should've never left the Bulls. The guard fidgeted, wanting to end his shift and get home.

Finally, the guard said, "I thought you were supposed to hurry."

"Well, now. I don't want to make no mistakes. I got to set up and check and recheck and do it right the very first time, don't I?"

"How long is this going to take?"

"Maybe twenty minutes." Nicco carefully removed all the components for the security camera and wall mount. He examined the threads on each screw. "Maybe a half hour."

"Okay," the guard said. "I'm off. Somebody will be up to check in twenty minutes. If you get done before that, just close the door and it'll lock automatically."

Nicco nodded. "Y'all have a nice day."

Overcoming security measures was almost too easy. Left alone in Daughter's office, he deftly assembled an explosive device. His wristwatch contained the timing device and coil. The plastique and detonator came from inside what looked like a camera in his workbox. The explosion would further unnerve Daughter. If fearful, she was more likely to cooperate later.

He fastened the plastique explosive beneath her desk and rigged the timer for fifteen minutes. From inside his padded stomach, he removed a manila envelope, which he placed near the door. His work done, he exited the office.

Passing through the lobby, he waved to the guards. "Sorry, y'all. My equipment don't work. I'll be back later."

The guards barely looked up as he strolled through the revolving door. In eleven minutes, the bomb would detonate, and the fools would realize they should have detained him. Nicco permitted himself a grin of satisfaction as he stepped onto the sidewalk.

Then he saw Daughter. From half a block away, she strode toward the Quantum Building. Her unbuttoned black trench coat swirled around her like raven's wings.

Nicco checked his watch. Ten minutes left. It was long enough for her to enter, ride the elevator and take her place behind her desk in time for the explosion. She'd be killed. Nicco had to stop her. Her death was not part of the plan. Not yet.

"Excuse me," he called out. "Ain't you Natalie Van Buren?"

"Yes?"

"Well, ma'am, I'm from Apex," he drawled slowly. "And I just been up in your office trying to put in a security camera."

She frowned. Her cheeks were as pink as the sunrise skies overhead. Her eyes flashed with impatience. "I don't need a camera, but I understand. You're just doing your job. Thank you."

She started to walk past him, but he stepped in her path. "Ma'am, could I ask you a few questions?"

"Not necessary."

She tried to dodge around him. Nine minutes left. It was still too much time.

Nicco might have to revise his plan, to grab her right now. But his escape route wasn't arranged. His van was parked more than a block away. Improvisations led to errors. There was too much at stake.

"Excuse me," she said. "I need to go inside."

A cab squealed to a stop at the curb. Cowboy stepped out. "Natalie," he said, "how's about some breakfast?"

She rolled her green eyes. "I really must get some work done. Come up to my office, and I'll make you a cup of coffee."

"That's hardly breakfast." He looked directly at Nicco and stuck out his hand. "Howdy, I'm Quint Crawford."

"Nick Beaumont," Nicco said. The alias was not dissimilar to his own given name. Nearly every language had a variation on Nicholas. And Beaumont meant "beautiful mountain"—a pleasant thought.

"Are you from the south?" Cowboy asked.

"Little Rock," Nicco said. "I was just telling this here lady about the security camera I'm supposed to install in her offices."

Cowboy nodded. Though his lazy grin seemed casual and friendly, his gaze betrayed a piercing intelligence, as though he might see through Nicco's disguise. Perhaps Cowboy was more dangerous than he seemed.

"Well, then," Cowboy drawled, "Nick Beaumont from Little Rock, don't you think Natalie should have eggs and sausage with me?"

Nicco glanced at his wristwatch. Seven and a half minutes. "I'd say it's the right time for breakfast."

"All right," Natalie said with obvious exasperation. "There's a diner around the corner. If you don't mind, I'll skip on the sausage cholesterol platter and have a fruit plate."

"Okay by me." Cowboy tipped his hat to Nicco. "Pleasure to meet you."

"You, too."

As Nicco walked in the opposite direction, he realized that his heartbeat had accelerated. With slow breaths, he calmed himself. Cowboy might be a more potent adversary than he had anticipated. Good, Nicco thought. He needed a challenge, a reminder to be cautious.

A block away—beyond the range of security cameras—he climbed into his van. With high-power binoculars, he focused on the twenty-fourth floor of the Quantum Building. Less than a minute to go…

Scout wiggled up close to his shoulder. The dog's wet tongue lapped at the makeup behind Nicco's ear.

Precisely on schedule came the bright orange flash from the initial explosion. It was exactly as Nicco had planned. He started his van. God, he loved his work.

TREMBLING, NATALIE STOOD in the doorway to her office and stared through a stinking miasma left by a fire that had triggered the sprinkler system. Firemen, security guards and plainclothes policemen tracked across her pale beige carpet with footprints of soggy ash. Their loud voices blurred into the mechanical sounds of walkie-talkies and beepers.

The firemen punched holes in her ceiling and walls to access the spiderwebs of wiring and insulation conduits. She wanted to tell them to stop. This was her office. This was the place she went to every day between nine and five. This was her career, the center of her life.

No more.

All that remained were blackened scraps of documents and splintered furniture. A gray, smoky film streaked the windows and walls. Her original painting lay on the floor, torn and smeared beyond restoration. Her desk and the chair behind it were reduced to charred rubble. If she hadn't gone to breakfast with Quint, if she'd been here working as intended, Natalie would be dead.

The stench of destruction coiled tightly around her. Her breathing constricted. Her eyes stung. Dizziness threatened to overwhelm her, and she inadvertently took a backward step, unwilling to go forward and face what might have happened.

Quint stood directly behind her, and she gratefully leaned her back against his broad chest, needing his support. He propped her up. His arm protectively encircled her waist.

He asked, "Should I take you home?"

In the numbed center of her brain, she wanted to acquiesce to his suggestion. At home, she could crawl into bed, pull the covers over her head and hide from those who might hurt her. But would she truly be free from danger at her condo? Someone had attacked her office in spite of the extensive security precautions. Oh God, how could she ever feel safe again?

Turning in his arms, she buried her face against his chest. Her eyelids squeezed tight, but no tears would come. She was too shocked to cry.

"You'll be all right," Quint whispered as he held her. "Nobody's going to hurt you. I won't let them."

Though she had no logical reason to believe him, Natalie felt comforted by his words and his embrace. Twenty-four hours ago, she hadn't even known Quint Crawford. Now, she couldn't imagine facing this disaster without him.

From the corner of her eye, she saw the plainclothes man gesture to Quint. He wanted them out of the way. *But it was her office.* She needed to be here.

Quint shepherded her into the outer office, where Maria Luisa stood, pale and frightened, still wearing her leather jacket from the street.

"Natalie," she said in a quaking voice, "what should I do?"

Quint answered for her. "I'm real sure the police are going to want to talk to you. Maybe we should go upstairs to Henry's offices."

Natalie was aware that her father had not yet arrived at work. It wasn't even eight o'clock. Most of the other executives wouldn't be in their offices for another hour. It was up to her to make the decisions.

Her sluggish brain tried to make sense of the moment. She blinked, willfully erasing thoughts of her devastated office. What came next? She shook her head. *Think, Natalie.* No one else was here. She was in charge. It was up to her to step forward and take responsibility.

If—as she had planned all her life—she would someday be CEO of Quantum, she couldn't be seen as a cowering, frightened victim. In the eyes of her employees, she needed to be strong and decisive. She had to be a leader.

Her spine stiffened as she stepped away from the warmth of Quint's embrace. Fighting the quaver in her voice, she said, "We won't be hiding in Henry's offices. I can handle this situation."

"Are you sure?" Quint asked.

"Yes."

His blue eyes deepened to a steel gray. Dead serious, he said, "You need to talk to the man who's heading up this investigation."

"Yes," she said.

"I'll find him for you."

During the few minutes while Quint was inside her office behind the closed door, she pulled herself together. A familiar mantle of poise settled on her shoulders. She took off her trench coat and carefully hung it in the corner closet behind Maria Luisa's desk. Natalie's hand, where she had touched the charred door frame, was smeared with soot, which she wiped off with a tissue. It seemed very important to clean every smudge.

When the plainclothes man came out of the offices with Quint, she was ready for him. He showed his badge.

"FBI?" She'd assumed he was from the Chicago Police Department. "Why?"

"Special Agent Yoder," he said. "I'd appreciate if you and your secretary step into the hall. We'll take care of things."

"I have concerns," she said. Why was the FBI already involved? What was going on here? "What caused the fire in my office?"

"We won't be able to say until the arson investigators have gone over the scene."

A loud crash echoed from inside her office, and Natalie shuddered. "Why are they doing that? Why are they knocking holes in the walls?"

"Possible electrical fire," said Agent Yoder.

Doubtful. The FBI wasn't called in because of faulty wiring. "The security guards downstairs said they heard an explosion. Was there a bomb?"

Agent Yoder hesitated. "I'm not ready to conclusively state the cause of the fire."

Natalie recognized evasiveness when she saw it. Her assumption, therefore, was that a bomb had exploded in her office. "I'm concerned about the safety of Quantum employees. Is there any danger?"

"I don't believe so."

"But you don't know," she said. "You can't guarantee that there won't be other fires or explosions."

"No, Ms. Van Buren, I can't guarantee."

Natalie turned to Maria Luisa. "We need to evacuate the building. Notify Security."

"Should I tell them why?"

"We don't know why," Natalie said. Until she knew the truth, she didn't want to alarm everyone with bomb threats. "When we have explanations, the information will be made available. In the meantime, I think it's best to close the building so the firemen and policemen can do their jobs. Everybody has the day off."

Agent Yoder cleared his throat. "You might be over-reacting. This fire was out before we even got here. Indications are—"

"I don't care," Natalie said. She was in charge. She knew the right thing to do. With swift determination, she circled Maria Luisa's desk and called the head of Security. "This is Natalie Van Buren. Evacuate the building. Now."

The fire alarm began to shrill.

During the next hectic hour, Natalie arranged for a communications headquarters for herself and a core staff in the banquet room of a nearby hotel. She made hundreds of decisions and fought nearly as many skirmishes with other vice presidents and executives who didn't approve of her actions. Gordon Doeller was particularly annoying.

He hovered over her. "Do you know what you're doing to my marketing plans? Quantum is supposed to be a solid bulwark. What kind of message does it send when we evacuate the building?"

"I can't be one hundred percent sure the building is safe," she said.

"We look like a bunch of damn cowards."

"We look smart," she said coldly. "And alive."

All around them, cell phones buzzed as employees contacted their families and assured them that everything was under control. Natalie hoped their assurances were correct. Though her high level of energy kept her own panic at bay, she kept remembering the devastation inside her office—the soot, the stench, the splintered remains of her desk. She couldn't forget that someone wanted to do her harm.

She thought of the man she'd met on the street, Nick Beaumont. He'd been in her office only moments before the fire. He was the most obvious suspect, and she'd been standing right next to him, talking as if he were a normal everyday person. Was he a terrorist? The very word struck dread in her heart. She couldn't allow herself to think about how near she'd been to danger; there was too much work to be done.

Whenever the fear began to rise, she glanced over at Quint, who had followed her to these makeshift headquarters. He'd been amazing. Subtly and calmly, he had helped direct the Quantum employees. To those who were frightened, he offered assurance. He diffused tension with his cornball jokes, and confronted hostility from people like Gordon.

As if on cue, Quint stepped forward and grasped Gordon's upper arm. "It appears to me that Natalie's got her hands full right now. How about you and me step outside for a talk?"

"Back off, cowboy!"

Gordon tried to pull free, but Quint didn't let go. Instead, he yanked the red-faced marketing director around. The two men were a total contrast. Gordon in his tailored suit and silk tie. Quint in his blue jeans and cotton shirt with the sleeves rolled up on his muscular forearms. There was no question in Natalie's mind about which of them would win this little battle.

Quint drawled, "There's no call for rudeness, Gordon."

"Don't push me! I don't care if you've got a crush on Natalie. You don't have to protect her every minute."

"Is there a need," Quint asked in a low, dangerous tone, "to protect her from you?"

He gasped. Gordon's mouth opened and closed like a fish under water. "Of course not."

"Well, that's real fine," Quint said. "If I found out you were responsible for causing one minute of trouble for Natalie, I would consider it my personal duty to change you from a stallion to a gelding."

He released Gordon's arm with a slight shove, sending

him backward a pace. "Find something useful to do," Quint said.

Retreating, Gordon snapped at Natalie, "Your father isn't going to like the way you've handled things. Did you even bother to talk to him?"

"He would've done the same thing," Natalie responded. "Our first priority is safety."

Soon, she'd find out if she was correct. Only a moment ago, she'd received word that her father had taken a suite at the hotel, and he wanted to see her.

After leaving Jerome Harris in charge, she exited the banquet room and walked to the elevator with Quint at her side. Quietly, she said, "Thank you."

"For pushing Gordon around? Hell's bells, I've been itching to do that."

They boarded the elevator with a group, but they were the only people left as they rode the last few floors to the penthouse level. She smiled up at him and said, "You've been incredibly helpful, Quint. I appreciate that you haven't once challenged my authority."

"I figure it's hard enough to make decisions without having a back-seat driver."

"Very sensitive," she said.

He visibly winced. "Let's keep that our little secret."

"Your sensitivity?" She teased, "Are you scared the other guys will call you a sissy?"

"They better not." He adjusted his belt buckle and stared up at the ceiling of the elevator.

"Quint, are you blushing?"

"No, ma'am. Men don't blush."

On the top floor of the hotel, he held the elevator so the door wouldn't close. They were the only two people in the hallway, and Natalie took her time, slowly brushing past him. It might be kind of wonderful for the two of them to spend some time alone. She'd enjoy peeling away the layers of Texan to find the real man inside.

Side by side they paced the rose-colored carpet. She was

glad for Quint's company as she went into this meeting. At least there would be one person in the room who was on her side.

When Natalie knocked, the door to her father's suite was opened by his secretary, who ushered them inside, then retreated to the bedroom where she was, apparently, working. Henry rose from the brocade sofa and rushed toward her. In an uncharacteristic display of emotion, he hugged her. "Thank God, you're all right."

"I'm fine." The tears she'd been holding back moistened her eyelids.

"When I first heard…" His voice caught in his throat. "I've never been so damn scared in my life."

"It's okay, Henry. I'm fine."

He held her at arm's length, staring into her face as if he hadn't seen her in years. "Are you sure you're all right?"

"Positive." She dabbed at the corners of her eyes. Even now, in a moment of intense emotion, she would not indulge in weeping. That wasn't the way her family worked.

Henry turned on his heel and stalked across the nicely furnished room. Though this wasn't a five-star hotel, the penthouse suite was ornately decorated with Queen Anne style sofa, chairs and coffee table. There was also a bar, and a dining table scattered with documents and a laptop computer.

Henry did not sit. His back was ramrod straight. "Sit down, Natalie. You too, Quint."

The atmosphere in the room had changed. In the blink of an eye, Henry had transformed from loving father to high-powered corporate executive, and Natalie knew better than to disobey. She perched on the edge of the sofa, while Quint sat beside her.

"May I explain why I decided to evacuate the building?" she asked.

"Please do."

"I suspected the fire in my office was caused by a bomb.

There might have been other bombs planted. To avoid putting Quantum Building employees in danger, evacuation seemed the only rational course of action.''

"Why the hell didn't you call me?"

"Everything was happening so fast. I had Maria Luisa keep you informed."

"Maria Luisa is not my daughter. It was your voice I wanted to hear. Natalie, you should have discussed the evacuation with me. You overstepped your authority."

The dual nature of their relationship had never been more obvious. Natalie loved her father. Deep in her heart, she yearned to be a child again, to sit on his lap and make up fairy tales about faraway places. At the same time, she desperately wanted his approval as the CEO of Quantum. She needed validation for her career. No one else's opinion mattered as much.

Lacing her fingers primly on her lap, she realized that she could've done better in this situation. She'd messed up. "I should have called you."

He rocked back and forth on his heels. "There are procedures to be followed in cases of emergency. For example, did it occur to you to close down the Quantum Research Facility?"

"No."

"The facility where your sister works? Did it occur to you that all of those employees, including Caroline, might be in danger?"

Appalled by her own lack of foresight, Natalie shook her head. Increased security measures for other Quantum facilities had not even crossed her mind. There were offices and installations worldwide. Any of them might have been subject to attack. Grudgingly, she said, "Caroline isn't at work."

"So I heard when I contacted the research facility. You don't happen to know where she went on her vacation, do you?"

Now was probably not the best moment to confide her

fears that her sister had taken off to join an eco-cult located somewhere in southern Illinois. What could have possessed Caroline? Natalie couldn't understand how her brainy scientist sister expected to find any sensible answers inside a cult, especially a cult that condemned Quantum and all other oil-related businesses. The Solar Sons might even be responsible for—

"Natalie," Henry snapped. "I sincerely hope your sister hasn't taken off on another one of her environmentalist crusades. Where is she?"

"She's all right. We've been corresponding on e-mail. I'll get word to her about the explosion."

"I can't even control my own daughters." Henry paced across the room to the bar. "How the hell can I deal with a possible bombing!"

Though it was only ten o'clock in the morning, he poured vodka into a shot glass. "Business used to be straightforward," he muttered. "You'd make the best deal, implement operations, and there you were. Now everything is politics, protests and threats. You let me down, Natalie."

Miserably, she said, "I'm sorry."

"Excuse me, sir." Quint rose from the sofa and stepped out from behind the coffee table with its silk flower display. "You're not seeing the whole picture."

Henry turned and faced him. "I'm not?"

"Natalie faced the charred remains of her office. She assessed the situation and took immediate action to protect the safety of your employees."

Henry sipped his vodka. "That's not the point. She should have contacted me."

"Quick action saves lives," Quint said. "Where I come from, Natalie wouldn't be called on the carpet. She'd be celebrated as a hero."

A swell of gratitude spread from her heart and warmed her entire body. It was her turn to blush. She never considered herself to be a hero or, more accurately, a heroine.

That lofty assessment applied to people like firemen or soldiers, not to a vice president in charge of public relations.

"I believe," Quint continued, "that Natalie is one of the bravest women I've ever known."

She watched her father swallow the rest of his drink in a single gulp. His gaze fastened onto her face, and his lips curved in a rueful smile. "Sometimes it takes a stranger like Quint to point out the obvious. I don't tell you often, but you're doing a good job. This morning, you were right to evacuate the building. Better to be safe than otherwise. I'm proud of you, Natalie. Very proud."

She wouldn't allow her tears to leak and spoil this moment. Her father believed in her. He had approved of her actions. "Thank you, Henry."

He set down his glass and rubbed his hands together, anxious to return to the less emotionally-charged arena of business. "Now, we have a lot of work to do."

She was right with him. "I assume you've talked to the security men and Special Agent Yoder about the explosion. Are we looking at a terrorist threat?"

Henry shook his head and frowned. "According to the preliminary investigation, the authorities believe that the fire in your office was caused by faulty electrical wiring."

"An electrical fire?" Natalie doubted that explanation. The destruction in her office centered on her desk and her chair. An electrical fire didn't make sense.

"Apparently," Henry said, "when the man from Apex Electronics came in to install the security camera, he crossed the wires or something."

She glanced at Quint. "We saw that guy on the street."

He nodded. "Nick Beaumont from Little Rock. Average height. Brown hair."

"And a Cubs cap," she said. "He was wearing a Cubs cap."

"We're not sure he's responsible," her father said smoothly. "You'll need to put together the press releases.

You should emphasize that this was an accident. Not an attack.''

"Is that the truth?''

"It's what I've been told,'' he answered.

A lie! For the past several days, Natalie had the off-kilter sense that someone was lying to her. Something at Quantum wasn't right.

Anger flared behind her eyes, burning with absolute clarity. She'd informed the press that the explosion in Quantum's Reykjavik offices was due to a gas leak. *Another lie!* When she asked her father why he was beefing up security, he claimed it was merely a routine update. *Lies, lies, lies!* The presence of an FBI agent at her office should have been the final tip-off.

Slowly, she rose to her feet to confront her father. "It's time for you to tell me the truth, Henry. I'll be careful about what I tell the press, but I need to know. You have to trust me enough to tell me.''

"I trust you.''

"Then, stop lying to me!''

Her father's lips drew into a thin, straight line as he stared at her across a chasm of silence. If he wanted to play a waiting game, fine. She'd stand like a statue for hours before she'd allow him to palm off another easy deception.

Her father expelled a deep sigh. Then he looked away from her. "I didn't want to put you in danger.''

"Too late for that.'' She reined her anger. It wouldn't do any good to snap. "Do we have any idea who's behind the terrorist bombing in Reykjavik and here? Is it Zahir?''

"We don't know,'' Henry said. "There's an undercover operation underway, and the FBI wants us to downplay this incident, to call it an electrical fire while they investigate.''

"Fine. I'll check with you before I issue the press release. Is there anything else I should know?''

Henry walked to the conference table. From the clutter,

he withdrew a sheet of paper. "This is a copy of a note found in your office after the explosion."

She stared down at the familiar stick figure. It seemed to be dancing. The message read, "You can't stop me."

Chapter Five

Even now, more than an hour after he'd seen the message, Quint couldn't forget the taunting image. The stick figure danced in the back of his mind. The crude grin on its face infuriated him. And the message? *You can't stop me.*

The hell I can't. He tensed, ready to attack, to retaliate with all his strength and will. He wanted to track these people down and make them pay. But that wasn't Quint's assignment. His undercover bodyguard job meant he must not draw attention to himself. He must appear to be an easygoing, slow-talking, Texan cowboy.

Fighting his ever-rising sense of frustration, he tried to fade into the background at the makeshift Quantum headquarters in the hotel banquet room. He waited, minute by minute, ready to protect Natalie if necessary. By damn, it was near impossible to hold himself in check.

Every time he looked at her, he wanted to fling her over his shoulder and carry her to safety, far away from this imminent peril. Her father had strongly suggested the same thing, ordering her to take a few days off and leave town. She'd refused. And that came as no surprise.

Natalie Van Buren was the most mule-headed woman he'd ever met. Her big trip to Washington, D.C. was coming up, and she intended to fulfill all her obligations before she boarded the corporate jet and took on an angry energy consortium.

Likewise, when Henry said he wanted her guarded, Natalie declined. After she'd studied the stick figure drawing, which pretty well confirmed that her office had been targeted, she said that she had a message of her own to send: She wasn't scared.

On that count, Quint didn't quite believe her. The way he figured, she didn't *want* to be scared. She wanted to face these threats with her head held high. But fear was unavoidable in the face of escalating danger.

Right now, she was working with her public relations staff, preparing a written statement for the press—pretending like nothing unusual had happened. Occasionally, however, she stood up straight as though startled. She tucked her shining brown hair behind her delicate ear and looked directly at him. And he saw the truth, the ragged edge of terror in her eyes, the slight tremor in her fingers.

He offered an easy grin, reached out to her with nonthreatening support. Her brave struggle filled him with determination. He'd find the bastards who'd done this to her.

At the moment, the hotel banquet room seemed safe enough. A quick survey assured Quint that Henry Van Buren had made good on one of his suggestions. There were four armed security men posted near the exits. Whether or not Henry's daughter approved, she was being guarded.

This might be a propitious moment for Quint to slip away. He exited into the hotel lobby, then to the street. Using his secured cell phone, he contacted Chicago Confidential headquarters, where the receptionist, Kathy Renk, put him through to Vincent Romeo.

"Vincent, I need information on the bomb."

"I don't have much," Vincent said. "From fragments, we're guessing that the incendiary was simple plastique explosive with a wristwatch timer, designed for a small explosion and fire."

"Similar to the device in Reykjavik?"

"On a much smaller scale, the pattern is there. We can

assume the terrorists are here in Chicago. It's the same guys."

Quint had suspected as much, but it was good to have confirmation. "Who are they?"

"Andy has discovered several explosions with the same M.O., but there's no common thread among them. It's his theory that we're dealing with a bomb-maker for hire."

A mercenary. Someone who killed and committed mayhem for cash rewards. In Quint's mind, a mercenary was the lowest of the low. Even a supposed freedom fighter like Zahir had some kind of ethic. "Have you got a name for this guy?"

"Nothing," Vincent said. "Our best lead is the guy who posed as an Apex Electronics technician, alias Nick Beaumont. He timed his arrival for the shift change of the security guards and grabbed a couple minutes alone in Natalie's office, which is when he probably set the bomb."

"We saw him," Quint said. "On the street before the explosion, he stopped Natalie from going directly inside to her office."

"Interesting," Vincent said. "Nick Beaumont didn't want her to be there when the bomb went off. Which is also why he set the explosion for an hour when nobody was expected to be in the building. Just like the explosion in Reykjavik, when nobody was hurt."

Quint couldn't believe the bomber's motivation was altruistic. "Why would he be concerned about casualties?"

"The explosion wasn't meant to start a battle," Vincent said. "It was meant as a warning."

"About what?"

"He'll let us know."

Demands were yet to come. The danger was never over in a campaign of fear waged by cowards. First came the anonymous threats. Now, the explosion had escalated to the next level: Destruction of property. What came next?

Quint asked, "Is Zahir involved?"

"I don't know," Vincent said. "Prince Zahir is under

constant surveillance, and he hasn't made any suspicious moves. If he's involved, it's at a distance.''

"How about Gordon Doeller? Anything on him?''

"We ran computer searches on his finances, and it doesn't look like he's received any payoffs. He's up to his ears in debt. Flat broke.''

Therefore, desperate. Quint had heard the bitterness in Gordon's voice when he talked about his ex-wife leaving him nothing but the family SUV. "Where might Gordon look for ready cash?''

"Telephone and computer records from his office indicate that he's in touch with several persons in the Middle East.''

"But that's his job," Quint said.

"He's also had contact with a man named Greely who is affiliated with that eco-cult in southern Illinois," Vincent said. "I've got Law looking into the Solar Sons. And we're considering the possibility that our bomber might be homegrown.''

"Why?''

"No identification. We had clear pictures of him on security cams at Quantum. When Andy ran the visual profiles, we couldn't find a record. There was nothing.''

An idea occurred to Quint. "Natalie and I had a close-up conversation with the guy. Maybe we could help in the identification.''

"You can't blow your cover, Quint.''

"No problem. I'll bring her over to Solutions to see Whitney. While we're there, we can try out a computer program.''

There was a moment's silence while Vincent considered Quint's idea. Like any government agency, Chicago Confidential didn't like to involve civilians. "I don't know Natalie the way my wife does. How's she taking all this?''

"Like she was born and raised in Beirut," Quint said. "She might look like a spoiled city gal, but she's tough.''

"Let me ask you something, Quint. Is your bodyguard

assignment turning personal? Are you developing feelings for Natalie?''

To be sure, he cared about Natalie. A man would have to be inhuman not to feel compassion for the targeted victim. But he knew Vincent was asking about deeper emotions. Love? Not likely. Quint had already experienced the one true love in his life, and Paula had died. He always believed his heart would stay buried with her…but that was before he met Natalie.

Quint drawled, ''I reckon that's none of your business.''

''Be careful,'' Vincent warned. ''But, yes, you can bring Natalie in to look at the computer imaging for Nick Beaumont.''

''We'll be there this afternoon.''

Quint disconnected the call, glad to have some kind of plan. As soon as he could drag Natalie free, he'd take her to Solutions, then he'd get her to go home where he would watch over her in a safe, self-contained setting. Nothing would harm her. He'd make damn sure of that.

THOUGH NATALIE HAD HOPED to deflect all questions from the press with a simple written statement, the media were not so easily appeased. In the heightened atmosphere of vigilance surrounding possible terrorism, they demanded more. And so, Natalie found herself standing before a podium in the hotel banquet room where a dozen reporters had gathered. Assorted microphones decorated the edge of the podium like a grotesque bouquet.

She glanced over at Quint. Though it wasn't strictly appropriate for him to be here with her, she was glad he'd insisted on staying by her side. Having him close made her feel safe.

Facing the glare of television lights, she was glad she'd combed her hair and applied fresh lipstick. Public speaking had never before frightened her, but right now, her stomach fluttered. She felt strangely vulnerable.

''Ladies and gentlemen,'' she said calmly, ''thank you

for your concern. After a thorough investigation, we have determined that the fire in the Quantum Building was due to an electrical problem, possibly caused by new security measures being installed in our facility. We ordered an evacuation in case the problems were more widespread. I'm very pleased to announce that the Quantum Building has been deemed safe, and we will be returning to our offices within the hour.''

''Who did the investigating?'' came the first question.

''The Chicago Fire Department, the police department's arson division and other experts.''

''Did they consider the possibility of a bomb?''

''The possibility has been considered.'' Natalie was careful not to use the word *bomb*, which could easily be turned into a sound bite on the evening news. Her focus was to downplay suspicions of terrorism without telling any direct lies.

''Has Quantum received bomb threats?''

''As you are all aware, Quantum is a powerful international corporation. As such, we receive our fair share of hate mail.'' Damn! She hadn't meant to refer to the messages. Hoping to avoid more questions along this line, she smiled and joked, ''I guess I ought to be grateful for negative publicity. It's job security for somebody like me in public relations.''

''Who have you received hate mail from?''

''Generally, the author is anonymous.''

''Have you received threats from the Middle East?''

Natalie was confident on this score. ''No.''

''Prince Zahir Haji Haleem is in town,'' said a reporter. ''Has he been in contact with Quantum?''

Though she was glad the questions had moved away from the bombing in her office, this topic was no less delicate. ''We welcomed Prince Zahir at an impromptu reception last night.''

''Does this mean Quantum will be buying oil from Nurul?''

"That decision will be left to our board of directors."

"On Monday, you're travelling to Washington, D.C.," said the reporter from the *Tribune*. "Can you tell us about your—"

"When I return from that trip," she interrupted, "I'll have more information. Again, thank you for your interest in Quantum. Now, it's time for us to get back to work."

She stepped away from the podium, deftly grabbing the briefcase at her feet. Immediately, Quint touched her elbow. They'd planned her exit ahead of time. One of the keys to a successful press conference was a speedy escape.

"Hey!"

At the loud shout from the *Tribune* reporter, Natalie turned.

The reporter demanded, "Who's the cowboy?"

Quint leaned toward the microphone. "My name is Quintin Crawford. I'm the owner of Crawford Oil, and I hail from Midland, Texas."

"What's your opinion on the Quantum fire?"

Natalie stiffened. Quint could blow her carefully worded statements with one offhand comment.

Quint leaned toward the microphones and drawled, "I'm here as a tourist, seeing the sights in your fair city."

"You must have an opinion," the reporter demanded.

"Yesterday at the Art Institute," Quint said, "I surely did like that picture called *American Gothic*. The old fella with the pitchfork reminded me of Uncle Jody, who always told me that if I wanted to stay out of trouble I should keep my nose clean and my mouth shut. I reckon, that's what I ought to do. But thanks all the same for asking."

He tipped his hat, stepped away from the podium and guided Natalie through the exit into the hotel kitchen. Though she appreciated his refusal to comment, she didn't quite believe his cornpone story. "You don't really have an Uncle Jody, do you?"

"Sure do. But he wouldn't appreciate being compared to a farmer."

"Why not?"

"He's a rancher," Quint said. "That's a whole different breed."

"Like you?" she asked, as he led her through the back door and into an alley. "What makes ranchers so different?"

"A farmer is ruled by the weather and the soil—like a city man runs his day by the clock. There's nothing that tells a cowboy what to do. He lives by his own wits, goes his own way."

Though she thought his description was highly romanticized, Natalie recognized a grain of truth. She couldn't imagine Quint taking orders or following rules. He was a law unto himself, whether he was riding the open range or taking long, aggressive strides through a dirty brick alley where the sun never shone. He was so tall that the top of his Stetson almost touched the lower rungs of the iron fire escape scaffolding.

She hurried to keep up with him, but the uneven pavement between Dumpsters snagged her heels. "Slow down, Quint."

"Sorry." He paused beside her and held out his arm. Transferring her briefcase to her opposite hand, she laced her arm through his. Leaning on him might become a habit.

As they emerged from the alley, he hailed a cab and hustled her inside.

"Where are we going?" she asked.

"Solutions, Inc." He gave the driver the address. "I talked to Whitney on the phone on account of she's worried about your safety. And she has a computer program that might be useful."

"No way!" A hundred objections raced through Natalie's mind—not the least of which was annoyance at being whisked away without so much as a decent explanation. "I have work to do."

"Not in your office," he pointed out.

"True, but—"

"Settle down," he said. "You've been racing around since six o'clock in the morning. Let me handle things for the next few hours."

"But I have to talk to Jerome Harris in Accounting about the Washington trip. And I should help Maria Luisa construct a list of what was lost in my office."

"It'll wait," Quint said. "If I were you, I'd give Mary Lou the rest of the day off. The Feds aren't likely to give her access to the office, anyway."

He was right. Natalie flipped open her briefcase and took out her cell phone. Everything could be rescheduled for Monday during the day. Monday night, of course, she and Maria Luisa would be on the corporate jet, winging their way to the meetings in Washington, D.C. Thank goodness, Natalie hadn't lost the important documents and information she needed for that trip. Papers that weren't in her briefcase were backed up on her laptop at home.

After leaving a phone message for Jerome Harris to call her on the weekend, Natalie locked the cell phone back in her briefcase.

"Done?" Quint asked.

"For now." She relaxed, leaning back. The plastic taxi upholstery was probably filthy, coated with germs from hundreds of other passengers. In normal circumstances, she wouldn't have touched it, but she already felt dirty. Her nostrils still stung from the burned stench of her office. All morning long, she'd felt herself perspiring—not from exertion but tension. Panic? Fear?

Natalie allowed her heavy eyelids to close, longing for the wonderful, mindless release of sleep, though it was the late afternoon—there was still too much daylight left.

When she felt Quint take her limp hand in his, she didn't resist. His quiet gesture pleased her. Without speaking, he indicated his uncomplicated, ever-present support. So simple. So gentle.

"You're a good man, Quint Crawford."

"I try."

No other man she'd ever known gave her such a deep sense of security. Instinctively, she trusted him. He asked no questions and made no demands. He was simply…here. At this moment, when she needed a shoulder to lean on, he was here.

"Thank you."

"No problem." He gave her hand a little squeeze, and settled back on the seat beside her.

As the cab jostled through traffic snags, Quint kept one eye out for other vehicles that might be following, but mostly he concentrated on Natalie. He was worried about her. Though her face in repose was lovely, there were signs of exhaustion even more obvious than her closed eyelids. Dark circles beneath her eyes were outlined by the black crescents of her lashes. Her smooth rosy cheeks had faded into a tired pallor. Even her thick chestnut hair seemed limp.

His gaze slipped lower, exploring the vee of her neckline that showed the slightest hint of cleavage from the swell of her breasts. Very nice. Her well-toned body showed the results of her workouts at the gym. He peeked at her stocking-clad legs, neatly crossed. Her calves were firm. Her ankles, trim. Beautiful legs.

She exhaled a deep sigh, drawing his attention back to her face.

When her small pink tongue crept out to moisten her lips, Quint felt an emotion other than concern. He wanted to revive her with a kiss. No words. Just the pressure of his mouth against hers. He wanted to take her into his arms and feel her body come to vibrant life. She'd kiss him back. He knew she would. There was a passion in Natalie that couldn't be hidden by perfect makeup and designer clothes. He knew she'd be a remarkable lover. Her sexy legs would wrap tightly around him and—

Whoa there, cowboy! Quint had no right to slide his fantasies in that direction. It was his job to guard Natalie, not to bed her. He reined in his desire as the cab came to a screeching halt outside the Langston Building.

"Here we are," Quint said as he paid the cab driver. "Solutions, Inc. is up on the penthouse floor."

Natalie peered at him through drowsy half-lidded eyes. "I wanna go home."

"Next stop," he promised. "Right after we try out this new computer program."

"Why?" She dragged herself out of the cab. "I still don't know why we're here."

"I'll let Whitney explain."

When they entered the elegant outer offices of Solutions, Inc., the first sound they heard was a woman's shriek. Alert to possible danger, Quint stepped in front of Natalie, shielding her. His right hand went to his belt buckle, but before he could palm his modified Derringer, Quint heard a male voice muttering, "Look here, Kathy. I didn't mean to—"

"How could you!" Kathy Renk, the receptionist, stormed into the outer office brandishing a stuffed leprechaun as if she intended to strangle the hapless little toy. The front of her white sweater was stained with a huge, wet splotch of kelly green.

As soon as she spied Quint and Natalie, her round face slipped into a chagrined smile. "You've caught me at a bad time. I was putting together a Saint Patrick's Day display and it spilled."

"Saint Patrick's Day isn't until tomorrow," Quint said.

"I know." Kathy gestured to the green decorating her large breasts. "Green food coloring. I was celebrating early."

A very handsome young man in a maintenance uniform strode into the office. He, too, was stained with green. "It wasn't my fault."

"Oh, no?" Kathy's eyebrows raised so high that they disappeared under her bangs. "Weren't you supposed to hold the vase? Weren't you?"

"You arrange flowers like you're chucking spears," he said.

"If I were you, Liam Wallace, I wouldn't tempt me to start throwing things."

Whitney appeared behind them. Though her eyes twinkled with amusement, her tone was cool. "Perhaps we could try for a more professional image, Kathy."

"Sorry." She shot a glare of pure hatred at Liam. "This won't happen again."

After Whitney sorted out all the introductions and sent the maintenance man on his way, she escorted Quint and Natalie into her office. Seated behind her cherry-wood desk, she studied Natalie. "Are you all right?"

"To tell you the truth, I'm dead tired. It's been one hell of a day at Quantum Industries."

"I heard about the…fire." Whitney glanced toward Quint, and he readily picked up the cue.

"Whitney," he said, "you already know about the threatening notes. So, I reckon you might be drawing some fairly logical conclusions about the cause of—"

"Quint!" Natalie interrupted. "I'd prefer not to burden Whitney. This is my problem."

"And I'm sure you'll handle it beautifully," Whitney said. "But let's not pretend that I'm an idiot. You've been getting threats. Then your office catches fire. I'm assuming it's sabotage."

"Might even have been a bomb," Quint said.

Natalie glared ferociously at him, then turned to her friend. "If you asked me directly, I would deny the presence of any explosive device. And so would Quint."

"But there's nothing to keep me from my assumptions," Whitney said. "And I assure you that my lips are sealed, and I have a computer program that might be useful in identifying the man you met on the street this morning."

"The man from Apex Electronics," Quint added.

"Nick Beaumont from Little Rock," she said. "Except

that's an alias, isn't it? My father said they didn't have a real identification for him.''

''Yep,'' Quint said. He knew they were on the verge of breaking cover, but he counted on Natalie's longtime trust of, and friendship with, Whitney to keep her from guessing that he and Whitney were part of an investigating force.

With her green eyes narrowing suspiciously, Natalie said, ''I think this sort of thing is better left to professional investigators.''

''With all due respect to the pros,'' Whitney said drily, ''Solutions, Inc. technology is way beyond state-of-the-art.''

She wasn't exaggerating, Quint thought. The Feds had turned to Chicago Confidential for backup on this investigation. He guided a reluctant Natalie into the prototype computer room, presided over by Andy Dexter. With his wild blond hair sticking up like a cockscomb, his enthusiasm for his work was palpable as he explained, ''Identification by facial features is nowhere near as accurate as fingerprints or DNA, but there are coordinates that don't vary. The distance between the eyes. Triangulation between eyes and center of the mouth and nose and ears.'' He rubbed his hands together excitedly. ''The ears are real important.''

''Don't you need a photograph?'' Natalie said.

''Got one,'' Andy said.

He sat behind the computer and punched a button. The face of Nick Beaumont from Little Rock appeared.

Before Natalie could voice a question, Quint said, ''I told your father about this computer, and he arranged for a photo from the security cam to be sent.''

Though Natalie's mouth pursed doubtfully, she didn't object. ''If you already have a photograph, I don't see how we can help.''

''Think about a disguise like cosmetics,'' Quint said. ''You and me saw this guy up close in the direct sunlight. Maybe you noticed something weird.''

"Maybe *you* did," she shot back.

He grinned. "I'm not real good at noticing another person's makeup, especially not when that person is another man."

Natalie turned toward the computer and stared at the photo. There was quiet in the room but not silence. The faint *whir* and *buzz* of the computers created an ever-present electronic noise. No wonder city folks were so tense, Quint thought. Their ears could never rest. They were always separated from nature by artificial sound and light.

If he could take Natalie to his ranch for a month, even for a week, he could put the roses back in her cheeks, and he'd see a real smile on her beautiful lips. She needed a rest. Like so many totally self-sufficient women, she needed somebody to take care of her.

Pointing at the computer photograph, she started giving Andy information about possible makeup and prosthetics that could widen the cheeks and adjust the shape of a nose. "His complexion is probably lighter than in this photo. He'd darken his whole face to blend the seams between his skin and the prosthetics."

"How do you know so much about makeup?" Quint asked.

"I volunteer at the Lyric Opera once a week." She glanced at her wristwatch. "In fact, that's usually where I am right now. Believe me, those dramatic divas look just like regular women before they put on their stage faces."

Using the mouse, she experimented with the shape of the face on the screen. With each new version, Andy clicked off a copy.

"He had a tattoo on his wrist," Quint recalled. "A bird, I think."

"An eagle with an olive branch," Natalie said, "but I think it was fake. The colors weren't exactly right."

Quint shrugged. Women were always better at colors than men. As far as he was concerned, blue was blue and green was green. Natalie could probably name a hundred variations in hue.

She stepped away from the computer. "That's all I can do."

"Excellent," Andy said. "I'll run comparisons. If I get any matches, I'll notify the authorities."

Whitney came toward Natalie. "Now, let's talk about you."

"What about me?"

"You need to get away from all this. Natalie, I'm worried."

"I can handle it." Her voice was firm. "Monday night, I'm leaving town, anyway."

"Maybe you should cancel your trip," Whitney suggested.

"Not a chance. It's my job, and I'm going to do it. Frankly, Whitney, I'd think you—of all people—would understand. I've never been someone who ran away from her problems."

Whitney's smile seemed hesitant. "There's a difference between being a coward and being sensible."

"I am sensible," Natalie responded. "And I will do my work. No matter what."

STROLLING ON Lake Shore Drive opposite Natalie's apartment building, Nicco wore a business suit and necktie as he casually walked his dog. He watched as Daughter and Cowboy exited a taxicab and entered the building.

Though he preferred not to strike inside such a well-guarded building with limited escape routes, he might be driven to take such chances. Or he might stick to the original plan.

He bent down to scratch between Scout's ears, and was rewarded with a look of pure adoration from the three-legged dog.

"Soon," Nicco quietly promised. "Soon we will live on a beachfront with palm trees."

He counted the time until his retirement in days rather than months. Very soon, it would all be over.

Chapter Six

By the time Quint entered Natalie's condo, his stomach had overtaken his brain. He was acutely aware of one pressing need: hunger. He hadn't eaten since breakfast, and it was nearly six o'clock in the evening. Like a hound dog on the scent of a raccoon, he trailed Natalie across the living room into the large kitchen, where she opened the refrigerator.

He groaned when he beheld the dearth of edibles. "Eggs, milk, olives, O.J., parsley and some tired lettuce," he muttered. "I don't suppose you've got T-bones in the freezer."

"We'll be fine," she said as she whipped open a full-length pantry cabinet beside the refrigerator. "I'm really glad you took me to Solutions. Playing with that identification computer probably won't solve anything, but it made me feel like I was doing something useful for the investigation. Do you think it's true that Whitney's computer is better than the FBI's?"

"Could be." He stared at the ingredients she placed on the black marble countertop. Pasta. Canned artichoke hearts. Albacore tuna. "I could run out and pick up a couple of burgers."

"Not necessary," she said. "Why don't you open the wine? I'd like a nice zinfandel."

He went to the breakfront in the dining room, placed

the satchel he'd been carrying on the glass-topped table and perused a wine rack. There were over a dozen bottles. Natalie was a gourmet who took the trouble of matching the right wine with the meal. He remembered Whitney saying something about how Natalie was a world-class chef, and Quint hoped her perfectionism didn't mean a dinner of snails doused in extra-virgin olive oil.

He eyed her across the pass-through counter that divided the pristine kitchen from the equally tidy dining room. Though she appeared to be in a domestic mode, she radiated the same competent attitude that characterized her work performance. Natalie never let down, always stayed in control.

When he returned to the kitchen with a bottle of wine, she handed him a corkscrew. "I know you're starving, Quint. But I must take a shower before I start cooking. I feel absolutely filthy."

His belly snarled. "Maybe you've got something I could munch in the meantime."

"Crackers," she said.

"Peanut butter?"

Again, she rummaged through shelves. "Here we go. Peach chutney."

Swell. He uncorked the wine and poured it into two crystal goblets, while she prepared a plate of pale white crackers and something that looked like his grandma's preserves and smelled like an old shoe.

Natalie raised her glass to him. "Here's to new friendships."

When his gaze linked with hers, Quint momentarily forgot his empty stomach. She surely was a beauty. He'd thought so from the first moment he saw her photograph at the briefing. "I'm real glad we met."

They clinked glasses. Still maintaining eye contact, they sipped the rosy pink wine. She licked her lips. Her eyes shone like emeralds, and Quint felt a different sort of hunger rising within him.

He fully intended to stay the night at her condo, not leaving her unguarded for a moment, but he hadn't dared to hope he could share her bed. The idea of sleeping with her tasted better than wine.

"This is nice," she said. "Almost like we're on a date."

"Then, I guess we should have some meaningless chit-chat." He cleared his throat. "What do you do to relax, Natalie?"

"I work out twice a week at the gym. Sometimes I jog."

"Oh yeah, that sounds restful."

"I read," she said, taking another deep taste of her wine. "And I listen to music. I go to the opera. I tried knitting but I wasn't good at it."

"And you always like to be the best," Quint said.

"I can't stand being in second place," she said. "How about you? Hobbies?"

"I play the guitar. I even brought my twelve-string along to Chicago."

"I'd love to hear you play." She refilled her wineglass. "I have got to take my shower. My whole body feels itchy."

He almost offered to scratch wherever she wanted him to. Quint was in dire need of distraction. "While you're washing off, I ought to go over your condo with that machine Whitney gave us."

"The bug detector." Natalie eyed him suspiciously. "What's really going on here, Quint? Why would my old friend from boarding school have access to a device that could detect bugs?"

For a moment, he considered telling her the truth about Chicago Confidential and his bodyguard assignment. Natalie was nobody's fool. She was going to figure this out, sooner or later. And she was going to be mighty ticked off that she hadn't been told from the start. She might just throw him out on his ear.

He couldn't take that risk. For now, it was best for him to stay undercover. He shrugged. "I don't know why your old pal would have this kind of equipment. Guess you'll have to ask her.''

"How much do you know about Solutions, Inc.?''

"Enough.'' He hated not being honest with her. "I'm not a high-tech kind of guy.''

"I guess you're not.'' But there was still an edge of skepticism in her voice. "And if there was anything strange going on, you'd tell me. Because we're friends.''

"There's nothing in the world I want more than for you to trust me.'' The deception tasted bitter in the back of his throat. "That's God's truth, Natalie.''

She still didn't seem completely convinced, but she nodded. "I'm going to take my shower now.''

Quint went into the dining area and took a rectangular box from the Solutions, Inc. satchel. Though he had used equipment like this before, he fumbled convincingly. Electronic devices weren't his thing. Given a choice, he'd always pick direct action.

While he started the sweeping for bugs in the dining area, Natalie headed toward her bedroom.

As soon as she disappeared, his hunger returned. There was no good reason why he couldn't start in the kitchen. Balancing the bug detector in one hand, he scooped up a dollop of the peach goo on a cracker. Not bad. It had a spicy flavor like jalapeño jelly. Next to steak, Quint liked Tex-Mex with blazing hot green chili.

The music of an opera wafted through the room as he scooped up more chutney. Apparently, Natalie had put on a CD, an overture by Rossini.

Quint's head bobbed to the energetic beat as he swept through the kitchen and moved to the dining room. In the living room, he was pleased to notice that Natalie had followed his instructions and kept the drapes closed. He found nothing in these areas to hint that her condo was bugged. Likewise, the guest bedroom, bathroom and home office were clean.

He paused at the closed door to the master bedroom.

Beyond this threshold he might discover a more secret part of Natalie Van Buren's personality. Poking his nose in this room made Quint feel like a voyeur.

After a light rap on the door, he slipped inside. Her four-poster bed was covered with a delicate, white eyelet cover that was feminine but not fussy. The walls were lilac, and a matching scent permeated the air. The bookshelf was packed with paperback novels, mostly mysteries and romances. One wall was filled with framed photographs.

Quint finished his sweep quickly and returned to the photos. Most were unposed snapshots. In a collage were several pictures of young Natalie and a smaller girl who had to be her sister, Caroline. They were wearing mouse ears at Disneyland; there were pictures at the beach, on horseback. Oddly, there was only one formal family portrait of the girls as adults. Natalie and her father, both wearing suits, stood behind the sweet-faced woman who must be her mother and a rebellious-looking Caroline with hair sticking out in all directions. Their smiles seemed forced. It looked like their all-American childhood had gone a little sour.

He heard the door to the bathroom open and turned to see Natalie in the flesh, wrapped in a fluffy pink bath towel. Her moist skin was pink from the hot shower. Her damp hair was slicked back from her glowing face.

Quint should have made a joke to disarm this embarrassing moment, but he was stunned into silence and could only stare. Feasting with his eyes, he forgot food. Forgot everything. He was aroused. He wanted to possess her, to make her his own.

She seemed to realize her incredible power over him. Instead of giggling, her voice was low, seductive and teasing. "Well, Quint, did you find any bugs?"

What the hell was she talking about? Insects? He looked down at the sweeper in his hands. *Oh yeah, that kind of bug.* Dumbly, he shook his head.

"If you'll excuse me," she said, "I should get dressed."

"Do you have to?"

Slowly, she walked toward him. Her hips undulated. The edges of the towel loosened. If that scrap of terry cloth fell away, he wouldn't be able to stop himself from—

"I have to get dressed," she said. "I'm sorry."

Not half as sorry as he was. "Natalie, this might not be the best time to mention this, but I don't think you should be alone tonight."

She nodded, then turned away from him. "You can stay in the guest bedroom."

In his role as an undercover bodyguard, he was pleased by her answer. As a man, he felt as desolate as a lone coyote on the prairie, howling at the unreachable silver moon.

THE NEXT MORNING—after a breakfast of homemade streusel—Natalie dressed in a kelly-green sweater, slacks and comfortable loafers. Today, no matter what the threat, she was determined to attend the Saint Patrick's Day festivities. Though she expected Quint to make a fuss about how unsafe it was to leave the condo, he readily agreed.

"It'll be good for us to get outside and blow off the dust," he said.

"Really?"

"Maybe we could pick up a few supplies," he added.

Aha! His real motivation for going out was a search for beef.

Last night, he'd eaten a giant portion of the fresh pasta with mushroom and artichoke sauce she prepared for dinner, but he seemed unsatisfied, repeatedly asking if there wasn't something more, like a burger or a steak or even some jerky. The man was a true carnivore with a voracious appetite. And she suspected he was hungry for more than food.

More than once, she'd caught him watching her with an unmistakable longing in his gaze. Either he'd been considering her as a potential tenderloin or he'd been thinking the same thought that had occurred to her with annoying regularity. Should she invite him to spend the night with her instead of in the guest bedroom?

Natalie wasn't quite sure why she insisted upon their staying apart. Of course, there were professional concerns; it wasn't good business to be intimate with Quantum associates. Also, Natalie wasn't the sort of woman who indulged in casual affairs.

However, late in the evening, while sharing another glass of wine with him, she'd weakened. She allowed her gaze to linger on his chiseled profile. When he turned toward her, she reveled in the breathtaking blue of his eyes.

"Natalie," he'd said. Even his Texan twang was beginning to sound pleasantly melodic. "What are you looking at?"

"You. You're a good-looking man, Quint."

A wry grin lifted the corner of his mouth. "This old cowpoke?"

"This very one," she said.

"Most people tell me I look like something who's been rode hard and put away wet."

A good description, she thought. With his intense—almost aggressive—masculinity, he looked like somebody who lived hard, who faced rugged challenges and didn't mind getting his hands dirty. And yet, he had an appealing streak of sensitivity. At that very moment they'd been sitting in the living room, listening to *Carmen* by Bizet. Quint not only appreciated the music, but was familiar with the arias.

"My late wife," he explained, "liked classical music. She taught this ol' guitar-picker a thing or two."

His late wife. "Tell me about her."

He cocked his head. "Why do you want to know?"

"I'm sorry," she said, cursing herself for being so clumsy. "I want to know you better, but I don't want to open old wounds."

"I don't mind talking about Paula," he said. He described how they met in South America where she was working for the Peace Corps. He laughed when he talked about how his new bride couldn't cook and how she'd plunged into the routine of ranch life, turning every day into a new adventure. His expression darkened when he described her murder.

As she listened, Natalie's wanton thoughts abated. It must have been horrible to lose the woman he loved so deeply. Natalie tried to imagine herself in the same position and failed. She'd never cared so deeply for, and then lost, another human being. The closest she could imagine was losing Quantum. Her job was her only real passion; she'd never allowed herself to fall in love. She envied that ability in Quint. It seemed that he had found his soul mate in Paula, and no other woman could ever take her place.

And that was the problem, the real reason she couldn't allow herself to sleep with Quint. He could never love her best. His one true love was dead.

Even if they made love, Natalie would be relegated to second place, and that wasn't good enough. A mere physical relationship with Quint wouldn't be enough to fulfill her. *What do I want from him?* During the night, the question had plagued her. In brief waking moments between dreams, she envisioned Texas prairies. Her ears echoed with the pounding of galloping horses, a rhythm that accelerated her heartbeat as she imagined herself at Quint's side, riding into endless sunsets.

Fully awake, she knew such a life wasn't realistic. Natalie was a city gal. She loved Chicago. Her idea of nature was a stroll in Grant Park, which was where they were headed this morning to watch the Saint Patrick's Day parade.

Before they left, she checked the weather and decided it was warm enough to wear only a turtleneck and sweater. Then as she headed toward the door, her telephone rang. She glanced at Quint.

"Should I ignore it?"

"Might be important."

She picked up. It was Prince Zahir.

"I regret we had no time together yesterday," he said.

"Regrettable." Though she had no desire to spend more time in his company, it was her job to keep relations on an even keel.

"How did you get my home phone number?"

"One of your staff," he said dismissively. "I don't recall which one."

She made a mental note to track down the culprit. "Was there something you needed from me? Would you like me to set up a meeting or—"

"Perhaps you could join me for dinner tonight," he said. "Or tomorrow."

"Tomorrow would be fine," she dutifully agreed. Until they knew all the particulars on the takeover of Nurul, she ought to maintain a good relationship with the prince.

After they arranged to meet at his hotel at seven o'clock, she added, "I will be accompanied by Quint Crawford. While he's in town, it's my responsibility to entertain him."

"You mustn't lead him on," Prince Zahir advised. "I understand the man has a crush on you."

How would Zahir know anything about her relationship with Quint? "Tomorrow at seven," she said.

Quickly, she hung up the phone and dashed into her home office. "I have one more thing to do, Quint. Then we're out of here."

"Fine." His voice took on that resigned tone that men affect when kept waiting by women.

But this was important. Last night, she'd sent an e-mail to Caroline, and now wanted to see if there was a response. On her home computer, Natalie booted up and clicked to her e-mail page.

There was a message from Caroline. It said:

Heard about the fire at Quantum. Dad must be really mad, losing a day's work from his corporate slaves. Hope you're okay. I'm great, never better.
Love, Caroline

Muttering at the screen, Natalie said, "Yeah, sure. I'm fine. Having my office blown up and getting threats is all in a day's work for us corporate slaves."

Had she mentioned the threat notes to Caroline? Probably not. And even if she had, her little sister was too preoccupied with her scientific research to notice anything else.

Natalie quickly typed a response, telling Caroline that the Solar Sons were creepy and she should plan to come back home as soon as possible.

She signed off, ran to the other room and grabbed Quint's arm. "Let's go."

As they left her building and stepped into the sunlit morning, she inhaled a deep breath of city air. Nothing in Texas could possibly compete with the mingled scents from hundreds of restaurants, the wind off Lake Michigan and sun-baked brick and concrete.

Natalie flung her arms wide to embrace the morning. For the next few hours, she'd try to forget her identity as a corporate executive and simply enjoy Saint Patrick's Day. Grabbing Quint's hand, she pulled him along Lake Shore Drive.

"Hurry up. We want to get a good spot for watching the parade."

He balked, staring across the street at three men wearing green derbies and leprechaun masks. "Is this a big parade?" Quint asked.

"Huge!" She grinned up at him. "With floats and bands and horses and Irish wolfhounds. And step dancers, probably two thousand step dancers."

"Maybe we should avoid the crowd," he suggested.

"No," she said firmly.

"Considering that you had your office blown up yesterday," he said, "dancing around in a huge mob with no special security might not be a good plan."

"It's the only plan," she said. "I'm not going to spend the rest of my life locked up in my condo. If they scared me into hiding, they've won."

"This isn't a contest, Natalie."

"But it is. This is a battle of wills. And I'm going to win."

She did, however, agree to take a taxi to the ornately sculpted Tribune Tower. They got out of the cab and walked over the Michigan Avenue Bridge. Halfway across, she came to a halt. "Now," she said to Quint. "Look down."

The water below was green—bright and beautiful and green as the hills of Ireland.

"I'll be damned," he said. "Does the whole city go crazy on Saint Patrick's Day?"

"Everything turns upside down," she said. "The Chicago River is green. People who walk with a shuffle are dancing jigs. It's a giant party. And did I mention the green beer?"

"And corned beef," he said. "That's an Irish dish, right?"

"Everything with you comes back to meat."

"I'm starving," he said. "Not to disparage your cooking, which is mighty fine, but I need something solid in my belly."

She guided him to a sit-down delicatessen where the celebrating had already begun. All the waiters wore huge shamrocks and green vests. Finally, Quint got his preferred daily portion of beef in a massive corned beef on rye. Though it was only eleven o'clock in the morning, Natalie ordered a green beer.

Between bites, he studied her. "I haven't seen you like this before."

"You really don't know me well," she reminded. "But

you're right. This isn't my typical behavior. I'm usually much more focused."

"Competent and efficient," he said. "I wouldn't have guessed you were a party girl."

"I'm not, but Saint Patrick's Day is different," she explained. "When I was a little girl, Quantum used to sponsor a float in the parade. One year, I got to ride on it and wave to the crowds. I felt like a princess."

Natalie took another swig of her beer. Though she generally preferred a more sophisticated beverage, there was nothing like green beer on Saint Patrick's Day.

"For me," she said, "celebration is required. My mother's maiden name was Murphy."

"But you got your green eyes from your father," Quint said.

"In his case, green is the color of money."

"Interesting comparison." It was the first time Quint had heard her say anything remotely critical of her father.

"Henry was born to be a CEO. He took over the family business when he was in his thirties, and it's the center of his life. There's nothing more important to him than Quantum."

Quint didn't exactly agree. In his opinion, Henry Van Buren's greatest concerns were twofold: doing the right thing, and taking care of his family, especially Natalie. It was tearing Henry apart to do the right thing—keeping their undercover operation secret until the root of the terrorist threat was destroyed—while his daughter was in danger.

"Your daddy is a good man."

"Of course, he is," she said, affronted that he thought *she* thought otherwise. "I'm a lot like him."

"That reminds me," Quint said. "Yesterday, you told Whitney that she ought to know you aren't somebody who runs away from her problems. What did that mean?"

Natalie shrugged. "When Whitney and I were in school together, one of the older girls accused me of trying to steal her boyfriend. A total lie. But I wasn't going to let myself get bullied. I confronted her. It wasn't much of a fight. My sister and I used to have way more vicious battles.''

"But nobody else at school ever again tried to push you around," Quint concluded.

She nodded. "I think it's best to face your problems head-on. Don't you?"

"In theory, I agree. But in practice, it isn't always so. When my wife was killed, I ran away like a scared rabbit. It took months for me to face what happened."

Then he'd gone to the opposite extreme, joining up with Texas Confidential to battle against people who hurt and terrorized innocent citizens.

"And now?" Natalie asked. "Have you accepted your wife's death?"

"I've made my peace," he said.

"But you still think of her. That's why you still wear your wedding ring."

"She was part of me." One of the best parts. He would never forget their love, the magic they had shared.

"Do you think there will ever be another woman for you?"

"Hell, Natalie. I'm not a monk."

"I wasn't asking about sex."

What was she asking about? He wondered if there was a coded feminine message in her questions. Then he decided that Natalie was more direct than most females. If she wanted to make love, she'd look him straight in the eye and tell him. He tried to be equally truthful.

"I'm moving on with my life," he said with more honesty than he'd felt in a very long time. "I've got to admit, Natalie, spending time with you is giving me a whole new outlook."

"How so?"

Because you're different from the other women who pitied me or tried to console me. There isn't a lot of flirting or game playing. You are brave and smart and tough. He smiled at her. "You give me hope."

Her green eyes brightened as she reached across the table and touched his hand. "And now, I'm going to give you a couple of hours of incredible fun."

As they left their table and joined the throngs on the street, Quint was plunged into a bodyguard's nightmare. No matter how often he turned his head and looked around, it was impossible to discover whether someone was tailing them. At any given moment, he and Natalie could be shoulder-to-shoulder with the man who'd bombed her office. Glancing at faces in the crowd, he thought he recognized the man named Greely who ran the Solar Sons' eco-cult. Another man's rectangular shoulders reminded him of Gordon Doeller. What about the so-called Nick Beaumont? Was he here?

Earlier that morning, Quint had used his cell phone to check in with Andy at Chicago Confidential headquarters. From all indications, the current theory with the many agencies involved in this investigation was that Natalie was in no immediate danger. If anything, the opposite was true. The profile and behavior of the bomber had been to protect her.

And if the experts were wrong? Quint knew that her safety came down to him. He couldn't fail. Damn it, all these people! He hoped the crowds would provide their own protection, making it difficult for the terrorists to get close to her.

At Congress Parkway, they crossed over to Grant Park, where the parade down Columbus was already under way. Everything was green, from the twenty-five-foot shamrocks to the blimp overhead. In addition to the fife and drums, there were bagpipers and high school marching bands. Everywhere, the Irish step dancers in colorful dresses or tartan plaids performed their fleet-footed tapping.

"I used to take step-dance lessons," Natalie confided.

"Looks a lot like clog dancing," he said.

"No, it doesn't," she scoffed.

"Sure does."

She stepped back on the sidewalk and struck a pose with arms straight down at her sides. In her loafers, she performed a quick series of intricate steps, then turned to him. "Show me your stuff, cowboy."

This was one challenge he didn't need to back down from. He settled his Stetson firmly on the crown of his head, hooked his thumbs in his belt loops and started up stomping in his cowboy boots.

The crowd around them took notice of their small contest and formed a circle as Quint ended with a *whoop*. "Top that, lady."

"No problem," she said. Natalie leaped high with toes pointed in a graceful jig. She tossed back her head, sending ripples through her hair. Her green eyes flashed.

He responded with a heel-and-a-toe and a do-si-do. The crowd applauded, and he tipped his hat.

A vendor in the crowd presented Natalie with a bumper sticker that read: Kiss Me, I'm Irish. She tossed him a dollar, peeled off the backing on the sticker and slapped it across her chest before she returned to her jig.

With her hair and makeup mussed, she was just about the cutest thing Quint had ever seen. He admired Natalie for her courage and decisiveness, but this giggling, dancing woman was purely adorable. "Excuse me," he said, coming closer to her. "Does that sign say, Kiss Me?"

"It says, I'm Irish."

"I'd better take a closer look."

She puffed out her chest. "Irish!"

"Kiss me." He grabbed her around the waist and twirled her around so fast that her feet left the ground. Around them, the crowd was laughing. Quint felt as if he had their blessing. Not that he needed approval from anybody else to kiss this vivacious lass.

He gazed into her upturned face and gently nuzzled her cheek. A harmless little peck.

But Natalie had other ideas. She held his face between her two hands and pressed her lips against his for a *real* kiss that sent an electric jolt through his body.

He could do better than that. A lot better.

Quint removed his Stetson. He wrapped his arms tightly around her, molding her body against his, crushing her breasts against his chest.

His mouth claimed hers with a hard, fierce possessiveness. Her mouth opened to him, and his tongue sought the slick sweetness within. His body came alive as she pressed against him, arching her back. Her legs tangled with his. This was more than a kiss; it was a prelude to something amazing, the dawn of a brand-new day. Excitement crackled through his veins. He was aroused.

The kiss continued, longer and deeper than he'd intended. His breath backed up in his lungs, and he felt he was going to explode, but he didn't want to let her go, didn't want this moment to end.

As if from a distance, he heard the crowd applauding and cheering them on. Far from sharing a private moment, he was making a public spectacle of himself and a corporate vice president of Quantum Industries. He ought to be ashamed. But nothing in his life had ever felt so right.

He ended their kiss with a sheepish smile, glad to see the bedazzled look in her eyes when she gazed up at him. He leaned toward her and whispered, "Is that what you wanted, Irish?"

"Oh, yes." She leaned away from him and waved to her new fan club. "Happy Saint Patty's Day!"

In Quint's eyes, the whole world was a beautiful green blur. The spring buds had begun to leaf on the trees in Grant Park. The streets and the rivers were green—the color of new life.

He watched with a grin as another troop of Irish step dancers paraded past them on Columbus Street. The music of marching bagpipers vibrated in time with his thrumming heart. He felt like singing.

Natalie held tightly to his hand, pointing at the revelers. ''Look!''

Before them on the street were a lovely group of long-haired, flower-draped Celtic maidens leading a handsome white steed with a horn fastened to his forehead like a unicorn. The horse stepped high and graceful, showing off dressage training.

Others in the crowd had started their own jigs, and Natalie was pulled away from him in an energetic polka. Quint didn't mind the intrusion. He enjoyed watching her as she danced and swirled, holding hands with one young man, then another.

They darted into the street with the costumed dancers, then emerged on the other side. Natalie's head was thrown back, and he heard her laughter above all the noise.

But they were moving farther away from him—

Sudden alarm streaked through him. He couldn't see Natalie.

Then he spied her green sweater. Between the thick tree trunks on the opposite side of the parade, two men were pulling her. A kidnapping!

Chapter Seven

From the parade route, the pipers' music played on. Natalie's Irish jig became a life-and-death struggle. She fought to break free from the two men who flanked her. Each of them clamped her upper arm in a tight grip. She couldn't move! There was a painful jab in her rib cage. She looked down and saw the gleam of a handgun.

"Come quietly," said the man on her right, "and no one will be hurt."

"If you scream," warned the other, "others will be killed."

My God! Is this really happening? Her frantic gaze took in the scene at Grant Park. Thousands of people—innocent men, women and children—celebrated Saint Patrick's Day. If the gunmen fired into the crowd, there would be panic. Death from their bullets. Death and injuries from the stampeding crowd.

Natalie couldn't allow herself to be responsible for these murders. "I'll do as you say."

"Very smart."

Her heart hammered wildly, driven by the surge of adrenaline through her veins. She felt light-headed and weak. *No good!* She had to be strong, to use her self-defense training. How could she? Her arms were helpless against the combined force of her captors. Her legs staggered. She couldn't remember a single move. Everything was a blur. *Focus, damn it!*

She'd always known something like this might happen. She'd prepared herself physically and mentally, but the brutal reality was far different from the safety of the gym with mats cushioning the hard floor. This was real life— and ultimately dangerous.

She willed herself to concentrate, to clear her mind of terror and visualize the techniques required to free herself. Her muscles tensed.

"Calm yourself," one of the men ordered.

Resolve flowed through her. She would escape. These men would be apprehended. The threats against her and against Quantum would cease.

Natalie studied her captor. Memorizing his features, she carefully searched for possible signs of a disguise. His hair was sandy brown and curly. Eyes, gray. His nose was crooked. Average height, average weight. He seemed to be in his late twenties and didn't look at all like a terrorist. The same was true for his companion, who had an olive complexion and a neatly trimmed mustache. Neither of them resembled Nick Beaumont from Little Rock. Was he the mastermind? The commander?

A technique she recalled from self-defense classes was negotiation. She should try to talk herself out of the situation. "Who are you?" she asked.

They said nothing. The fact that neither of the men was hiding his face did not bode well for her continued survival. If she could pick them out of a lineup, how could they release her? *Oh God, I don't want to die.* Fear crashed around her, shattering her tenuous grasp on clarity.

Suddenly clumsy, her feet stumbled over the root of a tree, and the men roughly yanked her upright, propelling her toward the booths that would be used for the celebration at the end of the parade route. They were headed across the park toward Lake Shore Drive. Most likely, a car would be waiting.

Again, she tried to talk to them. "If you let me go, I'll pay you. I'll forget this ever happened."

Again, no response.

"Tell me what you want," she said. "Please. Please tell me."

"You'll know soon enough," said the man with the mustache.

"Shut up," his companion snapped.

They were in an open area less than a hundred yards from the street where traffic streaked past. With her legs turned to rubber, it seemed like an impossible distance. At the same time, she might be taking her last steps and so she wanted the field to go on forever.

A sob caught in her throat. "Why me? What have I done to you?"

No answer.

The farther they got from the parade, the more the crowd thinned. Natalie and her captors were only fifty yards from the street, half a football field. If they got her into a car, she'd have no chance for escape. She needed to act now!

She gave vent to frightened tears that weren't entirely an act. "Please, stop! I can't take another step."

The gun poked against her side. "Keep walking."

"I can't," she wailed. "I'm afraid."

As her body sagged, she kicked hard. Her feet connected with the shins of the man on her right. As he went down, she used her leverage to pull the second man off balance. Linked together, they fell to the ground in a heap.

Her right arm was free. She flung her body back and forth, separating from the second man. Then she was standing, facing the man with the mustache. He was on his knees. He held a gun, aimed at her midsection.

Coldly and menacingly, he whispered, "You shouldn't have done that."

If he fired a shot, the sound would attract attention. There was a battalion of Irish cops marching in the parade.

On the other hand, if shot at point-blank range, she'd be dead.

"Don't move," he ordered.

Natalie froze. Though she'd learned all the requisite moves, she doubted her ability to disarm him with a flying karate kick. She'd already hesitated too long. "I fell," she said.

The other man groaned. "She kicked me. My knee—"

"Get up. Let's go."

She should act now! While the gunman's attention was diverted toward his partner, she should—

Bursting through the festival tents came a man on horseback.

Natalie's eyes widened as she stared at the gleaming white steed. The horse was draped in chains of flowers with a horn affixed to its forehead. A unicorn! The long mane flowed majestically. Quint rode toward them at a violent gallop.

The gunman turned, scrambled to his feet. He braced his weapon with both hands. Before he could fire, Quint charged into him, knocking him to the ground. As the second man took aim, Quint whirled on his horse and fired a pistol so small it was nearly hidden in his large hand. His aim was true. The curly-haired man dropped his weapon and gripped his shoulder.

Without firing again, Quint leaned down, grabbed her beneath her arms and scooped her off her feet. He dumped her facedown across the front of the unsaddled horse.

"Hang on," he shouted as they thundered across Grant Park.

At the sound of gunfire, Quint ducked low over her body. Somehow, he managed to ride bareback, hold on to her and talk on a cell phone simultaneously. His voice was crisp. "Headed toward Shedd Aquarium. Request pickup. One suspect down. Move in."

"What the hell is going on?" she demanded.

"Hold tight, Natalie."

Flopping on the unicorn's back like a sack of flour, she had no other choice. With one outstretched hand she clung to his thigh. The blood rushed to her head. Her cheek bounced against the flank of the horse. Had she really been rescued by a cowboy riding a unicorn? She must be losing her mind. This couldn't really be happening.

At the edge of Lake Shore Drive, a mounted policeman met them. Quint leaped from the horse and hauled her down. Her feet hit the ground with a jolt and she realized that she'd lost her loafers in the wild ride. Her head was spinning. Her stomach churned. Oh God, she was going to vomit.

Quint nodded to the policeman, who gave him a quick salute and accepted the flower reins of the unicorn.

Natalie glanced over her shoulder. Some distance away, she saw other officers—and someone who looked like Agent Yoder—converging on the injured gunman.

Gently, Quint took her arm and guided her into the rear of a limousine. Breathing hard, she slumped against the leather seat. Her eyes were wide open, staring.

"Are you all right?" Quint asked.

"None of this is real," she said. "It's impossible."

"But you're okay, aren't you? No broken bones?"

"I don't know." She moved her arms and legs. There were aches. There would be bruises. "It felt like I was going to throw up."

"Should we pull over?"

She thought for a moment. "I'm okay now."

Taking off his Stetson, he slipped on a headset and pulled out a retractable shelf equipped with a laptop computer. Tapping a few keys, he brought up a picture that looked like an aerial view of Grant Park. He zoomed in for a tight shot of the activity in the open field where the police were taking the man with the curly hair into custody.

Natalie was mesmerized by the computer screen.

"Where is this picture coming from? How are you doing this?"

"Satellites and other security cams. I don't know exactly how it works," he said. "In this situation, an overhead view isn't much good. There are too many trees in the way."

"Amazing."

"That's the right guy, isn't it?"

She stared at the video. It looked like something she might see at the movies, but she recognized the curly-haired assailant. Bitterly, she said, "That's one of them."

He spoke into the headset. "Second suspect might be limping. I hit him pretty hard."

He switched the zoom focus to the festival grounds, then to the parade itself. Into the headset, he said, "Negative. Can't pinpoint him."

"Who are you talking to?" she demanded. Something very odd was going on here, and she wanted some answers.

When he turned to her, there was no evidence of the laid-back cowboy. His attitude was all business. "You need to help me, Natalie. Can you describe the second man?"

"Average height, maybe five foot ten. Skinny. Straight black hair. A mustache. Thin face. Almost no chin at all."

Using a computer program similar to the one at Solutions, he created an approximate replica of the man's face. "That's pretty close," she said.

Quint again spoke into the headset. "Transmitting witness identification now."

As he concentrated on the task, Natalie observed the man she'd known as Quint Crawford—oilman and cowboy from Midland, Texas. To say the least, he was different. Efficient and capable, he performed with high-precision professionalism as he pounded the computer keys and gave crisp reports about surveillance and apprehension of suspects. Was he a spy? James Bond in a cowboy hat?

Gradually, the truth dawned upon her. Whenever she and Quint were on the street walking, his gaze was constantly busy, searching faces in the crowds. When he'd rescued her in the park, he'd been armed and amazingly capable. From the moment they'd met, he'd stuck to her side like Velcro. Why? Natalie had flattered herself by believing his attention was due to an attraction. Not so!

He stayed close to her because that was his job. Quint Crawford was a bodyguard.

And who did he work for? She glanced at the computer—so similar to the one in Whitney's office. Natalie remembered her suspicions about the bug sweeper and her old friend's concern for her safety. Solutions, Inc. was somehow involved.

A slow anger simmered in her belly as she added two and two. Her dear old friend Whitney and Quint and even her own father had conspired behind her back. Why hadn't they told her the truth?

Quint removed the headset and slid the computer to one side. As he turned his attention toward her, Natalie muttered, "I suppose this is the part where I'm supposed to fall into your arms, flutter my eyelashes and tell you that you're my hero."

He grinned. "I wouldn't mind one bit."

"Don't hold your breath, cowboy. You're a bodyguard, aren't you?"

"Sometimes."

Quint leaned forward, rested his elbows on his knees and rotated his shoulders to relieve the tension in his back. He hadn't rode bareback since he was a kid. Rescuing her like that had been a crazy stunt, and he was damn lucky that he'd succeeded. If he'd failed, they might both be dead.

"You lied to me," Natalie said.

"I suppose I did."

He leaned back against the leather seat, closed his eyes and allowed the enormity of what had just happened to sink into his consciousness. When he'd seen Natalie trapped between those two cowardly bastards, his blood had raced like wildfire through his veins. He hadn't thought of danger, hadn't worried about the proper procedure in contacting backup. He became a primitive, ferocious, single-minded hunter. A warrior. His only aim was to rescue her. If she'd been hurt, he would've rained death on his enemies.

Quint knew—better than almost anyone else—what it was like to lose someone beloved to violence. After Paula was killed in the white skies over Texas, he died a thousand deaths with every day he missed her, every morning he woke to an empty space on her side of the bed.

He felt Natalie's hand on his shoulder. "Quint? Are you okay?"

"Fine," he said.

"You're shaking."

From fear, the fear of losing her.

He swallowed hard, digesting the countless tears he'd shed over his wife's untimely death. But when he opened his eyes, it was Natalie's face he saw.

Her beautiful green eyes shone with concern. Her lips, slightly parted, seemed unsure whether to smile or growl. She was different from Paula in a hundred ways. Yet, the sight of Natalie, the scent of her perfume and the sound of her voice awakened a strange tenderness he'd never expected to feel again.

"I'm glad you're all right," he said.

"And you?" she asked. "Are you hurt?"

Looking at Natalie, knowing that she was alive and well, he felt the soul-deep pain beginning to heal. "I'm just fine."

"Good." She straightened her shoulders. "Because I'm going to kill you."

"Answer a few questions first." Though trying to be a good agent, he wanted only to brush a wisp of hair off her cheek and kiss her behind her ear. "What did those guys say to you?"

"Not much."

"Any hint of why they grabbed you?"

She shook her head. "They said I'd find out soon enough."

"I don't suppose they called each other by name."

"No." She peeked through the window. "Where are we going?"

"To your condo. Somebody will be waiting to take care of you."

"You're not going to get rid of me so easily, Quint. I'm sticking with you. And I expect you're going to Solutions, Inc. Correct?"

"How did you know that?"

"Logic." She tapped the side of her head. "If you people won't tell me the truth, I have to figure it out for myself."

"It might be better for you to rest," he said. "You're probably full of bumps and bruises. A doctor should check you out."

"I'm fine. And I'm coming with you."

Instead of arguing, he spoke through the intercom with the driver and gave instructions to drop them off at the garage level at the Langston Building.

As they rode in silence, Natalie continued to stare through the tinted windows at the happy faces of Saint Patrick's Day celebrants. Inwardly, she seethed. These lies were a slap in the face to her professionalism. All these people, even her own father, had treated her like a child who couldn't be trusted. Thank goodness she hadn't slept with Quint last night.

In the underground parking garage, she threw open the door of the limo and charged out, immediately stubbing her toe. Maintaining her dignity was difficult in her stocking feet, but Natalie held her head high as she strode across the concrete floor.

When the door to the elevator whooshed closed, she glared at Quint. "Aren't you even going to pretend that you're sorry?"

He adjusted his Stetson. "Nope."

Infuriating man! "Where'd you get the gun?"

He hitched his thumbs in his pockets. "Belt buckle," he said.

"Of course." She'd known that huge silver discus was lethal. "Any other weapons I should know about?"

"A knife in my boot heel. The silver band on my hat can be used as a garrote."

When other people joined them on the elevator, she noticed how Quint moved closer to her, subtly protecting her. An hour ago, she might have misinterpreted his actions, thinking he wanted to be near her for personal reasons. Now, she knew the truth.

At the Solutions offices, Natalie marched through the door, passed the empty receptionist desk and went into Whitney's office. Her friend popped up from behind her desk. Standing at the window was a dark, handsome man dressed all in black. He turned as they entered and approached her with his hand outstretched.

"You must be Natalie. I'm Vincent Romeo."

Though she shook his hand, Natalie made no pretense of friendliness. "You're the director of Solutions, Mr. Romeo. I demand an explanation."

He matched her bluntness. "There's nothing you need to know. We're handling the situation."

"Are you? Thus far, I've received seven threatening notes. My office has exploded. And I was snatched in Grant Park. If you think this is how to handle a situation, I suggest you think again."

"But you're still alive," he pointed out. "That might be considered a plus."

His dark, smoldering looks were the very opposite of Whitney's redhead complexion and her well-bred manner. At first glance, they seemed to be an unlikely match, but

Natalie understood why they'd been attracted to each other. He gave her sexiness. She gave him class. No doubt, their children would be gorgeous.

This was not, however, a social call to congratulate the newlyweds. Natalie repeated, "I want to know the truth about your operation."

Vincent reached across Whitney's desk, picked up a brochure for Solutions, Inc. and handed it to Natalie.

"Not that," she snapped. "Your other operation. The undercover work."

He challenged her. "Give me one good reason why I should tell you anything more."

From behind her back, she heard Quint clear his throat. "You know, Vincent, I think we should—"

"Excuse me." She cut him off. This was a battle she could fight on her own. "Here's your reason, Mr. Romeo. I'm in public relations. With three or four phone calls, I can have reporters crawling all over these offices, demanding to know the real job of Solutions, Incorporated. Gosh, I might even get you on Oprah."

"As I was saying…" Quint stepped up beside her. "We need to tell Natalie what's going on."

"Might as well," Whitney said. "She's going to be a pain in the butt until we level with her."

Vincent Romeo regarded her with a cool dark gaze. "You're different from Whitney's other friends."

"I'm smart. I'm tough. And I'm determined." Natalie stared back at him. "I'm also fair. If you cooperate with me, I won't cause trouble."

His gaze flitted between Quint and Whitney. Though they had both vouched for her, Vincent still seemed reluctant. Seeking to reassure him, she said, "As part of my job, I am required to keep certain information undisclosed. You can trust in my silence."

"Okay, Natalie." Vincent crossed the room and closed the office door. "You've already figured out that Solutions is a front."

"But not a fake," Whitney said. "Solutions does excellent work when it comes to computer consulting for businesses."

"I'll vouch for that," Quint said. "They really have updated and streamlined the systems for my ranch."

When she looked up at him, a burst of conflicted emotions flashed before her. She'd trusted him. She'd completely believed in his cornball cowboy act and had gone beyond his shield of humor to find a sensitive man—someone she cared about.

And it was all a lie.

Though she directed her question to Vincent, it was meant for Quint. "Who are you, really?"

"Chicago Confidential," Vincent said. "We're a branch of the Federal Department of Public Safety. The Confidential program started in Texas, operating strictly undercover to research and reveal illegal operations. Our agents are unique because most of them have other occupations, other lives. We call them in for specific assignments."

"Like Quint," she said. "He really is a Quantum supplier...and a cowboy from Texas."

"Was there ever any doubt?" Vincent gave a slight ironic smile. "Do you have other questions?"

"Specifically, what is your current assignment?"

"Terrorist activity."

"Based on threats against Quantum?"

"Yes," Vincent said.

"Starting with the explosion in Iceland."

"Correct."

Natalie inhaled a deep breath. Extracting information from Vincent Romeo was like reading the fine print on a contract—too much was left unsaid. "Who's behind these threats?"

"We don't know."

Whitney interjected, "Catching the guy in Grant Park could be a major coup. If he talks, he might point us in the right direction."

"Do the officers in the Park work for you?"

Vincent frowned and shook his head. "We're coordinating with the FBI, the Chicago PD and other antiterrorist units."

"I'm a little confused," Natalie said. "How is Chicago Confidential involved?"

"Through our specific research capabilities and our undercover agents, like Quint. Don't ask me to reveal other names."

His tone reminded her that she was still an outsider. Fine. Knowledge of the inner workings of an undercover investigation was beyond the scope of her job description. However, like it or not, she'd been targeted.

"Why are they coming after me?"

"Again," Vincent said, "we have conjecture, but we don't know for sure until we hear the demands."

Another possibility occurred to her. "Was I a suspect? Is that why I wasn't told the truth?"

Quint said, "Nobody ever doubted your loyalty to Quantum. But we reckoned there might be somebody inside the company who was tied in with the terrorists."

"Who?"

Quint shrugged. "We still don't have definite answers."

Damn him for being so reasonable! He never argued with her, never raised his voice above a low, sexy drawl. She glared at him. Did his eyes have to be so darn blue? Even now, a grin touched the corner of his mouth. Was he remembering their kiss in Grant Park? Was he laughing at her?

She turned away from Quint and spoke to Vincent. "Is Prince Zahir involved?"

"He's a suspect. So is Sheik Khalaf Al-Sayed. And Greely from the Solar Sons."

"The Solar Sons," Natalie said. That was the group Caroline had gotten involved with. "Do you seriously believe they're involved in terrorism?"

"We haven't ruled them out," Vincent said. "Listen,

Natalie, I can keep you updated on developments, but this is an ongoing investigation. I won't promise minute-by-minute reports.''

"What about the guy who might have set the explosion in my office? Nick Beaumont from Little Rock?''

"No positive ID,'' Vincent said. "Natalie, do you really want to know more?''

She paused to consider. At this point, she'd been given the basics. Her options were to walk away and allow these people to do their jobs or to become more seriously involved in their operation.

Frankly, she had more than enough to keep herself busy. Day-to-day operations at Quantum were a full-time job. Plus, there was the fallout after the fire, and the Washington trip coming up on Monday evening.

On the other hand, she might hold a key to rooting out these terrorists.

"A moment ago, you asked why you should level with me,'' she said. "Here's the best reason I can think of. I can help.''

Vincent's brow lowered. "Not necessary.''

"Nobody knows the inner workings at Quantum better than I do. Also, these people seem to be focusing on me, for some reason.''

"She has a point,'' Whitney said.

"Bring me into the investigation,'' Natalie said, "and you won't be sorry. I have only one stipulation.''

"What's that?'' Vincent asked.

She avoided looking at Quint. "I want a different bodyguard.''

The tension in the room was palpable to Natalie. She wondered if Vincent and Whitney could feel the crackling energy.

"Why?'' Vincent asked.

Because he kissed me. Because he made me care about him. Because he might be the man who could break my heart. "He's intrusive. It's just not a good fit, okay? We don't work well together."

She heard Quint chuckle. In his heavy drawl, he said, "Miss Natalie, that dog don't hunt."

"Spare me the down-home humor."

Quint opened the office door. "Vincent and Whitney, would you please leave us alone for a moment."

As the newlyweds left the room, Natalie gathered her resolve. This would be the end of what might have been a relationship.

Gently, Quint took her shoulders and turned her toward him. "What's this about? I want the truth."

"You're a fine one to be talking about honesty. Every minute we've been together has been a lie."

"Not exactly. I couldn't tell you I was your bodyguard because you refused protection. Also, when I'm under-cover, I play up the cowboy role so people won't suspect me of being anything else. But that's not a lie. It's part of who I am."

He touched her chin and tilted her head up so she couldn't avoid looking directly at him. "Natalie, where's the deception?"

"You led me on. I believed…" She'd believed he cared about her. She'd believed there was something deep and sensitive and—God help her!—romantic between them. How could she tell him those things? It was too humili-ating. "Let's just forget it. Vincent can assign another agent to be my bodyguard."

"I'm not dropping out," he said. "I'm accepted at Quantum. There are leads I'm pursuing, and it would hurt the investigation for me to quit now."

His words confirmed her fears. The only reason he wanted to stay with her was dedication to his job. "I don't want you around me."

"That's just too damn bad because I'm the best there is, and I won't entrust your safety to another agent. If anything happened to you, Natalie, I couldn't take it."

"As if you care about me."

"I tried not to. When my wife was killed, I swore I'd never allow another woman to touch my heart, but you reached inside my chest and grabbed me hard."

"I did?" A strange excitement fluttered inside her.

"From the first minute I saw your photo at a briefing," he said, "I knew you were special. Then I got to know your courage, your loyalty, your inbred sense of honor. I even like your snooty attitude."

"You do?" She felt like the office was suddenly awash in brilliant sunshine.

"I won't back off this assignment," he said. "I'm your bodyguard. And there is no way on God's green earth that I'm going to let another man spend the night in your condo. Is that understood?"

"Completely."

She threw her arms around his neck and kissed him for all she was worth.

Chapter Eight

Natalie had made such a big deal about learning the entire truth that she couldn't very well turn her back on Vincent and make a mad dash for her condo, where she could be alone with Quint, exploring this wonderful new connection between them. No matter how much she wanted to, she couldn't ignore the threats against Quantum or herself, couldn't disregard her responsibilities. And so, she tried to concentrate as Vincent and Whitney showed her the computerized marvels of Chicago Confidential.

The special-operations room—with interconnected laptop computers built into the conference table—was truly impressive. Natalie should have been amazed by the screens, switches and knobs, the state-of-the-art communications. But all she could think about was Quint. Being held in his arms made her feel truly feminine...but not in a ruffles and froufrou way. She felt like a real woman, a quintessential female, eager to offer herself to him and be overwhelmed, ravished, devoured....

"On this screen," Whitney explained, "we have instant satellite access, providing overhead surveillance based on longitudinal coordinates, similar to Global Positioning System technology."

Dragging her attention back to the matters at hand, Natalie asked, "Can you see anything, anywhere in the world?"

"Weather's a problem. We can't see through heavy cloud cover or storms." She gestured to another piece of equipment. "This provides updated intelligence around the world, sorted by topic and time. This computer provides its own hacking devices."

"With all this equipment," Natalie said, "it seems impossible that you still don't know who's coming after Quantum."

"That's why we use undercover agents," Vincent said. "No amount of technology can account for the unpredictability of human action. Like Quint rescuing you on horseback."

She smiled at him. Her hero! The tall, lanky cowboy with his honeyed drawl and his sexy blue eyes had none of the qualities she looked for in a mate. And yet, he was perfect.

His gaze locked with hers, steady and somehow possessive. She remembered the tremor that had gone through her when he said he wouldn't allow another man to spend the night in her condo.

But now he was more businesslike. "Our conclusion," Quint said, "is that the bomber who attacked Quantum is a hired contractor."

"Nick Beaumont?" she asked.

"He's numero uno on my suspect hit parade," Quint said. "First we apprehend him, then we go after the person or group who hired him."

"I still don't understand why they're targeting Quantum," Natalie said. "What do they want?"

"Until they make demands, we don't know what they want."

Whitney pressed a few computer keys and displayed a photograph of a man who was familiar to Natalie. "Hutch Greely."

"Leader of the Solar Sons," Whitney said. "Though they haven't been officially accused of eco-terrorist tactics, they've been suspected in a couple of bombing incidents."

Natalie frowned, immediately thinking of her sister, Caroline. "I can't imagine the Solar Sons are capable of something as complex as a bombing in Reykjavik."

"But they might have hired someone who would use such a tactic," Whitney said. "And they have a contact inside Quantum. Gordon Doeller."

"How do you know this?"

"We checked his phone records and his e-mail. He's been in touch with Greely."

Apprehension crept over her. Though Natalie had received an e-mail from Caroline saying that she was fine and would be back in Chicago soon, she hadn't spoken to her sister. Had Caroline's well-meaning passion for the environment led her into danger? "Now you've got me worried about Caroline. I know she went downstate with the intention of visiting the Solar Sons."

"So, she obviously knows the location," Whitney said. "The next time you e-mail her, ask exactly where she is."

But Caroline would never fall for such an obvious ploy. Nor would she willingly betray her eco-cult buddies to big, mean Natalie. She gestured to the knobs, dials and flashing lights. "Can we use this equipment to track down my sister?"

"We have an agent working on that angle," Vincent said. "Lawson Davies."

"Head of the legal department at Petrol?"

"Yes."

Her tentative uneasiness gave way to hostility. Though she hadn't been close to her sister since they were children, Natalie knew that Caroline had a history with the Petrol attorney. She'd had an affair with Law, after which he'd unceremoniously dumped her.

"On behalf of my sister, I think I can say—without any doubt—that Law Davies is an unmitigated jerk. Another agent should be assigned to the Solar Sons. Immediately."

Vincent regarded her coolly. He obviously didn't like to

have his decisions questioned. "Quint, is she always like this?"

"Yes, sir," Quint said.

"I'm trying to be useful," she said. "My sister has close ties to the Solar Sons. She could provide inside information, but she wouldn't say 'boo' to Law Davies."

"I'll keep that in mind," Vincent said. "Whitney, please bring up the next photo."

Gordon Doeller. He was shaking hands with Zahir.

"Wait a minute," Natalie said. "I thought Gordon was connected to the Solar Sons."

"He is," Vincent said. "And also to the prince."

Natalie scoffed. "There's nothing strange about that. Gordon is vice president in charge of marketing. He's familiar with the heads of most Middle Eastern nations. For that matter, so am I."

"We suspect Gordon has more intimate ties with Zahir and those ties lead to Sheik Khalaf Al-Sayed in Imad. Gordon might be brokering an oil deal that would ultimately be distributed through Quantum."

These were serious allegations. Though Imad wasn't technically under United States sanctions, Quantum had taken the lead in refusing to buy from the renegade sheik. It made Quantum look bad if there was an under-the-table deal.

Natalie sank into one of the chairs at the conference table. If Chicago Confidential had this information, the people she'd be seeing in Washington on Monday certainly possessed the same data. When she met with them, she might be walking into a lion's den.

"Do you have proof of these sales?"

"It's hard to trace," Whitney said. "Like money laundering. Imad has sold to someone else who sold to another and so on."

"And finally to Quantum. Are you sure Gordon is making the transaction?"

"No," Whitney said. "We've been monitoring his bank accounts and have seen no unusual activity."

"What about numbered Swiss accounts?" Natalie asked. "He could hide money there."

"We have limited access to offshore banking and Swiss accounts, but so does Gordon. If he's stashed his payoff money somewhere else, he'll have to leave the country to use it."

"Could his motive be political?" So much of the oil business had become political—from making complex deals with ever-changing Middle East governments to appeasing the ecology protesters in the United States.

"According to our profile," Whitney said, "Gordon Doeller's motive is pure greed."

"I can help with this." Tomorrow evening, Natalie was scheduled to have a private dinner with Zahir. Possibly, she could deduce his connection with Doeller or with someone else. "I need access to all the data you have on this oil-laundering scheme. I have a meeting with Zahir, and maybe I can—"

"No," Vincent said. "You're not an agent, Natalie."

"Quint would be with me," she said.

Quint spoke up. "It's a good opportunity. Natalie and I should go ahead with this meeting."

Before Vincent answered, the door to the special-operations room opened. Zahir himself stepped inside. He nodded pleasantly and said his good afternoons.

Natalie's throat constricted. Her natural instinct was to gape, but her years of training in public relations and protocol helped her maintain poise. In fact, her posture straightened as she leaped to her feet.

Quint touched the small of her back, guiding her toward the prince. "Natalie Van Buren, this is Javid Haji Haleem, the twin brother of Prince Zahir."

She'd been aware that Zahir was a twin, but she wasn't prepared for the startling resemblance. She was surprised when Javid approached her with hand outstretched.

"I'm glad to finally meet you, Ms. Van Buren. Anbar has been doing business with Quantum for many years."

"Yes," she said, regaining her composure. "We've always dealt with your minister of Commerce."

"Your dealings have been very efficient," he said. "There has been no need for me to interfere."

"Education," she remembered. "You travel as a good-will ambassador, promoting education and awareness of Anbar."

He nodded. "There's much to do in a developing nation."

As they conversed about education, literature and human rights, she decided that Javid and Zahir were like flip sides of the same coin. Both were gorgeous and charismatic. But Zahir was dangerous, and Javid was enlightened.

"I'm sorry we didn't know you were in Chicago, Prince Javid. Quantum would surely have arranged a reception for you."

"For now, I prefer to have my whereabouts unknown."

Another undercover person? "Is everybody in this office hiding something?"

"That's our job," Whitney said.

Natalie rolled her eyes. She felt as if she were standing on ever-shifting sands. These people changed identities as easily as normal people changed clothes. Nothing was as it seemed. "I don't think I'd like working here."

Quint gently took her arm and said, "I think Natalie and I should be heading out. We'll stay in touch."

She made no objection as he whisked her out of the room. In the reception area, she came face-to-face with a tall, handsome man dressed in kilts and a tartan. He was a little unsteady on his feet, obviously the result of too much green beer.

"I'm looking for Kathy Renk," he said.

"And who are you supposed to be? Mel Gibson?"

"I'm Liam Wallace, a Scotsman. And I'm honoring Saint Patrick's Day."

"The new maintenance man," Quint informed her. "I think he's a little infatuated with our receptionist. Is that right, Liam?"

"It's a possibility." The several syllables seemed to tangle on his tongue.

Kathy Renk, dressed in a green jumper, came into the room, scowled at Liam and then laughed when he swept her a bow and offered to escort her to the festivities. Together, they swaggered out the door.

Natalie turned to Quint. "This has been the most unbelievable day."

"Guess so," he said. "I'm surprised you never met Javid before."

"I've met with Anbar's ministers, but not Javid. He was probably too busy doing whatever undercover thing he does."

"Antiterrorism," Quint said. "He investigates terrorism."

Unbelievable! Everyone with this operation had a secret identity. She glanced toward an open office. "Do you think Whitney would mind if I used one of these computers to check my e-mail?"

"Worried about Caroline?" Quint guessed.

"A little." She sat down at the flat-screen computer and accessed her own e-mail account.

Caroline had responded. Her terse message said:

Natalie, you are totally wrong about the Solar Sons. All they want is what's best for the earth. Please try to understand. Love, Caroline.

Natalie stared at the computer screen, annoyed that her sister was so easily conned by eco nonsense. Then she thought of Javid and his evil brother, Zahir. Siblings were a pain in the neck.

NICCO WAITED at Union Station, standing below the ornately sculpted clock with white face and black Roman numerals. The clock hands measured one slow minute after another. Each *tick* echoed against the marble floors and the majestic vaulted ceiling. The relentless passage of time created order for the train passengers and commuters.

Today, Nicco's timing had been off.

He should have stayed with his original plan. Nothing good ever came from improvisation. But when he'd seen the crowd at the parade route and the relatively simple escape to Lake Shore Drive, he couldn't resist. The possibility of apprehending Daughter had seemed easy.

Nicco hadn't counted on Cowboy riding to her rescue. He had underestimated his adversaries. And he had failed. It wouldn't happen again.

He stared up at the clock. Today, his disguise included a baggy tweed suit, a valise and a beard. The spirit gum used to fasten his facial hair had begun to itch. Beneath his gray wig, he sweated like a pig.

In three minutes, he would deliver the first installment of the agreed-upon payoff for a well-connected mercenary. Twenty-five thousand dollars.

Although the expense was budgeted, Nicco had hoped to avoid payment. If the attempt to seize Daughter had succeeded, the services of this mercenary would have been unnecessary.

The clock ticked to the appointed time, and a tall, lean man with a prominent jaw and tight grin came toward him with arms outstretched. "Uncle," he said, "you've come to meet me. Is Monique well?"

Nicco replied with his half of the coded greeting. "Cold spring water agrees with her."

Side by side they climbed the stairs leading to the street. The battered valise dangled between them. The smiling mercenary said, "You had a change in plans today."

"An opportunity presented itself," Nicco said.

"Who is Cowboy?"

"Quint Crawford from Texas." Though he'd searched all sources, Nicco had found nothing unique or special about Cowboy, except for the death of his wife. "He's not important. Just a boyfriend."

"Your men were thwarted by an unimportant Texan. This causes me to worry."

"Don't," Nicco said. "All you need to know is how to play your part."

The mercenary closed his grip around the handle of the valise, taking it from Nicco with a slight tug. "One of your men was apprehended today."

"He won't talk."

"How can you be sure?"

"He's my brother."

At the corner, they separated. Nicco walked alone on the relatively deserted city street. On a Saturday, Saint Patrick's Day, the masses were elsewhere. Yet, Nicco could smell their sweat, their filth. He longed for solitude, for a place where no one would bother him. When this was over, he would seek quietude. Perhaps on an island. This would be his last mission.

ON THE TAXI RIDE to Natalie's condo, Quint maintained a bodyguard's natural vigilance—watching out for the people who were undoubtedly watching them. He assumed there was surveillance from the terrorists. Plus, he had backup. Other agents from other national security organizations, including the FBI, were tailing Natalie and Quint in the hope that they could get a lead on the wrongdoers. It was a regular web of deception.

Though there was a strong probability after his rescue of Natalie on horseback that the terrorists had pegged Quint as an agent, his assignment was basically unchanged. Still undercover, Quint played the role of a visiting Quantum supplier who had a crush on the vice president in charge of public relations. There was, however, a major development in his story: Natalie was supposed to like him back.

For now, they were posing as a couple. He glanced at her profile. Even when she was disheveled and shoeless, Natalie looked too sophisticated to fall for a dusty cowpoke from Midland, Texas. Feeling like a very lucky man, he grinned. "Do you think anybody's going to really believe we're dating?"

"Why wouldn't they?"

When she tilted back her head to gaze up at him, her neck arched so gracefully that he couldn't keep himself from touching her. Gently, he traced the line of her throat.

She caught hold of his hand. Instead of pushing him away, she raised his hand to her lips and lightly kissed his calloused palm. She said, "Zahir didn't seem to have a problem with the concept that you and I might be a couple."

The prince seemed like a very strange confidant. Most women chatted to a girlfriend. "When did you talk about us to Zahir?" he asked.

"You remember," she said. "It was this morning before we left for the parade. When he invited me to dinner, he told me that you had a crush on me."

"But he's only seen us together once. At the reception. And we weren't particularly lovey-dovey at that time."

A tiny adorable frown twisted the corner of her lips. "I don't know where he got the idea that we were having a relationship."

"Gordon Doeller," Quint said. "I bumped into him at the hotel, and I might have mentioned that I thought you were cuter than a newborn foal."

She was suddenly alert. "Quint, this means Gordon had a private conversation with Zahir. Like Whitney said, they have a relationship outside of regular Quantum business."

"It's just gossip." But Gordon had made a point of bumping into Quint and probing his background. It seemed likely that he'd been working to gather information for Zahir. "I wouldn't call this proof."

"Nonetheless, this is significant," she said. "We should contact Whitney and tell her. Then she can focus on Zahir and stop worrying about the Solar Sons."

"It's better to investigate all leads," he said.

"I can't imagine anything useful will be discovered by Law Davies."

She said his name with a snarl, which made Quint wonder about Natalie's personal history with the Petrol attorney. "You don't like Lawson."

"He dumped my sister. The creep." Her little frown deepened. "I don't want to think the Solar Sons are anything more than an overly zealous eco-cult. Caroline really respects Greely."

Quint wished he could reassure her that her sister was fine. It must be hard for Natalie to have a sister who had given her loyalty to the foes of Quantum Industries.

Hoping to distract her, he returned to an earlier topic. "We're going to have to work on our cover story. I'm not the type of guy you usually date."

"You're right. I tend to get involved with professional men who wear three-thousand-dollar suits, drive Jaguars and eat Brie." She laughed. Her green eyes flashed. "Obviously, those men haven't worked out very well for me."

"Why not?"

"They're too much in love with themselves to notice I'm around."

He couldn't believe that. "Any red-blooded American male who could overlook your assets has got to be gay."

"Possibly, it's my fault that relationships don't work," she said. "I'm a very high-maintenance woman."

"High-maintenance? What's that mean?"

"I require a lot of attention. I'm demanding and never settle for second best. I hate being bored. And, as you know, I require total honesty."

Quint had never given much thought to the inner workings of his relationships with women. Or men. Or horses, for that matter. He relied on his instincts. Either it was right or it wasn't.

"Given all this maintenance, what does the man get in return?"

She leaned so close to his ear that her breath tickled when she whispered, "I'll show you tonight."

He kept his voice calm as he said, "Fair enough."

Inside his chest, his heart danced with anticipation. Tonight he would share her bed. It seemed too good to be true. Quint had never expected a second chance at love.

When they reached her building, the doorman turned over Quint's suitcase and his guitar case, both of which had been delivered from his hotel. Though Quint pressed a five-dollar tip in the man's hand, he carried the luggage himself. Natalie was already toting the laptop from Solutions.

At the door to her condo, Quint entered first. Now fully armed, he pulled his Glock automatic from his shoulder holster and went from room to room, searching. Nothing appeared to have been touched or tampered with.

While Natalie set up the computer on the kitchen table to send a traceable e-mail to Caroline's laptop, he swept again for bugs. This time, he found one in his suitcase. He held up the small metal disk for Natalie to see.

She mouthed the words, *A bug?*

He nodded and signaled for her to follow him into the bathroom where he flushed the object and waved bye-bye. "I reckon the hotel security wasn't so hot."

"Are there others?" she asked.

"I think we're safe."

"No one can hear us," she said.

"Not unless we're real noisy." The thought appealed to him. "It might be good for our cover story if you did some loud moaning in the bedroom."

"Like this?" She braced her hands on the edge of the

marble sink, arched her spine, threw back her head and loudly groaned, "Oh, baby! Oh, yes!"

Though she was only teasing, her pose reflected double in the bathroom mirror and aroused him.

She closed her eyes. "Baby, don't stop. Oooh."

He came up behind her and fitted his body against her delectable backside. His hands glided under her arms and cupped her breasts. With the tip of his index finger, he teased her nipples hard.

Her eyelids snapped open. Staring at their reflection in the mirror, she gasped. For real.

He murmured, "You won't have to fake it with me."

She wriggled, making a halfhearted attempt to get free, and he pressed more firmly against her, wanting her to feel his hardness.

In the mirror, he saw her eyes begin to glaze over. He felt her melting.

"You're pretty sure of yourself," she said.

"Just stating the facts, ma'am." He nuzzled beneath the silky brown hair at the nape of her neck.

"Do you like your women to be loud in bed?"

His gaze lifted and met hers in the mirror. Right now he didn't want to think about any other woman. No other lover would be like Natalie. "I want you to be yourself."

"Then, I need to take a shower."

He groaned. "Another shower?"

"Sorry, Quint. It seems like I'm always running off to the shower, but attempted kidnappings are dirty work. And, possibly, I'm a bit of a neat freak."

"Definitely a neat freak."

This time, when she pushed away from the sink, he stepped back.

She looked up at him. "I'm worth it."

"I expect you are."

Paula had often said the same thing: *I'm worth it.* Though Natalie hadn't meant to summon the ghost of his dead wife, Quint couldn't help thinking about her. They'd had a great sex life, and he'd never expected to find such intense fulfillment again. "Go ahead," he said.

"You could use the shower in the other bathroom," she suggested.

"Sure."

He turned on his heel and left her alone in the bathroom of the master suite. Paula had never minded making a mess. Some of their best lovemaking had been in the barn at his ranch. Her memory followed him into the guest bathroom, where he peeled off his clothes and ducked under the hot steaming water of the shower.

As he lathered his hands, he noticed the gleam of the ring he'd worn since Paula's death, a symbol of his devotion. During the past two years, he hadn't been one-hundred-percent true to her memory. He'd had sex a couple of times, but those occasions hadn't been particularly satisfying or personal. He was just scratching an itch with a partner who didn't expect to see him in the morning. Natalie was different.

He had real feelings for her. With her bravery, she'd earned his admiration. Her vulnerability had touched his heart. Paula would've liked her. Paula would approve of Quint finding someone he might be able to love. Damn it, she wouldn't want him to end up a withered, bitter, old hermit at age thirty-five. But was he ready to make this move?

It wasn't fair to Natalie for him to make love without the possibility of a real relationship. He lathered his chest hair and rinsed. Natalie deserved a man who would treat her right.

He could be that man. He wanted to be the one.

Leaving the shower, he dried himself off. Thinking about relationships made him confused. He should act on his gut feelings, and his instincts were telling him that Natalie might be the woman who would change his life.

He wrapped a towel around his waist. He needed to make a decision.

Slowly, he eased the gold-and-silver wedding ring off his finger.

Chapter Nine

After her shower, Natalie lingered in the bathroom. Gingerly, she checked her body for injuries. Both knees were bruised, as was her left upper arm where the man with the mustache had held her. Somewhere in her struggles, she'd picked up a light scratch below her cheekbone.

As the overhead fan in her bathroom sucked the steam from the air, she viewed her reflection in the mirror. She didn't look too much the worse for wear after her ordeal this afternoon. To be completely honest, her appearance had improved.

Her spine had straightened. Her chin had lifted. Her gaze was direct and proud. She'd been attacked and had survived, which somehow made her less fearful than facing unexplained threats and senseless terrorism. Though she didn't know the enemy, she knew the truth. She was, in fact, a target. Someone had set out to terrorize her. However, more importantly, she wasn't alone, fighting shadows in the night. Natalie had a bodyguard.

Her cowboy. As she dusted herself with a light talcum mist, she considered the sheer irony of her attraction to him. Definitely not the type of man she usually dated. Definitely…he was better. Strong, brave and undeniably masculine, Quint never ceased to amaze her. Today, he'd been incredible when he took charge in her rescue. He *was* James Bond in a Stetson.

Somewhere between blow-drying her hair and applying lip gloss, Natalie realized that she wanted a serious relationship with him. She didn't want to go to bed with him if this was just a passing fling.

Was a serious relationship possible?

First, she had to take their geographic problems into account. She was based in Chicago. He was in Texas. She wrapped herself in a silky, thigh-length black robe and pulled the sash tight around her waist. Working out the logistics of a long-distance romance was doable. She rather liked the idea of spending time on his ranch. Riding the range at his side. At night, they would count the stars. In the morning, she'd brew espresso and serve him on a table decorated with a fresh-picked bouquet of wildflowers. No more grits and gravy for him. With Natalie in the kitchen, the menu would change. Chuckling to herself, she imagined how he'd complain about the switch from beef to tofu. They'd work it out. Distance wasn't really a problem for their potential relationship.

What about his undercover work with the Confidential outfit? She didn't like to think of Quint being in constant danger. Not unless she was right there at his side. Like Whitney and Vincent. That could work.

Facing the door that led from the bathroom to the bedroom, Natalie confronted the real issue, the major obstacle to a relationship, the knockout punch. Was Quint ready for a relationship with her? Or had all his love been consumed by his first wife? He still remembered Paula. When he spoke of her, there was an ache in his voice. He wasn't over Paula, possibly he never would be. And where did that leave Natalie? She hated being second best, competing with a ghost who would always be perfect in his memory.

Could he ever truly love Natalie?

Still unsure, she turned off the fan in the bathroom. From the bedroom, she heard music. Natalie opened the door.

Quint sat on the edge of her bed, wearing a towel round

his waist and nothing else. On his lap, he held his twelve-string guitar.

When he looked up at her and grinned, she realized she'd never seen a more sexy, handsome man. His thick brown hair fell rakishly across his tanned forehead, and his blue eyes shone with a warm, welcoming light. His shoulders were broad and well muscled from working outside. His splayed legs were long and lean.

He struck a few chords and began playing, ''When Irish Eyes are Smiling.'' When he sang, his rich tenor vibrated through her.

She'd meant to discuss their relationship with him, but he'd taken her breath away with his tender serenade.

''Did you like that?'' he asked.

She nodded dumbly.

''I didn't think you were a country-western gal,'' he said. ''Let me try this.''

He picked out the opening notes to ''Greensleeves,'' then segued into a more intricate version. Mesmerized, she stared as his fingers plucked and strummed the delicate melody. His left hand slid up and down the neck of the guitar, changing chords.

There was something different about him, about his hand. Then, she saw it. He wasn't wearing the wedding ring. Tonight, there would be no memories. No ghosts. By taking off his ring, he'd made a commitment to Natalie. Tonight, he would be hers alone.

She snuggled up beside him on the bed. ''Put the guitar away, cowboy.''

''Thought you'd never ask.'' He set his instrument aside.

Then his skillful fingers loosened the sash on her robe. As he slipped the black silk from her shoulders, his blue eyes regarded her reverently, as though her body was more than mere flesh. She felt like a magnificent sculpture.

''Beautiful,'' he whispered.

Masterfully, he played her with gentle caresses and

sweet attention to every sensitive inch of her body. His kisses were light at first, then harder and more demanding.

Natalie abandoned herself to his sensual challenges. She matched his rising passion, touch for touch. Wanting to be part of him, needing to be possessed by him, she stretched the length of her body against his. He kissed her hard.

They tangled in a passionate embrace, clinging to each other with all their strength. They rolled across her four-poster bed, tearing apart the bedclothes and the sheets.

Gasping, she found herself lying on top of him as though she'd been washed ashore by tumultuous waves. She sat astride his naked torso, looking down on him, catching her breath. He was perfect. The perfect man. Her buttocks pressed against his hard arousal. He raised his knees, and she leaned back against them, displaying herself. He pushed up on his elbows and watched her with fire in his laser-blue eyes.

Before she was fully aware of what had happened, he had turned her over and pinned her flat on the sheets. He rose above her and entered. With slow, hard thrusts, he drove her toward fulfillment. Shuddering, she groaned. No need for faking. This was the real thing.

Her self-control disassembled. She'd never felt such a mind-numbing burst of sheer animal lust. Caught in a frenzy, she rocked back and forth, clutched at his shoulders, clawed at his back. And then...

Spasms of deep, perfect pleasure reverberated through her in a widening echo, leaving her tingling and at peace.

She lay beside him, breathing deeply as the tremors subsided. "You didn't lie."

"About what?" he asked.

"When you said I wouldn't have to fake it." A soft smile spread across her face. It felt like her whole body was smiling. "You weren't lying."

"You're an amazing woman, Natalie." He leaned over and nuzzled behind her ear. "You're the best."

But am I number one? Will I ever be number one?

Somewhere in the back of her mind, she wanted to hear those three little words. *I love you.* But it was too soon. Forgetting any other question, she cuddled against his chest and wished she could stay in this moment forever.

ON SUNDAY NIGHT, it was a very different Natalie Van Buren who strolled into the five-star restaurant for her scheduled dinner with Prince Zahir. After a full night and day of lovemaking with Quint, she knew that she was glowing more brightly than a ton of uranium.

Quint had chosen the dress that she wore beneath her simple black blazer. It was a sleeveless, rayon sheath in royal blue, detailed in black. She'd never had the nerve to wear the dress before because the neckline showed a positively decadent amount of cleavage.

Quint guided her across the restaurant to the table where Zahir was waiting with two fawning female companions. The prince stood, separated himself from the other women and took her hand. The animal in him responded to Natalie's radiant physicality. Avidly, his dark eyes searched her face, looking for a hint that she might be sexually available to him.

In response, Natalie slowly turned her gaze toward Quint. She was taken, held in thrall by her magnificent Texan. "You remember Quintin Crawford?"

"Yes," Zahir said curtly. He'd gotten her message and didn't like it. Too bad. Zahir was supposed to be engaged.

Quickly, he seated himself between his two lady friends and lavished them with little caresses to show Natalie that he, too, was a sexually desirable creature.

But not for her. For Natalie, making love was more than a physical act. She needed honesty, strength of character and sensitivity. She needed Quint.

In any case, she hadn't come to this dinner to play a sexy game of one-upmanship with Zahir. She wanted to take this time to figure out, once and for all, if his connection to the notorious Sheik Khalaf Al-Sayed of Imad had resulted in the campaign of threatening notes. "Tell us about your home country, Zahir."

"I was born in America and spent part of my childhood here and in Anbar, but I consider the world to be my home. Anbar is too small for me." He glanced toward Quint. "A well-traveled man such as yourself must understand."

"I know that Anbar doesn't have a lot of acreage. It's nowhere near as big as Texas. But I don't think a man ever really escapes his roots."

"By birth, I will always be Prince of Anbar," Zahir said. "But my vision is much larger than Texas."

Natalie glanced toward Quint. To a loyal son of the Alamo state, those were fighting words, but her cowboy maintained his cool. "I heard somewhere that you've got a twin brother. Do you ever see him?"

"As little as possible. Family is so tedious." He winked at the blonde on his right, and she giggled, launching into a chatty story about an incident on her family's yacht.

After she was finished, the first course of their meal arrived. "French onion soup," Zahir said. "I've taken the liberty of ordering for all of us. Hope you don't mind."

Natalie minded. A lot. She hated when men ordered for her. But she nodded and said, "I'm sure it will all be delicious. Tell us more about your twin. Do you have that kind of mysterious twin 'connection.'"

"I have nothing in common with my brother. How's your soup?"

"But don't you resemble each other?"

His voice was gelid and cold as aspic. "My brother is treacherous. He turned our father against me and caused me to be cut off without a cent."

"Oh dear," Natalie said. "Then, how do you finance your glamorous lifestyle?"

"By my wits." Again, he used his female companions as buffers. Turning to the brunette on his left, he asked, "Am I not witty?"

She regaled them with an anecdote about the cleverness of Zahir.

During the main course of stuffed pheasant, Quint returned to the pertinent topic. "I reckon your financial problems are pretty much over, Zahir. From what I've heard, you're fixing to be the next ruler of Nurul."

"Allah willing," he said smoothly. He turned to Natalie. "It will be most vital for Nurul to sell oil to Quantum."

"Well, of course," she said. "There are very few Middle East nations we don't deal with on a regular basis. Imad is one. It's very close to Anbar, isn't it?"

"The neighbor to the north." He eyed her suspiciously.

"Are you acquainted with Sheik Khalaf Al-Sayed?"

"We've met."

Zahir's gaze was guarded, but she could see the anger building within him. His jaw was set hard. He seemed to be gritting his teeth.

"Is the sheik as dangerous as everyone says?"

"I find him to be a patient man."

"Biding his time until he gets what he wants," Natalie translated. "I've heard he's cruel, even threatening."

"Only to those who betray him."

"Or those who stand in his way." Purposely taunting, she laughed. "I wonder what this little sheik wants? To take over the world?"

On cue, Zahir's two companions giggled.

"Stop," he said quietly. There was no mistaking the hostility in his dark eyes. "To disrespect Khalaf is to disrespect me."

"So sorry," Natalie said lightly. "I didn't realize you were so close to Khalaf."

"There is much you don't realize. Khalaf is closer to me than my own father. I would do anything for him."

"Anything," she repeated. "That covers a wide spectrum."

"Yes," he said coldly.

"Does it cover bombings? Kidnappings? Threats?"

Realization flared in Zahir's eyes. He had said too much, and he seemed to know it. Instead of backing off and spewing denials, he accepted the fact with a quick nod. He leaned back in his chair and stared at her.

"With all due respect, Natalie, has anyone ever told you that you have a big mouth?"

That had been the message in most of the primitive threat notes she'd received. Zahir was as much as acknowledging that he'd been behind the threats. She was about to accuse him, when Quint weighed in on the conversation.

"Zahir," he said, drawing the attention to himself, "I'll thank you not to insult this lady."

"And what are you going to do, cowboy? Challenge me to a shoot-out?"

The chiseled lines of Quint's profile told her that he'd like nothing better.

In a calm voice, he drawled, "I wouldn't need a six-gun to take you."

"Oh?" Zahir sneered. "Should I be afraid?"

Quint stood and helped Natalie rise from her chair. "In any fair fight, a coward will always lose. But I don't expect that for you fairness has much relevance. Otherwise, you wouldn't be going after a woman."

Zahir sprang to his feet. He seemed ready to leap across the table and strangle Quint. "Do you call me a coward?"

"Heck, no. I was just talking in general terms. Do you think of yourself as a coward, Zahir?"

"Please excuse us," Natalie said as she shoved Quint toward the exit. "It's terribly late, and I need to work in the morning. Thanks so much for the enlightening dinner."

As she linked her arm with Quint's, she felt the tension coursing through him. Quietly, she murmured, "Not here. It won't do any good to get into a fistfight at one of the better restaurants in Chicago."

On the street, he inhaled deeply and exhaled slowly, bringing himself under control. "I didn't mean to get so worked up."

"You were protecting me." Though his behavior bordered on uncivilized, she loved it. "Zahir practically admitted that he was behind the threatening notes. Can we have him arrested?"

"Not on the basis of a dinner conversation." Quint draped his arm around her shoulder. "But don't you worry, Natalie. I won't let him hurt you."

She absolutely believed him. Though she had never been more under siege, Natalie had never in her life felt more safe and secure.

IT HAD BEEN a long, hard Monday. All day long, Quint had trailed Natalie around while she dealt with the aftermath of the bombing of Quantum and prepared for her trip. Now, she was ready to leave, and he didn't want to let her go.

At Midway Airfield, far from the passenger terminals, Quint stood outside the hangar where the Quantum fleet of corporate jets was housed. It was dusk. To the north, the lights of the city outlined distant skyscrapers.

He spoke into his cell phone. "Okay, Whitney, tell me again why I should let Natalie get on this plane without me."

"There's nothing to worry about," Whitney said. "The terrorist cell in Chicago is falling apart. The guy they picked up in Grant Park says there were only three of them, and one contact inside Quantum, who we suspect was Gordon Doeller."

Gordon was a dead end, literally, permanently erased from the picture. This morning, they'd gotten the news from FBI sources that he'd been killed.

Though Gordon Doeller's murder would probably go down in the books as an unsolved crime, it had the earmarks of an execution. He'd been burned alive in his SUV. Though Quint had no love for Gordon Doeller and the part he likely played in terrorizing Natalie, he hoped the traitor had been unconscious before his horrifying and agonizing demise.

"Any new information on the investigation into Gordon Doeller's murder?"

"Time of death," Whitney said. "Doeller was murdered last night at the same time you were having dinner with Zahir. You and Natalie are his alibi."

"Convenient," Quint said. But not unexpected. Zahir was pretty careful about covering his butt. "I don't expect the guy in custody has said that it was Zahir who hired him."

"Not yet."

"And he hasn't said why he grabbed Natalie."

"His only motivation," Whitney said, "was money. He's a very small fish. A cut-rate terrorist."

"Which is all Zahir can afford. I hope you're right about their operation falling apart."

Whitney said, "Natalie will be okay in Washington. And we need you here at the Confidential office. Your buddy, Daniel Austin, is coming to town."

"You need me?" Quint asked. "Why? To translate Daniel's Texan accent?"

Quint liked and respected Daniel Austin, a former member of Texas Confidential and the founder of the Montana Confidential operation. But he didn't feel a need to get together with Dan. Not when he had concerns about Natalie.

He saw her signaling to him as she came out of the hangar. The wind caught hold of her black trench coat and the fabric swirled around her. Underneath she was wearing a black pantsuit over a pale pink turtleneck that almost matched the color of her skin. Her long scarf was a swirly pink-and-gray pattern with long fringe, like something a gypsy princess would wear. God, she was pretty.

"Quint?" Whitney's voice came over the phone.

"I gotta go."

"We'll see you back here in an hour."

He disconnected the call and slipped the cell phone into the pocket of his suede jacket. Today, he had opted not to wear his shoulder holster. With newly installed metal detectors at Quantum and at the airfield, being fully armed wasn't worth the hassle. Besides, he still had the Derringer in his belt buckle, and the Quantum contingent had acquired two bodyguards as escorts for the duration of this trip to Washington, D.C.

Natalie grasped his hand and tugged. "Let me show you around the corporate jet."

"I'm coming. Hold your horses."

When it came to planes, he didn't expect to be impressed. His attitude was, been there, done that, bought the T-shirt. During his traveling years while he was on wildcat oil explorations, Quint had been transported on every imaginable type of aircraft, ranging from a glider to the transatlantic SST. Also, he was a fully qualified small plane pilot, though he hadn't been in a cockpit since Paula was killed in his Cessna.

Natalie stopped outside the hangar and looked up at him. "What's wrong?"

Being this close to the planes, inhaling the smells of oil and grease, brought back memories. If Paula hadn't taken her first solo flight that day, she'd still be alive.

Though he was trying not to compare the two most important women in his life, he couldn't help thinking of the similarity in this situation.

"I'm worried about you," he said.

"I'll be okay," she promised. "We've got two bodyguards. The security at Midway is excellent. And this jet has an outstanding safety record."

He pulled her close. Her body relaxed against his. After two nights of intimacy, her shape was pleasantly familiar to his touch. His hand slid easily along her slim torso. He could almost circle her tiny waist with his outstretched fingers.

There was so much more about her that he wanted to

explore. He wanted to see all the shadings of her many moods, to hear the full range of her voice and her laughter. If anything happened on this flight...

He couldn't stand to watch as she flew away from him. "I should come with you."

"There's plenty of room," she said. "Now, come inside the hangar and take a look at this jet. It's my father's pride and joy."

"Sure," he said. Quint didn't want their last moments together before she took off to be ruined by his groundless fears. He had to stop acting like a nervous old woman, finding trouble where none existed. "Okay, what kind of aircraft is this? A Falcon? An Aerobus?"

"No way. My father always buys American."

"Gulfstream," he said.

"It's a Boeing, a variation on the 737. Ultralong range. Twin turbojet engines so we can land practically anywhere and a special wide-body construction. It has over nine hundred square feet in the passenger cabin."

Quint was beginning to get interested. A 737 was large enough for airline use. "Specially outfitted?"

"Oh, yes," she said. "Henry is usually a prudent businessman, but he went a little crazy on this jet. After he saw what the Sultan of Brunei did with his private transport, my father wanted something bigger and better."

She pulled him inside the domed, open-beamed hangar, where the ground crew loaded luggage and the pilots made final safety checks. Two smaller Gulfstream jets were dwarfed by the modified 737 with the Quantum corporate logo emblazoned on the tail.

Quint stood and stared. "Your daddy did himself proud when he purchased this aircraft. It is a thing of beauty and a joy forever."

Eagerly, he followed Natalie up the stairs to the front entrance behind the flight deck. She played tour guide. "This is the rest area for the crew. Two pilots. We have two attendants on this trip because there'll be nine of us."

"Who all is going?"

"The only people you know are Maria Luisa and Jerome Harris from Accounting. Two bodyguards. And the others are from Legal and Marketing." She lowered her voice to confide, "Gordon Doeller would've been on this flight."

"What about the crew?" Quint asked. "Can they be trusted?"

"Relax. They've all been on the Quantum payroll for years."

She pulled him into the lounge area, where leather sofas the color of melted butter and matching recliner chairs surrounded wooden coffee tables that were bolted to the floor.

"Nice," Quint said. The interior cabin height was over seven feet, so he didn't have to duck his head, and the furniture was full-size with plenty of leg room.

He followed her through a narrow hallway past a closed door. "What's in here?"

"That's the last place I'll show you."

At the end of the narrow corridor was a conference room with a large wooden table encircled with comfortable-looking chairs. Jerome Harris and two other people were seated there, working on laptops, papers scattered across the table.

Though Quint maintained his friendly attitude when he was introduced, he eyeballed each of them carefully. Nobody looked dangerous, but you never could tell. The guy from Marketing had been working with Gordon Doeller, and Quint had to wonder if the second in command had any idea about his late boss's activities.

The next area was a standard two-seat, single-aisle area that resembled the first-class section of a commercial airliner. Maria Luisa and the other passengers, including the bodyguards, were back here.

"Behind these seats which, of course, fold down into sleepers," Natalie said, "is the service area with galley modules and fully-equipped kitchen for gourmet meals."

"I noticed them loading the food through the rear cargo hold," Quint said. "I expect you'll be having some kind of fancy pasta with gravy."

"Sauce," Natalie corrected. "I eat pasta with sauce. *You* eat biscuits and gravy."

Maria Luisa flopped into the chair next to where they were standing. As soon as she'd realized that Quint and Natalie were a couple, her flirting came to a halt. Glancing between them, she shook her head. "You two are positive proof that opposites attract."

"Me and Natalie," Quint said, "we're not all that opposite."

Behind his back, Natalie made a squeaking noise. Either she was stifling a giggle or she'd sprung a leak. He turned to her and raised an eyebrow. "Did you have something to say?"

"We are so totally different." Her eyes lifted as if reading from a billboard over his left shoulder. "I shop at Saks Fifth Avenue, and you go to the feed lot. If I mentioned Rodeo Drive, you'd think I was talking about a horse show. I like Spago. You like spaghetti with big meatballs."

He snugged a hand around her waist and pulled her close. In a low voice, he said, "I know one thing we agree on."

Her green eyes took on that dazed sheen that drove him crazy. "You're right, Quint. We're not different in the ways that count."

"Please," Maria Luisa said, "get a room."

"My thought exactly," Natalie said. "There's one place on the aircraft I haven't showed you."

They backtracked through the conference room into the narrow hallway. She opened the door and led him into a private office, decorated in dark rosewood with blue patterned wallpaper. After pointing out the private lavatory and the shower with endlessly recirculated hot water, Natalie took off her trench coat and hung it in the closet. She slipped behind the desk and sat in a subtly patterned chair that faced a matching sofa. She touched a button.

Automatically, the desk disappeared into the floor. The sofa flipped back and the wall descended, creating a queen-size bed.

"Wow," Quint said. "I got to get me one of these jets."

In a few steps, she crossed the private cabin and stretched out seductively on the bedspread. "We can share this one."

He didn't need more invitation to lie beside her, his hand shaping the voluptuous swell of her hip. How could one woman be so slim and so curvy at the same time? It was like she'd taken all the best parts of femininity and put them together in one succulent package. "You look good enough to eat."

She touched his lips. "Taste me."

His mouth claimed hers. He kissed gently, not wanting to become too aroused. Though they were in the private cabin, thin walls separated them from the rest of the Quantum staff and the flight crew.

"Come with me on this trip, Quint. We can spend the whole flight in here."

"I'm sorely tempted." Oddly enough, her tour of the airplane had reassured him. Nothing bad could happen on such a magnificent aircraft. Quantum security was top-notch. He'd been needlessly worried. "But I promised Whitney I'd be back at the Chicago Confidential offices in half an hour."

"I'll miss you," she said. "It's only three days, but that seems like a long time to be apart."

"I can fly to Washington and join you." He stroked the satiny bedcover. "Then we'll come back together on this sexy aircraft."

"After I've taken care of business." She nodded. "Perfect."

He kissed her once more. Oh, how he wanted to stay. Reluctantly, he rose and offered his hand to help her off the bed. "Would you be so kind as to escort me off your fine corporate jet? It's so big, I'm afraid I'll lose my way."

Together, they strolled through the lounge and down the stairs, where they met the pilots who were preparing to enter the flight deck. Natalie introduced a rugged-looking older man with gray streaks at his temples. "Chuck has been with Quantum for almost thirty years. He learned how to fly post-Vietnam."

Quint shook the pilot's hand. "Pleased to meet you, sir."

Chuck introduced his co-pilot. "My regular co-pilot is sick, so I called on the reserves. This is Ted Jackson, former U.S. Air Force captain, otherwise known as Smilin' Jack."

Quint could easily see where the nickname came from. Smilin' Jack had a lantern chin and a tightly stretched grin. His handshake was firm. A substitute pilot? Was he trustworthy?

Quint said, "Y'all take good care of Natalie."

"Don't worry," Chuck said. "We just completed safety checks and expect to be ready for takeoff in just a few more minutes."

Smilin' Jack held open the safety door to the flight deck. "Would you care to take a look in here, Quint?"

"Another time," he said. He would definitely enjoy studying the mechanics of this aircraft, but right now his focus was Natalie. He wanted to say a private goodbye.

They descended the stairs and stood beside the aircraft. Through the opened hangar, the night poured inside. He held her, kissed her. "I'll miss you, darlin'. Be careful."

"You, too." Reluctantly, she stepped away from him. "See you in Washington."

"Count on it."

Though Quint should have hightailed it back to Confidential headquarters, he wanted to prolong these moments when Natalie was near. He might still change his mind and join her right now. That bed in the private cabin had been mighty seductive.

Casually, he circled the belly of the plane. Most of the loading had been done, and the door to the rear cargo hold was closed and latched. None of the baggage handlers were nearby.

Quint climbed the ramp leading into the forward cargo hold. In the back of his mind, he considered the possibility of stowing away down here and climbing out to surprise Natalie midflight. He could make a dramatic entrance. But with the chases and threats and bombs, there had already been too much drama in their relationship.

Instead, he explored deeper in the belly of the plane. Some of the luggage was stacked behind mesh to keep it from sliding around, and there were a couple of large containers that locked to the floor. The ceiling height in the cargo hold was lower than in the cabin; he had to take off his Stetson to walk standing up.

A sound caught his attention, and he turned. Inside the mesh, sitting on top of a large trunk, was a shipping kennel. Quint moved closer.

A friendly dog peered out at him. Black and white, it looked like a Border collie.

"Hey, fella. What are you doing here?" He must belong to one of the Quantum employees or maybe somebody in the flight crew. Seemed strange to bring your pet on a short trip to Washington.

The dog circled inside his cage.

"You want to get out of there, don't you?"

The dog pressed up against the front of the cage. He was missing his front leg. A black-and-white Border collie with three legs.

"Damn."

Quint finally had his answer. He knew what had happened to the dog in Reykjavik.

Chapter Ten

Along with the other passengers and flight attendants, Natalie took her seat; hers was in the rear area with the standard first-class airline chair arrangement—double seats by the windows and an aisle in the middle. The two bodyguards—big, stalwart men—claimed the seats nearest the door that led into this section. Their presence seemed excessive for only seven Quantum employees on this flight, but Natalie wouldn't complain. Her previous stance on refusing protection had gotten her attacked in Grant Park.

As the flight attendant in a rear jump seat politely requested that they fasten seat belts for takeoff, Natalie eagerly peered out the window, hoping to catch a last glimpse of Quint before they were airborne.

Nose pressed against the glass, her gaze searched the tarmac in front of the hangar, expecting to see his tall frame, wide shoulders and ever-present Stetson. But he wasn't there; he must have hurried off to his meeting at Confidential headquarters. A little disappointed, she faced forward as they taxied toward the runway.

Maria Luisa, sitting beside her, smiled and said, "I'm happy for you, Natalie. Quint is a terrific guy."

Which was why it would hurt so much if she lost him. "I hope this relationship works."

"I'd bet on it. The way he looks at you…" Maria Luisa

knotted her hands above her breasts. "That man is head over heels in love."

"It's too soon to talk about love. We've only known each other for a few days. It takes months, sometimes even years, to know if you really care deeply enough to call it love."

"So careful!" Maria Luisa teased. "Don't you believe in love at first sight?"

Shaking her head, Natalie recalled her first impression of Quint. She'd thought he was an annoying jerk—handsome with a great body, but definitely not for her. "The first impression wasn't so good for me and Quint."

"Maybe not from your side," Maria Luisa said. "But I think he liked you from the very beginning."

A rumbling vibration shook the aircraft as the two powerful turbofan engines geared up for takeoff. Through the porthole window, Natalie watched as the glittering lights beside the tarmac blurred. With a little bump from the wheels drawing up into the belly of the plane, they left the ground.

In the distance, she saw the magnificent glitter of Chicago. At night, the glow from millions of lights reached as high as the clouds. In her eyes, the sight was beautiful, enchanted. Would Quint appreciate her city the same way? Could he ever call Chicago home? Perhaps that was a bit much to ask of a loyal Texan. She'd be wiser to cherish their differences.

As they soared above Lake Michigan, Jerome Harris unfastened his seat belt and turned to her. "If you don't mind, Natalie, there are a few figures I'd like to check with you."

"Of course." A few days ago, her entire consciousness had been absorbed with preparation for this meeting in Washington. Every waking moment was devoted to creating exactly the right speech, memorizing the data to refute any accusations regarding the way Quantum did business. Now, her presentation didn't seem nearly so earthshaking.

Nonetheless, she followed rabbity little Jerome into the adjoining conference area, where they were joined by three others. The other passengers sat in the comfortable easy chairs in the conversation area in the forward lounge, or stayed in their reclining seats at the rear.

The bodyguards, she noticed, had split up. One was at the front, near the door to the flight deck. The other stayed in the rear where the flight attendants were busily preparing food and drink.

Natalie stood at the head of the conference table. She focused on the man from Marketing who was in line to be promoted to vice president. His name was Gregory Walsh. A husky blond guy with a permanent tan, he had the reputation of being an outdoorsman and an outstanding golfer, which was a useful talent for a marketing man.

Natalie nodded to him and addressed the assembled employees. "Before we get started, I'd like to take a moment to remember Gordon Doeller. He gave many good years to Quantum, and he will be missed."

There were nods and quiet murmurs, but no tears were shed.

She turned to Jerome. "I believe you had some numbers to run."

His head jiggled up and down as he passed out sheets of paper filled with a dizzying array of neatly typed columns. Distribution figures. Profit and loss. Margins. Percentages.

At one time, Natalie had found these numbers to be as compelling as a fast-paced thriller. She sifted through the sheaf of papers, and found herself thinking of Quint. What was he doing right now?

INSIDE THE FORWARD CARGO HOLD, ducked down beside the luggage, Quint felt the aircraft level off as they attained cruising altitude. In the cabin above his head, the passengers would soon begin moving around. And then, the Reykjavik terrorist would strike.

On the ground, when the cargo hatch had closed and Quint had realized he was about to be locked in, his first impulse was to alert the bodyguards to the approaching danger. Then he'd thought again. There was the possibility that those bodyguards were in cahoots with the terrorists. Sure, they'd been approved by the Feds, but mistakes had been made before. Quint wasn't prepared to trust anybody. Not when there was so much at stake. Natalie's safety. Her life.

When he thought of her being in peril, a burning rage churned in his gut. He wanted to charge up into the cabin, grab her and kill anybody who dared to get close. That was his second impulse. His fists clenched. He wanted action, but he needed to be smart. Right now, he had the element of surprise in his favor. Nobody but the three-legged dog knew Quint was on board the Quantum jet.

By the dim illumination of work lights, he crept toward the sliding door that led to the rear cargo bay behind the wheel well. There was a considerable amount of junk down here. A folded-up display booth. A couple of office machines. And sports equipment. Apparently, when Henry Van Buren traveled in his luxurious corporate aircraft, he wanted to be prepared for anything. Quint was glad for the extra bit of height in the cargo bay. He could walk standing up, whereas in a typical 737, he'd have had to duck way down.

As he came up to the fire door separating the two cargo hatches, he wished he'd paid more attention to the mechanics of this aircraft instead of gaping at the padded leather seats and the mechanical fold-down bed. All he could deduce from prior experience was that there were two insulated cargo bays to the fore and aft, separated by a wall and the wheel well. The belly of the plane was pressurized but not heated. The temperature down here would stay between fifty and sixty degrees—chilly but not ice-cold. Much more annoying was the lack of soundproofing against the constant loud hum of the turbojets. As he picked his way toward the rear of the plane, he noticed auxiliary fuel tanks. They ought to be empty for a short trip like this, but this was still a dangerous place to be firing a weapon.

Where were the terrorists hiding? Where was the owner of that three-legged Border collie?

If Quint himself had been planning a hijacking, he'd divide his forces. He'd position men in the rear cargo hold with access to the cabin through the service kitchen. Then, he'd have another force to attack from the front. But there was no one else in the forward cargo bay. He had to wonder if other terrorists were already on the flight. Maybe the bodyguards or the flight attendants. Maybe Smilin' Jack, the substitute pilot.

There weren't many other hiding places on a plane like this. There was a crawl space in the ceiling above the cabin. There was a bay underneath the flight deck that held some of the override computer avionics. Only one man could fit in that tiny space, and he'd need help from the pilots to get out.

Counting on the constant engine noise to cover the sound of his movements, Quint slid back the door leading to the aft cargo bay. He slipped through and closed the door.

Through the shadows, he saw three armed men, poised at the steep metal stairs leading up to the service area, where the flight attendants were probably preparing food.

Three of them. Somehow, Quint had to disable three armed terrorists with his one-shot Derringer.

There wasn't time for him to come up with a plan. They were already on the move. The first one climbed the steep metal stairs leading to the cabin.

Quint lowered his head and scrambled across the cargo bay.

The second man disappeared up the stairs.

Number three climbed more carefully. He was limping.

Quint made a dive and caught the guy by the leg, pulling him down the stairs. His weapon fell from his hand and clattered into the shadows as he staggered to his feet. Quint recognized the man with a moustache from Grant Park. He was also the guy with the Vandyke beard who had shadowed them in the Art Institute.

He squinted toward Quint. "You!"

From the heel of his boot, Quint removed the switchblade. It snicked open. The handle fit neatly in his hand.

The terrorist looked at his knife and sneered. He reached inside his jacket and unsheathed a long, wicked-looking blade.

Quint was damn good and ready for a fight. He gestured the other man toward him.

STIFFLY, NICCO EMERGED from the cramped space beneath the flight deck where he'd been hiding for nearly forty-five minutes. Though the wait should have been only a minimal test of his endurance, his body ached. A cold sweat dampened the clothing he wore under his ground crew jumpsuit.

He had no need for worry. According to brief walkie-talkie transmissions, he'd been assured that every phase of the hijacking had gone as planned. His men had hidden in galley modules from the catering truck. When loaded onto the plane, they released themselves and hid in the aft cargo bay. Their weapons had been placed in the hangar earlier by the ground crew employee, the smoker, who Nicco had eliminated and then been hired to replace. Nicco himself carried the weapons onto the plane.

No one had questioned the credentials of Smilin' Jack, the mercenary who was paid excessively to replace the co-pilot on this flight and compromise his otherwise sterling reputation.

Nicco stood erect at the rear of the flight deck.

The pilot was slumped over in his seat. Smilin' Jack stared through the windshield at the night sky.

"We're on autopilot, cruising at an altitude of twelve hundred meters," he said.

Nicco nodded to the pilot. "Is he dead?"

"Unconscious. I used the stun gun, then whacked him so he'd stay quiet."

"Good." Though Nicco had no aversion to killing when necessary, he preferred to keep his hostages intact to use as bargaining chips.

He stretched his arms and legs. This would be the most risky part of the operation—eliminating the bodyguards and taking control of the aircraft.

He and his three men were armed with pistols, but Nicco preferred the Taser stun guns with a striking distance of fifteen feet and an ability to immobilize the target without permanent harm.

Before giving his men the order to attack over the walkie-talkie no larger than a cell phone, Nicco felt a strange need for reassurance. After all these years of working alone and underground while he constructed sophisticated explosive devices for other terrorist groups, he wished for validation.

He would not expect congratulations from Smilin' Jack. To ask for support would be perceived as weakness.

Nicco thought of Scout, his beloved dog whom he'd loaded earlier into the forward cargo bay. When this was over, he and Scout would be rich enough to live anywhere. They would no longer take orders from fools. They would walk together on sunlit beaches.

Inwardly, Nicco smiled. His plan would not fail.

Lifting the walkie-talkie to his lips, Nicco gave the order. "Go! Now!"

SITTING IN THE AIRBORNE conference room, Natalie stared at the sheets of paper Jerome Harris had distributed. The rows of numbers blurred before her eyes, and she struggled to concentrate.

From the rear of the plane, she heard a shout, a scream. *Gunfire!*

Natalie leaped to her feet. Similar noise came from the front of the plane. Apprehension rushed through her. The worst possible scenario was an attack on the airplane. There was nowhere to run, nowhere to hide.

Frantically, her gaze scanned the walls and the portholes as though she might suddenly discover a magic corridor for escape. No chance. She was trapped. Unarmed. Helpless.

A flight attendant rushed into the conference area. "It's a hijacking."

Jerome Harris backed up against the portholes. Trembling, he whispered, "We're all going to die."

"Stop it!" Natalie commanded. Where were the bodyguards? There were two bodyguards—special agents—on this aircraft. Where were they?

The other flight attendant who had been in the rear of the plane staggered into the conference room. Her face was white with terror. Tears streaked down her cheeks.

Two armed men followed. One of them held Maria Luisa with a knife to her throat.

"Go." He shouted the order to all of them. "Single file down the hall to the lounge. Move it. Fast."

The other hijacker—a huge grizzly bear of a man— hauled slackers to their feet. Rudely, he shoved them forward. "Go. Now. Go."

Through her fear, Natalie still needed to resist. These were her employees, her responsibility. She could not stand idly by and watch them being herded like sheep. Bracing herself, she demanded, "Who are you? What do you want?"

"Move it!" The hijacker slashed his blade across Maria Luisa's bare arm. She screamed. Blood oozed from the wound.

Natalie couldn't bear seeing the fear and horror in her secretary's dark eyes. Just a moment before, they'd been giggling about her relationship with Quint. Now, their futures were over, gone.

Stalking toward the corridor, Natalie joined the line.

In the lounge area, a third armed man waited. At his feet lay the body of one security guard. His wrists were handcuffed behind his back. His ankles were tied together.

The third man barked an order. "Everyone sit."

His two companions enforced the order. Roughly pushing and prodding, they made sure all the passengers were seated on the plush leather sofas and chairs. The luxurious comfort of the furnishings mocked their fear.

"Thank you," the third man said. The tenor of his voice seemed familiar to Natalie. "I want all of your cell phones and anything that might be used as a weapon. Swiss Army knives. Nail files. Toss them on the floor."

Jerome Harris was the first to comply. He dropped his cell phone with shaking hands.

"You will be searched," the hijacker advised. "If we find any of you have held back, the consequences will be severe."

They quickly disarmed themselves. Natalie didn't have her cell phone; it was in her purse.

When the hijacker looked directly at her, Natalie recognized him. She'd thought about his face often enough after her office had been bombed. "Nick Beaumont from Little Rock," she said.

His eyes glittered. "And you are Natalie Van Buren, daughter of Henry Van Buren, CEO of the most powerful oil distribution company in the world."

He was obviously the leader. Could she negotiate with him? "Please tell your man to release Maria Luisa."

"Of course." Nick nodded to his companion, who placed the sobbing Maria Luisa on a sofa beside a flight attendant. "I apologize for the injury," said Nick Beaumont. "It is not our intention for any of you to be harmed. We are not fanatics."

Natalie couldn't help thinking of their destination: Washington, D.C. The horror of recent hijackings was all too fresh in her mind. "Why have you done this?"

"We have demands." All eyes focused on Nick as he strutted among them, proud as a rooster. He seemed to take pleasure in their fear and confusion. "We're not terrorists. We're old-fashioned criminals."

His men laughed. He spoke to them in German, a language Natalie understood well enough to know that he was asking about another person, another of his men who was not with them. One of the others replied in German that he had never left the cargo bay. His leg had been bothering him.

"Coward," Nick said in English. He turned toward Natalie and her co-workers. "You are our hostages. To gain your safe release, we will need to be paid a very substantial sum."

This plan would never work. Natalie said, "The United States government doesn't negotiate with hijackers."

"Of course not." He stopped in front of her and bent down to look directly in her eyes. "But your wealthy father will negotiate. And he will pay a princely sum to have his dear little daughter safely returned."

He was right.

Clearly, she saw the fiendishly simple logic to this campaign. First came the written threats to start the engine of fear. Then, the bombing escalated the threats into the promise of danger. Real peril struck when she was attacked and nearly abducted on Saint Patrick's Day. Now the hijacking. Her father would believe that Nick and his men were serious in their threats. And her father would pay.

But why had they targeted Quantum? There were other captains of industry who were more wealthy, more powerful, more vulnerable. Why Quantum?

"Who do you work for?" she asked. "Who financed your operation?"

Without answering, he turned away from her. "Ladies and gentlemen, your comforts will be provided for. This ordeal should be over in less than two hours. You will not be harmed."

"How can we believe you?" Jerome Harris asked nervously. "You've already stabbed one person."

"Again, I apologize to Maria Luisa," said Nick.

She gasped and looked up. "How do you know my name?"

"I know all of you," Nick said. "I've researched your petty, boring lives. I know your salaries. I know what cars you drive. I know you are soft, spoiled and too self-indulgent to withstand pain or sacrifice. I also know you are intelligent enough to obey my commands."

"The bodyguard," Jerome said. "Is he dead?"

"Merely stunned." Nick held up a small rectangular device. "This is an Air Taser. The range is fifteen feet. When hit, you are paralyzed for several minutes, but the effect wears off. Much safer than guns for use on an aircraft. I'll demonstrate."

He whirled and fired at one of the men from the legal department. He cried out, then stiffened and fell from the sofa. On the floor, his body shuddered as he curled into a fetal position.

"Any questions?" Nick said smoothly.

All were silent.

"Keep in mind that we are also armed with conventional automatic firearms and will not hesitate to shoot if you don't obey. Shall I demonstrate the effect of a bullet through flesh?"

"We understand," Natalie said quickly. "Hold your fire."

"Very well." He withdrew his hand from his holstered pistol. "Natalie, please come with me."

Though it seemed that she should stay with the others,

she didn't dare to disobey. Yet, as she followed him down the narrow corridor, she considered attacking him from the rear. Possibly she could grab his gun or the Taser. But if she failed, the consequences might be terrible.

At the door to the private cabin, he turned to face her. His eyes pierced through her, seeming to read her mind. "You've decided to do as I tell you. Clever girl."

Inside the cabin, she noticed that the bed was back against the wall and the desk was in place. She hadn't left the room this way.

"Sit," he ordered.

She circled the desk and sat in the bolted-down swivel chair. Trying to take charge, she said, "Let's get these negotiations started. I assume you have a way to reach my father with your demands."

"In a moment." Reaching into the pocket of his flight crew jumpsuit, he produced a roll of duct tape. "Place your arms on the arms of the chair."

He came close, so close that she noticed the disgusting stench of his sweat. He smelled like fear. Though he appeared to be in complete control, the man who called himself Nick Beaumont was nervous. How could she use that information? How could she turn this situation around?

"You don't have to go through with the hijacking," she said. "Stop right now, and I'll make it all go away. You won't be arrested."

"Why would I stop now?"

"You're taking all the risk, but you're working for someone else," she guessed. "Someone else financed this operation."

He cocked his head and regarded her curiously. "Explain your logic."

"The bombing in Reykjavik. The surveillance time in Chicago. The costs of hijacking this plane. A lot of expenses. Someone else paid those bills, and they'll be the ones who reap the reward from extortion money. I'll double any amount they're paying you."

Quickly, he wrapped the tape tightly around her forearm, fastening her to the arm of the chair.

"I'd make the payment directly to you," she said. Though she was desperate, her voice remained calm. "Call this off right now, and I won't press charges. You'll be paid."

"I will be paid," he said. "My way."

Natalie strained against the tape. "It isn't necessary to tie me up. I won't do anything that would endanger the lives of my employees."

"Think about those lives," he said as he backed away from her. "Their survival depends upon you and your father."

"What are you doing?" Her muscles tensed as she pulled against her bonds. "Are you leaving?"

"Patience, Natalie. I'll be back soon enough."

He closed the door. She was on her own. Helpless to do anything. Frustrated, she clenched and unclenched her fists. Even if this was only an extortion scheme and not a terrorist action, she foresaw no good outcome.

"Don't scream" came a whisper from behind the wall sofa.

In two softly spoken words, she knew. "Quint!"

He stood and squeezed himself out of the narrow space between the sofa and the wall. "Natalie, keep your voice down."

But she wanted to yelp for joy. Her heart leaped. They were going to be all right! Quint wouldn't let anything bad happen to her. Then she saw it. His white shirt, untucked and unbuttoned, was spattered and smeared with blood.

"My God, Quint. Are you all right?"

"I'm fine," he whispered. "But you should see the other guy."

There was an automatic pistol tucked into the waistband of his jeans. He flipped open a switchblade to cut the tape holding her arms. "Don't," she said. "Don't untie me."

"Honey, this ain't the time to get kinky."

"I can negotiate with this guy. He's not going to hurt me. I'm his meal ticket."

Quint closed the blade with a *click*. He peered into her eyes with ferocious intensity as if he were absorbing the sight of her. And she gave herself gladly to his scrutiny, wishing she could melt into him, that she could be a part of him.

Damn it, why had he come back? Their situation was hopeless. Quint would be killed, too.

Gently, he touched her cheek. He kissed her forehead lightly. "You're the bravest woman I've ever known."

"I'm not." She desperately wanted to believe they'd survive, but she feared the worst. "I'm scared, Quint. I don't want to die."

"Hush now." He kissed her mouth, taking away her sadness and giving her every reason to go on living. "Nobody's going to die."

He stood up straight, looking every inch the hero she needed. For the first time in her life, she felt she wasn't alone. Quint would be with her. He would support her and protect her.

With one last caress, he moved away. "Go ahead with your negotiating. You were doing good."

"What are you going to do?"

"I'm going to kick some hijacker butt." His grin was almost gleeful. "Then I'm going to take back this plane."

He slipped into the bathroom adjoining the private suite. Though she couldn't see what he was doing, she heard the *click* of a latch, shuffling noises and then silence. Quint had vanished into the bowels of the plane.

Natalie had to believe she'd see him again.

IN THE FORWARD CARGO BAY, Nicco released Scout from his carrier and held him. Wagging his tail, the dog licked his master's face.

"Good boy," Nicco said. He couldn't leave Scout down here. The belly of the plane was too cold.

The Border collie hopped down to the floor and started toward the rear cargo bay. Very likely, they'd find the coward who'd been afraid to charge the passenger cabin back here, hiding in the dark.

"Alex," Nicco called out. "Where are you?"

He slid open the door to the rear cargo bay. Alex's participation was not necessary. Nicco's plan did not require four men and a pilot. Three could handle the hostages easily.

But he didn't like loose ends. "Alex?"

The fool must be hiding with the luggage, afraid for his miserable life. He should be frightened. This was the second time he'd failed. First in Grant Park on Saint Patrick's Day. Now on the plane.

Nicco unholstered his firearm. For a moment, he considered firing into each container until he heard the scream of his comrade. But he thought better of that action. These walls were insulated but it was best not to shoot inside a plane.

Scout paused at a spot on the floor and gave a soft bark.

"What is it, boy? What have you found?"

Nicco knelt. Blood on the floor?

He glanced toward the metal stairway leading up to the rear galley. In the shadows, he saw a black Stetson.

Chapter Eleven

Quint wedged and twisted to fit his long body through plumbing underneath the shower in the private suite. Legs dangling, he dropped into the forward cargo hold. He crouched, arms spread wide and gun in hand, ready for an assault. But no one appeared. So far, so good.

Surrounded by semidarkness and the constant hum from the turbojet engines, he peered into corners as he moved cautiously. It was cold down here. He noticed the dog's carrying cage was empty. The dog's master—alias Nick Beaumont—had been here.

Moving as quickly as possible, he went to the aft cargo hold, to a built-in storage locker. Carefully he opened the locker. The guy with the mustache was inside, barely moving, still unconscious. He was bound and gagged. No need to tie his feet. One of his legs had been broken in their knife fight. Later, Quint would get first aid for his victim, but he wasn't in a rush. There were a whole lot of other things to do.

He found his jacket where he'd left it behind a storage trunk, and slipped it on to ward off the chill in the cargo hold.

Then he looked for his hat. Nowhere to be found. If Nick Beaumont had picked up his Stetson, Quint had lost his only advantage—the element of surprise. That was…not good.

In spite of his boast to Natalie that he'd take care of everything, Quint had no idea what came next. If he'd been alone on the aircraft, without hostages, he might have tried a surprise attack. By reputation among the Confidential branches, he was known as the Lone Ranger, taking on a gang of bad guys with only his six-gun and his horse. Not this time. Too many other people would be hurt. Besides, he couldn't overpower three armed men. Actually, there had to be four men, because another hijacker must be in the cockpit, piloting the aircraft.

At the very least, he needed technical assistance. Quint pulled the cell phone from his pocket and speed-dialed Chicago Confidential. When Kathy Renk answered, he spoke softly. "I'm in deep trouble. Hijacked."

Within seconds, he heard Vincent's voice. "Quint, where are you?"

"Hijacked on the Quantum corporate jet, headed toward the nation's capital."

"I'll contact the FBI."

"No," Quint said quickly. In these perilous times, the Air Force was likely to shoot down a hijacked plane rather than taking a chance on more deaths from a targeted crash.

"How many hijackers?"

"Four, maybe five," Quint said. And he was sure one of them would always be with Natalie. If he thwarted their mission but failed to eliminate all of them, she'd surely be their first victim. He imagined a gun to her head, fear and resignation in her beautiful green eyes. *Don't go there!* He couldn't start thinking about the danger to Natalie, or his rage would overtake his smarts.

"What can we do to help?" Vincent asked.

"Have Andy start tracking the flight."

"Done," Vincent said. "What else?"

"Line up an expert pilot. I need somebody who knows how to fly a modified Boeing 737."

"I've got just the guy. Anything else?"

The flight deck was equipped with the new security doors, and that presented a problem. If he was going to take over the plane, he needed to be at the controls. "I want to create a malfunction to draw the pilot off the flight deck. Have Andy look up specs so I can manually disconnect the autopilot."

"Better yet," Vincent said, "we'll figure out how to reset the course away from D.C."

Apparently, Vincent was also thinking of national security. Even if they didn't alert the Feds, Chicago Confidential couldn't be responsible for allowing a hijacked jet to enter Washington, D.C.'s airspace.

Quint was about to disconnect, when Vincent said, "Somebody here wants to talk to you."

A familiar voice boomed over the phone. "Hey, Quintin Crawford."

It was Daniel Austin, the founder of Montana Confidential—Quint's good friend. "Hey, Dan, you sorry son of a sheepherder. How the heck are you?"

"Can't complain. I understand you got yourself in a heap of trouble."

"Nothing I can't handle," Quint lied. He'd never felt so overwhelmed.

"Whitney's been telling me you found a girlfriend—that pretty girl I asked you to keep an eye on. Is that true?"

The sheer incongruity of gossiping about his social life while he was stuck in the cargo hold of a hijacked aircraft amused Quint. Dan Austin had never been one to acknowledge danger, even when it was staring him in the face. "Yep, I hooked up with her—she sure is a real pretty, real smart woman."

"I got a question." Daniel's voice turned serious. "Do you love her?"

Quint recognized the deeper meaning. During his first days with Texas Confidential, Quint had been in a transition from his grief back to life. He'd been learning how to accept his wife's death, had done a lot of talking about her. Dan Austin was the only man who'd ever seen him cry.

Quint remembered saying over and over that there would never be another woman for him. His heart had died with Paula, and he would never love again. But Natalie had changed that. She'd taken his sorrowful words and shredded them by demanding everything he had to give. No holding back. She pushed him to the limit, which was okay because she applied the same standard to herself.

"I love her like there's no tomorrow."

"Then, you'd best get that aircraft down in one piece. I intend to be best man at your wedding."

"You sound like Natalie," Quint said. "She's always got to be the best, too."

"Henry's told me that about her." He paused. "Good luck, partner."

The call ended. Quint pocketed the cell phone just as the hatch leading to the rear cabin opened. Quint hunkered down. Somebody was coming to take a look around. Looking for him? Had Nick Beaumont sent out the forces, knowing that Quint was in the cargo hold?

A foreign-accented voice called out, "Alex, you coward. Come out! I don't want to waste time looking for you."

Quint angled around to get a clear shot at whomever might come down those stairs. He switched the semiautomatic pistol to single shot. The last thing they needed was a hail of bullets in the belly of an aircraft.

A stocky man lumbered down the stairs. With thick shoulders and neck, he looked like a weightlifter. In his right hand, he held an automatic pistol. He grumbled in a language Quint couldn't quite understand. Maybe German.

Up in the cabin, Quint had overheard Nick Beaumont speaking German. Another of the hijackers spoke in French. This crew seemed to be drawn from several different nationalities, which might indicate that their goals weren't politically motivated. They truly were in this for the money.

In English, the weightlifter said, "You're like a little girl, Alex. Come upstairs and you can help the ladies bake fresh cookies."

As he shuffled around the perimeter of the rear cargo hold, Quint had a clear opportunity to shoot. But if he did, the others would be alerted. They'd know for sure that Quint was on the plane, and would come gunning for him before he had time to adjust the autopilot. It was better to wait.

The weightlifter came closer, shoving at the various containers, banging on the metal storage lockers. A few more steps and they'd be face-to-face. Quint was pretty sure it'd take more than one bullet to bring this guy down. Better to use the Taser.

"I give up!" The weightlifter bellowed, "Stay down here and freeze in the dark, coward."

He turned back toward the steep metal stairs. Heavily, he climbed them.

Quint hoped he hadn't made a mistake in letting this big guy walk away.

He speed-dialed Confidential headquarters. Andy Dexter came on the line. "Okay, Quint. Go through the forward cargo bay, close as you can get to the nose of the plane. You'll find a rectangular panel, something like a fuse box. It's labeled EQUIP, and it's going to be hard to open. Have you got tools?"

"Just a switchblade. I'll call back when I find it."

Quint returned to the forward hold through the sliding door. His step was steady, but his nerves were tight. He had to pull off this maneuver. It had to work. He couldn't fail. He would not lose the woman he loved in an airplane incident. Not again.

STILL TAPED TO THE CHAIR in the private cabin, Natalie shifted uncomfortably as Nick Beaumont tossed a black

Stetson on the desk in front of her. Was this his way of telling her that Quint was captured? Or dead? Though panic screamed inside her, she kept her lips sealed. The first rule in any negotiation was to make the adversary speak first.

"Your boyfriend," Nick said. "I didn't see him among the other passengers."

He hadn't seen Quint! Good! Natalie lifted her chin. "He's not here. He was going to meet me tomorrow in Washington."

"But he left his hat." Nick's voice was dangerously low. "A cowboy never leaves his hat."

"I don't know anything about it," she said truthfully. Indeed, she didn't know how or why Quint had dropped his hat. "Maybe he gave his hat, or one like it, to one of the other people on the plane."

The ring of truth in her voice must have convinced him, because Nick relaxed. He strolled to the sofa, sat and made a summoning motion with his hand.

A dog responded. The black-and-white Border collie hopped spryly onto the sofa, though missing a front leg. It seemed a bright-eyed animal, intelligent. Why would a hijacker bring his pet on the flight?

"His name is Scout," Nick said. "And when this is over, my dog and I will retire to a quiet place where there are no jets flying overhead and no fools to bother us."

Why was he telling her his plans?

"You see, Natalie, I wasn't raised in a privileged home with ponies and swimming pools and yearly vacations to Disneyland. When I was fourteen, I was on my own. Fortunately, I discovered my particular genius—a talent for handling explosives, building bombs." He scratched behind his dog's ears. "I worked alone. And I learned to disdain the people who used my services. All of them, fools. Black or white. Christian or Muslim. They're all the same. Beneath contempt."

She nodded, encouraging him to continue. The more

time he wasted in self-reflection, the more time Quint had to perfect a plan.

"My brother," he said, "was apprehended in Grant Park. I don't blame you or your cowboy friend. My brother was clumsy, and he will pay the price in prison."

She thought of her sister, Caroline. If anything bad happened to her, Natalie would move heaven and earth to help her. To abandon his brother, Nick Beaumont must have ice water in his veins.

"Human life means nothing to me," he said.

Through her fear, she tried to analyze this man who still wore the ground crew jumpsuit. If she understood him, she might have an edge in negotiating. What could she deduce? He was bitter. Apparently, he hated everyone equally. Emotion played very little part in his self-absorbed, egotistic thinking. He must be a true sociopath, a man without conscience.

Though she only knew the psychology she'd learned in college textbooks and in years of sitting around conference tables, Natalie figured her diagnosis made sense. A sociopath. That might explain his audacity. Nick Beaumont needed blind arrogance to think he could get away with a hijacking in a climate of heightened national security.

"If you don't care about anyone or anything, why did you target Quantum?"

"The opportunity presented itself. You have many enemies. They were willing to finance my operation."

"Zahir?" she asked. "But that couldn't be. He doesn't have ready cash. It must have been Sheik Khalaf Al-Sayed."

His bemused smile neither confirmed nor denied her conclusion. "Does it matter?"

"I should think it matters to you. How can you be sure they'll pay you for your efforts?" This might be the logic she needed. She could promise him real cash. She wouldn't go back on her word. "You can't really trust Zahir or the sheik."

"Your reasoning is backward," he said.

She frowned. Backward? "Are you telling me that the sheik and Zahir can't trust you?"

He nodded. There was a hint of triumph in his smug expression. "A double cross," he said.

"You're going to keep the ransom money for yourself." It was a dangerous plan. In a way, brilliant. "Surely, those who financed you will seek revenge."

"Unless they are unavoidably detained in one of your fine United States prisons." Giving his dog one final pat on the head, he rose and came toward the desk. "I tell you these things so you will understand, Natalie, that I have no moral reluctance to betray anyone. Without a single qualm, I will kill every person on this plane."

She believed him. The depths of his blue eyes held no expression. In a rush, she reminded him, "But we're useful as hostages."

"Essential," he agreed.

"And you've been careful not to harm anyone," she said. "No one was hurt by the explosion in Reykjavik. Or in my office."

"I find it expedient not to create martyrs."

"I don't understand."

"It's simple. Your father can accept the loss of this aircraft. But if he lost an employee, he might be more aggressive. And if he lost a daughter…"

"He'd never forget." She despised this rational yet evil logic. "He'd devote the rest of his life to hunting you down."

"Now you understand why you're still alive." He gripped her chin and forced her to look up at him. "You and I, Natalie, we have the same goals. If my demands are met, you and the others will survive. You must convince your father."

"I will," she said.

Natalie didn't point out the most serious flaw in his sociopathic reasoning. Hijacking was a serious crime for which he would be prosecuted in every nation in the world. And there was another, more immediate flaw. "After you release the hostages, you have no more bargaining power. What will you do then?"

"At least one hostage must stay with me until I am safe."

"Me?"

"Smart girl."

"And then," she asked, "what happens to me?"

He took a knife from his pocket. Lightly he drew the tip of the blade across her throat. Then, he released her chin. Quick and businesslike, he cut the duct tape he'd used to fasten her arms to the chair. Pointing to the telephone on the desk, he said, "Get your father on the phone. Say nothing of the hijacking until you have reached him."

Natalie flexed her numbed fingers, shrugged and bobbed her head from side to side as if a few simple stretches would relieve her gut-wrenching terror. There was very little chance that she would make it through this ordeal alive. Quint was her only hope. Realistically, what could he do? He couldn't overpower these armed men.

"Do it," Nick said. "Do I need to bring one of your little friends in here and hurt them to remind you of the consequences for disobedience?"

"No," she said quickly. "I'll make the call."

She was about to bargain for the lives of the other passengers on board, and she didn't feel up to the task. With all her heart, she wished the weight of this horrible responsibility rested upon someone else's shoulders.

She punched in her father's private cell phone number. At this hour, he ought to be home, probably in his office.

"Use the speakerphone," Nick said.

She longed to be rescued from this nightmare, to wake up and find herself safe in Quint's strong arms. She wanted a future with him—a loving and endless series of tomorrows with children and a dog.

Glancing over at the sofa, she saw Scout innocently

wagging his tail. He cocked his head, seeming sympathetic.

She heard her father's voice, distorted by the speakerphone. "Hello?"

"It's me, Natalie. Are you alone?"

"As a matter of fact, I am. I'm in my office, digesting a very dull chicken dinner. You know how your mother is about cholesterol."

With a stab of pain, Natalie thought of what this would do to her mother. All Mom had ever wanted was for her daughters to be happy.

"Natalie? What's wrong?"

"Oh, Dad, I love you so much." A tremor broke her words. Quickly, she swallowed her panic. "I need you to do something for me."

"Name it."

"The corporate jet has been hijacked by the terrorists. But they're not really terrorists. They have no political statement. They're not on a suicide mission. You can't notify the authorities."

"The hell I can't. If I—"

"Henry, you're on the speakerphone."

"What do the bastards want?"

"Money," she said. "They know they can't negotiate with the government. They only want to talk to you. If you don't pay them, they'll kill everyone on the plane. Do you understand?"

There was silence. She imagined her father standing, gripping the phone with a white-knuckled fist. When he spoke, his voice was strong.

"I'll pay."

"You can't notify anyone," she said desperately.

"I understand. Let me talk to them."

Nick Beaumont leaned across the desk. "Good evening, Henry Van Buren."

"Who are you? Who do you work for?"

"Know this, sir. I hold the lives of your employees and your daughter in my hands. You will do exactly as I say."

"One condition," her father said. "I want to stay in contact with Natalie at all times. If she's harmed in any way, I will contact the FBI."

"Your daughter is well," he said.

"How much do you want?"

"Ten million dollars."

"Impossible," Henry snapped. "It's night. The banks are closed. How can I come up with that kind of—"

"Somewhere in the world," Nick said, "banks are open. I wish for this money to be exchanged in a series of computer wire transfers."

Natalie had to admire the cleverness of this ransom scheme. There would be no messy exchange of cash or gold bullion or bearer bonds. By the time the U.S. banks opened in the morning, the money would be long gone, transferred from one point to another until it vanished into an unreachable secret account.

"I'll pay," her father said. "But I don't know the mechanics of this kind of transaction. I need help."

"Jerome Harris," Natalie said. "The head of Accounting is on the plane. He can facilitate the transfers."

"I know," Nick said. He stepped into the corridor and shouted toward the front lounge. "Bring Jerome Harris in here."

The nervous little man walked in stiffly. He'd peeled off his suit coat and loosened his collar. Never before had Natalie seen Jerome without a necktie.

Though she'd been terrified to conduct these negotiations herself, the idea of handing the transaction over to Jerome was even more frightening. He didn't look as if he could remember his own name, much less perform the complex tasks before him.

Under the watchful eye of Nick Beaumont, she left her desk chair and guided Jerome to the seat. Her voice was gentle. "My father is on the speakerphone, Jerome. He has a job that requires your expertise."

His eyes darted to her face. "I can't."

"We need you to facilitate the ransom payment."

"I can't." He held up trembling hands. "I can't."

Irritation flashed through her. Did she need to tell Jerome what would happen if he failed? Did she need to remind him that they would all die if the ransom wasn't paid?

She forced herself to smile. Jerome looked like he might crack into a million pieces if one more ounce of pressure were applied.

"It's just a task, Jerome. A money transfer. It's the kind of work you do every single day."

"Jerome." Her father's voice came over the speakerphone. "Are you there?"

"Yes," he squeaked.

"We need to access several different accounts."

"Can't think." Jerome's breathing was shallow. He looked as if he might hyperventilate.

Standing by the door, Nick Beaumont removed the safety from his automatic pistol. "We don't have time for this."

"Wait!" Natalie had an idea. She leaned close to Jerome. "Do you like dogs?"

His brow furrowed, but he nodded.

She called to the black-and-white Border collie who still sat obediently on the sofa. "Here, boy. Come here, Scout."

The dog hopped down from the sofa and came toward the desk. Scout was just tall enough to rest his chin on Jerome's knee.

"He's a great dog," Natalie said. "Give him a pat on the head, Jerome."

Tentatively, the little accountant reached down. As he stroked the soft fur on the top of the dog's head, Natalie continued talking to him in a soothing voice. "Everything is going to be all right. As soon as you take care of the money transfer, we'll all be safe. We'll get off the plane and have a nice dinner. I'm so glad you're here, Jerome.''

Behind her back, she heard Nick Beaumont scoff, but she continued with her reassurances until she could see the high-strung Jerome Harris begin to relax. His constant stroking of Scout seemed to be having an effect.

"All right," Natalie said. "You can do this, Jerome."

"I guess I don't have a choice."

"You're okay." She lightly patted his arm. "I won't leave the room. I'll just sit over here on the sofa."

"Can Scout stay by me?" he asked.

"Yes," said Nick Beaumont as he took Natalie's place. From an inner pocket he produced a sheet of paper with a column of numbers. "When the transaction is successfully completed, I will receive a signal. Until that moment, you must do exactly as I say."

"How much money are we talking about?"

"Ten million," Natalie's father said over the speakerphone. "Don't quibble, Jerome."

"Yes, sir."

While Jerome tapped computer keys on a laptop, her father supplied additional code numbers and Nick Beaumont oversaw the routing. Though Natalie tried to concentrate, this was not her area of expertise. The transaction was beyond her comprehension.

Her thoughts traveled a dangerous path, thinking of what came next. Even if they managed the money transfer and landed safely at the private airfield near Washington, D.C. customarily used by Quantum, even if the other hostages were released, she would still be on the plane with Nick Beaumont and his crew. They would have to refuel and take off again. Then what? An unknown destination. It seemed impossible to keep the hijacking a secret. They would never find a place to land the plane.

Even if the hijacking scheme went off without a hitch, would her life be spared? Though she wanted to cling to that thin shred of hope, there were too many ways it might unravel.

Could she escape? Her gaze drifted toward the bathroom. Quint had somehow managed to disappear in there. He'd gone through a hatch. She might be able to do the same.

Without warning, the jet lurched violently. Shouts of surprise echoed from the lounge. Natalie felt herself being thrown back against the sofa. The aircraft banked left, making a sharp turn. She saw Jerome's hands fly off the computer keys. Nick Beaumont barely stayed on his feet.

"Don't stop," he ordered Jerome. He gestured to Natalie. "You. Come with me."

"Natalie!" Her father's voice boomed over the speakerphone. "What's happening? Are you all right?"

Nick Beaumont informed him, "She's coming with me."

"I had one condition," Henry Van Buren said. "My daughter stays in touch with me on this phone. If she's gone, the whole thing's off."

There were more shouts from the lounge area. Nick didn't have time to argue. His hand grasped the doorknob. His cold eyes made contact with hers. "Don't be a fool," he said. "You know how I deal with fools."

The instant he left, she went toward the bathroom where Quint had found a hatch. "Come on, Jerome. There's a way out. Tell my father that I'm okay."

"Sir," Jerome said meekly into the speakerphone, "your daughter is trying to escape."

"Natalie, stop it," her father ordered.

She dashed back into the room. "I'm not going to sit in this cabin and wait until that sociopath decides it's time to shoot me."

"Excuse me," Jerome said, "I've got some more numbers. Should I enter them?"

"Do what he says," her father ordered. "Natalie, I forbid you to take this risk."

Somewhere on this aircraft, Quint was doing his best to rescue them. She had to help him. "Henry, I'm going. I'll be okay."

"Excuse me," Jerome repeated a little more loudly.

"What?" Natalie yelled.

"The numbers," Jerome said. "I recognized some of these sequences. The initial routing of the money transfer is through Zahir."

"That bastard," her father snarled. "I'm calling the Feds."

"Don't," she said. "Please don't. They'll blast us out of the sky before they allow a hijacked plane to fly into Washington airspace. Don't do anything until I talk to you again."

"Natalie," he snapped.

"What is it, Henry?"

"I love you, honey. Be careful."

"I love you, Dad." She didn't intend to die. Not for a very long time.

Chapter Twelve

A warning light flashed on the avionics panel in the cargo hold. Quint didn't know what he'd done wrong, didn't know how to fix the error. He'd followed Andy Dexter's instructions precisely. He'd adjusted switches and copied a series of numbers into a keypad. The autopilot should've been manually reset to change the course of their flight.

Something had changed, all right. The whine from the turbojets ratcheted louder and louder. They were losing altitude. The aircraft bucked. They continued to bank steeply left.

"Andy," he said into the cell phone. "This isn't right. Feels like we're in a downward spiral."

"The manual override was correct," Andy said. "I'm sure it was."

Quint might have felt a little more confident if Andy had been a certified pilot instead of a computer jockey. "This isn't a simulator. We got a real aircraft here and it's—"

"Human error," Andy said. "Your pilot hasn't turned off the other autodrive instructions. Give him a minute to figure it out."

The floor beneath Quint's feet dropped as the aircraft took another swoop. It felt as if they were standing on one wing. He'd never heard of a jet this size attempting a roll-over and didn't want to be the first to try. "I can't wait. What can I do?"

"Get to the flight deck," Andy said. "Hit the autopilot switch."

Easier said than done. The whole point of this diversion was to draw the pilot away from the controls so Quint could get past the security door into the cockpit. There was no guarantee the pilot would come down here to check on the manual avionics, even though the warning lights on the flight deck instrument panel had to be flashing like Las Vegas on a Saturday night.

Given his druthers, Quint would have preferred to regain control of the aircraft in a more subtle fashion, luring each of the hijackers separately into the cargo hold. But he had to play the hand he'd been dealt—to handle an aviation emergency and to eliminate the hijackers at the same time.

Fighting the force of gravity that propelled him to the left, he went to the forward hatch and pulled down the hinged metal stairs. At the top of the steep stairs was a door with a circular handle. If twisted clockwise, a push would open it.

With pistol in hand, Quint prepared to open that door and emerge into the passenger cabin. He had to move fast. His training in close combat taught him that his best chance was to charge head-on, giving himself an instant of surprise before his enemies reacted. But when he got to the passenger cabin, he'd be outnumbered. And the hijackers were armed. Quint reckoned his chance of survival was worse than Custer at Little Big Horn.

A mental picture of Natalie flashed across his brain. Clear as crystal, he saw her smart-alecky smile and the ever-present challenge in her green eyes. She was an incredible woman. Losing her would be his greatest regret. Silently, he wished her goodbye—

"Quint, where are you?"

Either he was hearing things or that was her voice. "Natalie?"

Through the semidarkness of the cargo hold, he saw her. A combination of dread and sweet relief flooded through his veins as she rushed toward him. Sure-footed and strong, the list of the plane didn't slow her approach. She crashed into his arms, and he held her tightly, buried his face in her fragrant chestnut hair.

She shouldn't be with him. The risk was too great. "How'd you get here?"

"Squeezed through the plumbing under the private cabin." She beamed up at him. Her face was smudged, but her expression was alert. "What do we do next?"

"I'm running up those stairs. By myself. When I get up there, I'm going to take out a couple of hijackers and somehow get onto the flight deck."

"Bad idea," she said. "Charging up at them puts you at a disadvantage. Wait until they come down here to fix the autopilot, then we can pick them off."

"I can't wait." If he didn't get to the controls and stabilize the aircraft, they'd crash.

As he spoke, the handle on the hatch turned. *They were coming.*

Against his better judgment, he placed the Taser in her hand and positioned her to the side of the stairs. "Zap the first person who comes through the hatch. The Taser range is only fifteen feet."

"Got it," she said. "What will you do?"

He took the safety off the handgun. "I'll be ready for the second guy."

There was no more time for planning.

With a crash, the first hijacker charged down the metal stairs. It was the weightlifter. He got off a couple of shots before Natalie zapped him. As he was falling, Quint climbed over his body to confront the second man—Smilin' Jack, the co-pilot.

With a grin as tight as a corpse in rigor, Jack stared, recognized his adversary. He'd hesitated too long. Quint aimed and fired his handgun twice. Two hits. One in the arm. One in the leg.

Smilin' Jack went down.

Brutally, Quint shoved Jack out of the way, grabbed Natalie by the hand and pulled her up through the hatch. They raced into the bright lights of the cabin. To their right was the lounge where the passengers were screaming and tumbling in chaos.

To the left was the flight deck. The security door was wide open! Finally, he'd caught a break. He rushed inside, dragging Natalie with him.

Handing her the gun, he said, "Shoot anybody that walks through that door."

The pilot, unconscious, was safety belted into the jump seat at the rear. No one was at the controls. The aircraft continued its crazy rolling tilt.

Quint leaped into the pilot's seat. He stared through the windshield at a sheer black night, which made it impossible to visually navigate. Though he'd flown small planes and knew the basics of rudder and yoke, this was a full-size jet with a whole lot of flashing lights and dials and gears. He pulled back on the yoke to regain altitude. Nothing happened. He tried to counter the spiraling left descent. None of the instruments responded.

He punched speed dial on the cell phone. "Andy, I'm on the flight deck. We're losing altitude. The horizontal direction indicator is going crazy. Still banking hard left."

"Turn off the autopilot."

"Where is it?"

"Look for a switch on the upper right of the overhead panel."

When Quint hit the switch, the massive turbojets seemed to sigh with relief. He grasped the yoke and felt the jet respond. Using skills he thought he'd forgotten, Quint managed to level the plane's descent and control the tilt.

Reading the altimeter, he could tell they were lower than the standard cruising speed but not dangerously near the earth. They were still above the cloud cover.

He glanced over at Natalie in the co-pilot's seat. Her hair was mussed. Her cheeks flushed. Bracing the barrel of the automatic pistol on the back of the chair, she concentrated on the door to the cockpit with savage intensity. Nobody in their right mind would mess with this woman.

He grinned. "That's my gal."

"What comes next, cowboy?"

"Hell, I don't know. I didn't think we'd get this far." Picking up the cell phone, he said, "Are you tracking us, Andy?"

"You're on radar," said an unfamiliar voice. "This is Colonel Robbie Roberts, U.S. Air Force, retired. Currently with Chicago Confidential."

The sweet sound of practical experience! Colonel Roberts sounded better than Garth Brooks and Pavarotti combined. "Glad you're with me, Colonel. No offense, Andy."

"None taken." He snorted a laugh. "Over and out."

Colonel Roberts said, "Daniel Austin tells me that you used to be a damn good pilot. Right?"

"Roger," Quint said. "But flying my little Cessna was like riding a tricycle. This jet is a Harley-Davidson hog."

"The principles are the same," the colonel said. He proceeded to give Quint the fast course on the layout of the instrument panel. "When your altitude is twelve hundred meters, I've got the new numbers you need to feed into the autopilot computer."

Mindful that he still had two hijackers on the loose, Quint adjusted the tillers and increased vertical thrust. "Where's the autopilot going to take us?"

"You're coming back to Chicago, man."

"Good." To Quint, Chicago sounded like home, sweet home.

WHEN THE AIRCRAFT STABILIZED, Nicco left a man in charge of the passengers in the lounge and returned to the private cabin, where the idiot accountant still cowered behind the desk with Scout at his feet.

Natalie was nowhere in sight, but Nicco couldn't worry about her now. His carefully laid plan was falling to pieces.

"The transaction," Nicco demanded. "Is it complete?"

"I've done everything you told me."

"Out of my way." He pushed the little man aside.

With a fearful yelp, Jerome Harris scurried into the lavatory and closed the door.

Nicco plugged one last set of numbers into the computer and stepped back. The seconds passed like hours. He bent down and stroked Scout's black-and-white fur. His plan would change, but success was still within his grasp. The next moments would require every bit of his ingenuity.

On the computer screen, a message flashed: Received. *Ten million dollars. Received.* In a secret account beyond any regulating agency. By the time they caught up to him, he'd have the money in cash or gold bullion.

His challenge now was to get off this damn aircraft.

He signaled Scout to follow as he went toward the door. As an afterthought, he fired a spray of bullets into the closed lavatory door. Jerome Harris was one witness he could do without.

Leaving the private cabin, Nicco shouted instructions in French to his man in the lounge. Then he hurried toward the rear of the plane. He passed the seating area and went through the galley with Scout right behind him.

In the belly of the plane, he would make his final move.

WHILE QUINT HANDLED maneuvers with the aircraft, Natalie kept her focus on the door leading into the cockpit. Her assignment was to shoot without hesitation. The automatic handgun felt impossibly heavy in her hand.

Could she shoot another human being in cold blood?

When she'd zapped the hijacker with the Taser and he fell, there hadn't been time to think. And she knew the man would recover from the stun gun assault. If she fired lead bullets, she would commit murder.

Though she could aim for the arms or legs, her marksmanship wasn't that good. In every self-defense training session she'd ever taken, the instructor encouraged them to aim at the largest target. The torso.

From inside the cabin, she heard gunfire and screaming. Her heart jumped. Those were her people inside the plane. They were her responsibility. All her life, she'd groomed herself for leadership. If she had to commit murder to defend them, Natalie would.

Stealing a glance at Quint, she admired his unflappable calm. "Do you ever get afraid when you do this Confidential stuff?"

"Oh, yeah." He stretched his arm to reach across the center panel and touch her shoulder. "There was only one time in my life when I could face danger without fear. After my wife died, I didn't feel like I had anything to live for."

"Were you suicidal?"

"Never," he said. "But if I'd happened upon death, it wouldn't have mattered. I guess I'm lucky the grim reaper didn't stop by."

"Why?"

"I never would've met you. Being with you makes all the pain worthwhile. You give me a reason for living."

A warmth surged through her. "Even now?"

"Especially now," Quint said. "We're going to get through this, Natalie—"

From out of nowhere, the hijacker lunged through the doorway. His gun blazed. Bullets ricocheted through the flight deck.

Natalie fired back. She should have gone for his torso, but her aim centered on his arms and legs.

He dropped the gun. He stumbled. With disbelieving

eyes, he stared directly at her. Then, he toppled backward to the floor.

"Get his gun," Quint ordered. "And the Taser."

She leaped into action. With all her strength, she rolled the man to his back. He was the smallest of the hijackers, and she thought she'd heard him speaking French. Blood seeped from his wounds, spreading dark stains at his shoulder and thigh. His eyes winced tightly shut but he was still breathing. She hadn't killed him.

With his weapons in hand, she said, "He's not dead. We've got to start first aid."

Through the door of the flight deck, she saw Maria Luisa. Her left arm was bandaged. In her right hand, she held a golf club, ready to attack.

"It's okay," Natalie called to her. "Come here. Quickly. I need help."

When Maria Luisa stepped into the flight deck, her dark eyes widened in her ashen face. She gasped.

Natalie turned and looked over her shoulder. She saw, for the first time, the damage wrought by the hijacker's bullets. Sparks danced across the instrument panel like Saint Elmo's fire. Some of the dials had been shattered. The center panel between the seats appeared to have sustained most of the damage. Though Natalie smelled smoke, there was no discernible fire.

Quint's hands were busy, flipping switches, adjusting the dials.

Natalie shuddered. This was all her fault. If she'd fired more quickly, they wouldn't be in this danger. "Quint, what can I do to help?"

"Give me room," he said. "I think we're okay. Looks like the transponder is out."

"What does that mean?"

"We've got no way to communicate with the airport control towers." His hands gripped the yoke as he peered through the windshield into the darkness of night. "Should be okay as long as I can keep Colonel Roberts on the line.''

"I'm sorry," she whispered.

"For what?" He shot a swift glance over his shoulder. "You're the best damn backup I've ever had."

"Really? The best?"

"Number one," he said. "You're always number one with me."

She intended to occupy that position permanently. Turning back toward Maria Luisa, Natalie asked, "What's the situation in the cabin? There was one more terrorist in the cabin."

"The guy with the dog," she said. "He went to the rear of the plane, and I haven't seen him since."

Natalie counted up the threats. There was the huge guy she zapped with the Taser and Smilin' Jack—both of whom were in the front cargo hold. Now it sounded like Nick Beaumont had gone into the rear hold with his dog. "Okay, Quint. What do we do next?"

He asked, "Is there anybody back there who's got experience flying a plane?"

"Maybe one of the flight attendants," Natalie said.

Quint thought for a moment. Smilin' Jack had turned out to be working with the hijackers. There might still be a ringer among the flight crew. "What about one of the regular Quantum employees?"

"Gregory from Marketing," Maria Luisa said. "I know he does skydiving on weekends."

"Get him up here. Pronto."

After one last consultation with Colonel Roberts on the cell phone, Quint was fairly sure that the modified Boeing 737 was running all right. Miraculously, despite the hijacker shooting up the flight deck, their only real loss was the transponder.

According to tracking, the autopilot was keeping them on their new course toward Chicago. Right now, the danger from crashing due to mechanical difficulties was not imminent. It was more important to find and subdue the hijackers, especially Nick Beaumont.

When Gregory from Marketing came into the cabin, Quint got him seated in the pilot's seat. Maria Luisa would be beside him as co-pilot. Unless something happened, their job was to sit still. They needed to keep a watchful eye on the altitude, thrust and stabilization.

Gregory cleared his throat. "I've been taking flying lessons, but I'm not a certified pilot."

"It's okay," Quint said as he handed over the cell phone. "We're on autopilot. You shouldn't have to touch anything."

"And if I do?"

Quint patted him on the shoulder. "It'll be your first solo."

Gregory swallowed hard and gave him a thumbs-up. "You're coming back. Right?"

"Soon as I can," Quint assured him. "Don't worry, man. If you run into a problem, just do what Colonel Roberts tells you."

When Quint and Natalie left the flight deck, he closed the security door behind him. The flight deck was secure.

Gun in hand, Quint searched the crew lounge at the front of the plane. Assured that the area was safe, he closed the hatch leading to the cargo hold. He recruited another Quantum employee and armed him. Quint's instructions were simple. "If anybody pokes their head up from the cargo hold, shoot. Understand?"

Nervously, the guy nodded. His eyes flickered.

"Say it." Quint moved directly into his line of vision. "What are you going to do if somebody tries to come into the cabin?"

"I'll shoot."

"That's good," Quint said. "Again?"

"I'll shoot."

Maybe he would and maybe not. All these people were in shock, barely able to function. Their reflexes weren't sharp. Their wits had been paralyzed by terror. Somehow, he needed to force them back into functioning reality.

After he was sure the lounge was safe, Quint pulled Natalie to one side. "We got a problem."

"What's that?"

"The passengers are acting like a bunch of zombies. They need to stay alert. They've got to be smart. To toughen up."

"So sorry." Her eyebrows arched. "Hijacking is most definitely not part of their job description."

"Let's give them something to do," he suggested. "We need to set up an infirmary. Get everybody fed. Somehow, we need them to make the mental transition from hostages to warriors."

A grin lifted the corner of her mouth. "Leave it to me."

He'd seen her in action when the Quantum Building was evacuated. Natalie was a leader; she could whip her team into shape. "Fine. You take care of the strategy and planning. I'll hunt down Nick Beaumont."

"Consider it done," she said.

While Natalie returned to the lounge to organize the group, Quint completed his search of the seating area. In the aft galley, he closed the hatch door leading down to the cargo hold and slid a galley module on top of it. It wouldn't stop the hijackers if they made a concentrated assault, but it would slow them down.

The last place he searched was the private cabin. Nobody there. On the desk, the computer screen flashed a message: Received.

Quint reacted to a muffled noise from inside the lavatory. The door was pocked with bullet holes.

"Who's there?" Quint demanded. He stepped to one side so he wouldn't be directly in the line of fire from someone behind that door.

"It's me. Jerome Harris."

"Come on out, Jerome. Everything's okay."

The door creaked slightly open, then was flung wide.

Jerome sat on the closed toilet seat. There was blood everywhere. At least fifty paper towels were streaked with red. Jerome's white shirt was splattered with blood from a head wound, but his eyes were clear. He seemed charged with a new vigor as he bolted to his feet.

"I'm okay. It's only a superficial cut," he said. "But it's going to leave a scar."

Quint grinned. The little accountant seemed to have found his courage. "Women like men with scars."

"Do you think so?"

"When you tell the ladies that you got scarred in a face-to-face struggle with a hijacker, they'll be mighty impressed."

"I suppose they would be." His nose twitched as he grinned. Then he glanced toward the computer on the desktop. "I hope you cancelled the transaction."

"What transaction?" Quint asked.

"Oh dear, ten million dollars." Jerome ran to the computer and punched a series of keys. "There. Those hijackers will get nothing from us."

The message on the screen now said "Abort."

"Good work," Quint said. "Come on out here with everybody else. We'll get one of the ladies to take a look at that head wound."

As they stepped into the hall, Natalie intercepted Jerome and directed him toward the makeshift infirmary at the front of the plane. She stepped back into the private office with Quint. "We're trying to put together something to eat," she said, "but it's the strangest thing. There's practically no food. The galley modules don't even have trays."

"That's got to be how the hijackers got onto the plane," Quint said. "They were loaded on from the catering truck."

She nodded. "Except for that Smilin' Jack character who was posing as a co-pilot. Here's what I don't understand. Our regular pilot knew him, and didn't question his presence."

Quint nodded. In every field of expertise, there were traitors who could be bought to perform a specialized task. "Smilin' Jack probably is a real pilot with real credentials and history. If this hijacking had gone off as planned, he would've found a way to wiggle out of the charges against him."

"How?"

Good question. Quint tried to put himself in Smilin' Jack's mind. If Smilin' Jack received a gigantic payoff, he might disappear along with the other hijackers. On the other hand, there might be some twist Quint hadn't yet figured out. If Smilin' Jack landed the plane safely, he'd be acclaimed a hero. But how would the other hijackers escape?

"I'm missing something," he said, thinking aloud. "If nobody died in the hijacking, it would be nothing more than simple extortion."

Her eyes widened. "Oh my God, I've got to talk to my father. I need to let him know we're okay."

She raced to the office. Behind the desk, she punched numbers into the speakerphone. As soon as her father answered, she said, "Henry, it's me. We're okay. There are injuries but everybody is coming around. We have a little infirmary set up, and we're fine."

"Thank God you're all right."

Quint heard the tremor in his voice. This ordeal would be hell on a father. He leaned across the desk. "Sir, this is Quint. Have you been in contact with the Confidential office?"

"Yes. I spoke with Vincent and Dan Austin."

"We're flying back to Chicago," Quint said. "Ought to be there within the hour."

"Take care of my little girl."

"I'll try, but Natalie's real busy taking care of everybody else." He set his gun on the desktop, stepped back

and folded his arms across his chest as he studied her.
"Mr. Van Buren, you raised a hell of a fine woman."

"And a darn good executive," she said and sinuously
walked toward Quint.

"Natalie," her father said, "that sounds like you're
looking for a promotion."

"Actually, I thought I might take some time off." She
gazed up at Quint. "I'd like a vacation, Henry. And I've
never spent much time in Texas."

Quint wrapped his arms around her. His hands rested on
the small of her back, and he pulled her against him. He
was ready to kiss her beautiful lips, but it didn't seem
proper while her daddy was on the phone.

"Don't worry about a thing, sir. We'll be back home
directly."

"'Bye, Henry." Still in Quint's arms, she leaned back
and disconnected the call.

His hands slipped lower, cupping her firm buttocks. Already, he was aroused. "Someday," he promised, "we're
going to use the bed in this suite."

He kissed her hard, replacing his tension with a strong
pure passion. Her breasts rubbed against him. He could
feel the tight nubs of her nipples.

Lifting her onto the desk, he stepped between her legs.
"When this is over," Quint said, "you're taking that vacation and coming to Texas with me."

She wrapped her legs around him and looked up with a
sly, sexy smile. "I hear everything is bigger in Texas."

He laughed. "I'm going to make sure you have a long
time to figure that out."

"Maybe a week," she said.

"Maybe a month." *Maybe forever.* He kissed her again.

The door to the private suite flew open and Maria Luisa
burst in. "Come quick. We have a problem."

Moving fast, they untangled themselves. Together, they
raced to the flight deck, where Gregory was still sitting in
the pilot's seat.

"What's wrong?" Quint asked.

"I'm not sure." Gregory gratefully relinquished his seat. "Colonel Roberts wanted to talk to you."

Quint grabbed the cell phone as he sat in the pilot's seat. "Yes, Colonel, what's up?"

"You've got an escort. A wolf pack of F-14 fighter planes."

Full protection from the United States Air Force sounded like the cavalry riding in to save them. "Why is this a problem?"

"They need to talk directly to someone on the plane, and you need to convince them that you aren't terrorists."

Quint reached for the headset before he realized their problem. "Our communication is out. What happens if we can't talk to them?"

"They'll shoot you out of the sky."

Looking through his left window, Quint saw the lights of the spear-shaped jet, a lethal shadow in the night.

Chapter Thirteen

For those few fleeting moments in the private cabin, Quint had felt he was in control. He'd held his woman in his arms. The hijackers had been trapped in the cargo hold. The injured were being cared for. Their biggest problem seemed to be a lack of haute cuisine. Now, they were safe no more.

The arrival of the F-14s initiated a whole new disaster scenario. In an atmosphere of heightened national security, Quint was well aware that the United States was willing to sacrifice the lives of a few Quantum employees rather than risk a targeted suicide mission with a modified Boeing 737.

Once again, the Quantum corporate jet flew on the razor's edge of danger.

Speaking into the cell phone, Quint asked, "Why are the fighter planes with us? How'd they find us?"

"They've been tracking you ever since you went off the flight plan and turned back to Chicago," Colonel Roberts said. "That was considered a suspicious maneuver. When you failed to respond to the calls from air traffic control, they sent out the guard."

"I reckon we're damn lucky they haven't already shot us down."

"We patched through and explained."

Though the windshield, Quint watched the fighter plane

in the night sky. With moonlight glinting off its sleek, sharp wings, the F-14 looked like a bird of prey, hungry to attack. "I wonder how long your explanation is going to keep us safe."

Colonel Roberts cleared his throat. "Give me a complete situation update. I'll relay the information and see what I can do."

"I'm in control of the flight deck," Quint said. "The hijackers are in the cargo hold. Most of them are injured."

"But not apprehended," the Colonel said. "They're still able to move around and cause trouble."

"Yes, sir."

Therein lay the problem. The hijackers could easily screw up avionics. Quint himself had already done the painstaking work of removing the safety cover, making it easier for them. The plane could be sabotaged in the air.

But that wasn't the worst possibility. Quint knew that the people on the ground and in the fighter jets were considering that there might be a bomb on board. Nick Beaumont had shown himself to be mighty proficient at creating incendiary devices. He'd blown up a building in Reykjavik. He'd set a controlled explosion in Natalie's office. Maybe his initial hijacking plan hadn't included an explosion, but he was no fool. He seemed to have prepared himself for nearly any complication.

Quint decided not to remind Colonel Roberts of Nick's bombing expertise. Instead, he said, "They aren't terrorists, sir. They're hijackers, working on an extortion plan. All they want is money."

"But you foiled their escape."

"Yes sir, I did." And he couldn't predict how the hijackers would take their revenge.

"I'll coordinate with Air Force and get back to you. Over."

Quint sagged back in the pilot's seat, staring blindly at the multitude of dials. Had his interference been a terrible mistake? If he'd allowed the scheme to carry through, would all the hostages have been delivered safely?

He looked over at Natalie, who perched on the co-pilot's seat with her legs tucked under her.

He said, "I stuck my nose where it didn't belong."

"What do you mean?" she asked.

"If I let the hijackers have what they wanted, we might not be in this danger."

She held out her hand, and he reached across the center panel to grasp it. She squeezed hard.

"You did the right thing."

He shook his head. "They could've landed safely, let the hostages go, refueled and taken off. Neat and simple."

"Think again, cowboy." There was steel in her voice. "If they'd taken off without hostages, the plane would be subject to attack. They couldn't have released everyone, and I know who would have been stuck on board. Me."

What she said made sense. In the back of his mind, Quint had drawn the same conclusion. The person least likely to survive was Natalie. The minute she left the plane, the hijackers would be vulnerable.

"And here's another issue," she said. "Where do you think they could've landed after they released the hostages? Nick Beaumont planned to double-cross the person who financed him—perhaps it was Zahir. He was going to keep the ransom money for himself."

Quint digested this bit of information. "He must have another connection on the ground."

"Definitely," she said. "Somebody facilitated the money transfer from the other end. But how powerful is that somebody?"

"Could be just a broker," Quint said. "All the hijackers seem to be pulled from different backgrounds. There isn't a common thread."

"Or a common nation. Which presents another problem. What nation would allow hijackers to land without immediately taking them into custody?"

She made a good point. Even if somebody unfriendly to the United States, like Iraq or Libya, allowed the plane to land, they had no investment in keeping the hijackers under protection. "That means they must have been planning another escape route."

"Parachute," she suggested.

"Like D.B. Cooper," he said.

"Who?"

"The original skyjacker. Must have been twenty-five years ago. He took over a plane and demanded a ransom. After the plane took off again, he strapped the money to his chest and parachuted through the cargo hold. They never found him or the money."

"Our hijackers," Natalie said, "could have planned the same thing. They might still jump."

"Not at this altitude," he said. "Some of them are wounded. There's not enough oxygen and they'd probably freeze to death. We'd have to be under fifteen thousand feet."

Any kind of jump from a jet with a cruising speed of Mach 0.82 would be nearly impossible. Even when they slowed for approach, they'd be going over a hundred and fifty miles per hour.

If Smilin' Jack had been at the controls, he might have made a jump easier. He could have circled and slowed and dropped to an appropriate altitude. It all made sense to Quint. The hijackers would jump, and Smilin' Jack would land the plane. He could claim that he'd been forced to do what they instructed and could point to the rescued hostages as validation for his actions. More than likely, he'd get off with little more than a slap on the wrist. And the hijackers would be long gone.

"Their plan is still possible," Natalie said. "When we come in for a landing, they could use parachutes to escape."

"If it was up to me, I'd let them try it."

But the decision wasn't Quint's. Those F-14s wouldn't

allow them to approach a landing with hijackers on board, especially not after they figured out there was the possibility of a bomb on the plane.

Another explosion. The old familiar dread crawled over him. Still holding Natalie's hand, he closed his eyes, expecting to see the nightmare flashback of white Texas skies and a sweet little Cessna bursting into a ball of flame. He waited for the memory of violence to rock his soul. And he waited. But the vision didn't come.

Instead, he saw a black sky—dark as velvet and dotted with flickering silver stars above a moonlit cloud cover. He was flying this jet. He was here in the present. This time, it was up to him to bring her down safely.

He opened his eyes and saw Natalie, pretty as an angel with green eyes and a spunky attitude. He had to protect her, to keep her safe so they could have their chance at a life together.

He should ask her now to marry him, to share his life. "Natalie, I never expected to—"

The cell phone rang, and he grabbed it.

"Bad news, Quint." Colonel Robert's voice was firm. "Unless the hijackers are apprehended and pose no possible threat, you won't be allowed to enter Chicago airspace."

"Tell me more."

"You have twenty-two minutes to completely secure the aircraft."

"What's to stop me from lying, Colonel? I could tell you that I've got them under control right now."

"But you won't," he said. "The only reason you've got any time at all is your record on previous successful missions and your reputation for honesty. Yours and that of Dan Austin. Twenty-two minutes. Godspeed, Quint."

He turned to Natalie and said, "You need to handle the plane for a while. Stay on the phone with Colonel Roberts and he'll tell you what to do."

"Where are you going?"

He didn't want to alarm her, but there wasn't time to be sensitive. "I need to go into the cargo hold and apprehend the hijackers. Otherwise, the F-14s won't allow us to land."

Uncomprehending, she shook her head. "Why not?"

"With hijackers loose on the plane, we're considered a hostile aircraft. They won't take a chance on letting us near Chicago. Or anyplace else for that matter."

"You can't be serious, Quint. We'd be shot down by the United States Air Force?"

"Remember September eleventh," he said. "They can't chance that happening again."

As he rose from the pilot's seat, she caught his arm. "I'm going with you. Gregory can take care of the plane."

"No," he said firmly.

"I won't let you risk your life. Not without me."

They didn't have time for this discussion. "If I get killed, you still have a chance. Maybe you can talk them into letting you land the plane."

"If you die, I don't want to live."

Her simple declaration tore a hole in his heart. He'd been where she was now, watching the unstoppable approach of danger to a beloved. He knew the terrible emptiness of bereavement. It was a searing, soul-deep pain he wouldn't wish on his worst enemy.

He pulled her from the co-pilot's seat and embraced her warm body. "I won't die, Natalie. I promise."

He left her on the flight deck.

Twenty-two minutes. Not a lot of time, but it was all he had. Twenty-two minutes to make a difference, to set the foundations for his future. Or twenty-two minutes until death.

He would not fail her.

IN THE AFT CARGO HOLD, Nicco had packed five parachutes for his men and himself. Placing these had been the easiest part of his plan. While he was posing as a part-time baggage handler, he produced a Quantum requisition for parachutes. No one questioned it. Parachutes on an aircraft were a logical precaution. But now, who would use them? He'd lost two men. Another was barely recovered from the Taser. Smilin' Jack hobbled into the rear of the plane. His left leg was virtually useless.

"I can make it," he said. "Give me a chute."

Coldly, Nicco regarded him. For once, the mercenary wasn't smiling. "You never should've left the flight deck."

"The instruments weren't responding. It's been a while since I've flown this type of aircraft. I didn't know what to do. Everything went wrong."

"Not everything." Nicco had received the ransom money. His job had been accomplished to perfection. "Of course, you won't expect to receive the rest of your payment."

"The hell I won't." A spectre of the pilot's former grin distorted his face. "We had a deal."

"And you failed to deliver."

Nicco unholstered his pistol and fired twice into Smilin' Jack's chest. The man staggered before his good leg collapsed. His jaw went slack.

At the sound of gunfire, Scout scampered away and hid. How ironic that his dog hated loud noises. Nicco called for him, "Come on, Scout. We need to get ready."

He had a special pouch for carrying his dog when he parachuted from the plane. Determining the timing would be difficult. He would have to guess the rate of descent, opening the cargo hatch at just the right moment.

Originally, he had planned to stage a small explosion in the cargo hold that would touch off residual fuel in the auxiliary tanks. All witnesses on the plane would have been killed.

Unfortunately, it would now be too difficult to properly rig the timer and still make the jump safely. Nicco would have to forgo the satisfaction of blowing these fools to hell.

Oh, how he wished them dead! Pretty Daughter with her perfect, coddled life. The mindless drones who worked for her. Cowboy, who rode to the rescue. Big hero! Big deal!

The big man who had been stung by the Taser paced clumsily. "Dizzy," he mumbled in German. "Stiff. Walk it off."

"Stay here if you want."

"I won't go to jail. I'll come with you."

Nicco didn't care one way or the other. "Your choice."

After he strapped the chute onto his back and fastened the pouch for Scout on his chest, he removed a small satchel containing plastique explosive from the locker where he'd stored the parachutes. Longingly, he handled the makings for this bomb, the tools of his trade. No one was better than Nicco at precisely timed explosives. Did he dare to risk it?

Vengeance was a dangerous game. He shouldn't allow himself to be drawn into precipitous rage. If his timing was off by even ten seconds, he might die along with them and never have the chance to enjoy his reward.

Yet, it seemed vital to kill these witnesses and maintain the secrecy of his identity.

Tenderly, he fondled the coil and the timer.

The level of noise inside the aft cargo hold modified slightly, and Nicco looked up. The door from the forward hold was open. Was someone else down here?

The big German lumbered back and forth, muttering and stretching his huge limbs.

"Quiet," Nicco ordered.

The man stared blankly. "What is wrong?"

From the corner of his eye, Nicco saw a shadowy figure charge toward him. Before he could react, the cowboy was upon him. With the butt of his gun, he struck Nicco on the skull. All went black.

QUINT HAD CHOSEN to strike the most dangerous adversary first. When he saw the makings of a bomb in the hands of

Nick Beaumont, he knew he'd made the right decision. But the big guy was going to be a serious problem.

He felt himself being lifted off his feet and flung across the hold. Quint's spine crashed hard against a baggage container. He dropped his gun. His knees weakened, but he shook off the pain and shoved himself upright to face the next assault.

Neither of them had a weapon at the ready, which meant the hijacker had the physical advantage. He was as tall as Quint and twice as wide. But he'd been stunned. His movements were clumsy as a bear's.

In the shadowy dark of the cargo hold, Quint glanced at his wristwatch. Sixteen minutes left. Not enough time for a knock-down, drag-out fight.

The big man approached. Quint couldn't allow himself to be caught by those huge arms, capable of constricting his body and squeezing the last breath from his lungs.

Quint braced himself and flicked out two quick jabs that appeared to have little effect. He needed to get away from the walls to throw a good hard punch.

Dodging to the left, Quint moved into open space. The big guy charged at him, heavy as a freight train. Using his forward momentum and the unsteady motion of the plane, Quint sidestepped and pitched the big man to the floor of the cargo hold.

In the heel of Quint's cowboy boot was a knife, but he didn't have time to grab it. The other man rebounded to his feet. Surprisingly nimble, he circled like a wrestler, watching for the opening when he could make his move. He lunged.

Quint fired a one-two punch to the gut. The big guy bent double, allowing Quint to gather all his strength for a roundhouse right to the jaw that sent the hijacker sprawling. He hit the floor so hard he bounced. Then he didn't move.

Quint checked his wristwatch. Eleven minutes. Plenty

of time to tie up Nick Beaumont and get back to the flight deck. He was going to make it—

"Not so fast," said Nick Beaumont. He held the two parts of the plastique explosive in his hands. "I can touch this off right now. We'll all go down in a blaze."

His eyes shone with a frantic light. Clad in a parachute and leather jacket, he looked like a soldier in a dangerous army, taking his orders from unreasoning hatred.

Quint tried logic. "You don't want to die."

"It won't happen. I didn't come this far to die." He edged toward the cargo hatch.

Holding the explosive was going to be a problem for Beaumont, Quint realized. If he let go of either piece, he'd be vulnerable. He needed one hand to turn the knob and open the hatch.

Biding his time—time he didn't have to waste—Quint hooked his thumbs in his belt. He still held the one-shot Derringer in his belt buckle, but he couldn't risk firing so close to the explosive.

"We can cut a deal," Quint said. "You're a smart guy. You know there's no way you could survive a jump from this altitude."

"Don't worry about me."

He laughed. The sound grated against Quint's eardrums, driving the tension up another notch. There wasn't time for subtle negotiation, but he didn't want to spook his adversary. How the hell was he going to pull this off?

Just as he thought the situation couldn't get any worse, he saw Natalie creeping through the shadows with a gun in her hand. If she fired, they'd be blown to bits. Trying to alert her, Quint said, "What kind of bomb is that?"

"All you need to know," said Nick Beaumont, "is that if I touch these pieces together, it detonates. Not a large explosion. Just enough to start a fire here in the cargo hold, igniting the fuel tanks."

He peered into the semidarkness toward Natalie. "Step

into the light, Natalie. Know that if you shoot me, we will all die.''

''I understand.'' As she stepped forward, her arm dropped to her side.

''Put the gun down,'' he ordered.

She allowed it to clatter to the floor. Her attitude was calm; she showed no fear.

Though Quint would have preferred to have her farther away from danger, her presence was a distraction, forcing Nick Beaumont to divide his attention between two of them. Quint eased a few inches closer to him.

Natalie said, ''I have to ask you something. For my own satisfaction, I want to know who financed this hijacking and the acts of terror? Was it Zahir?''

''The handsome prince. Yes, he needed the money to finance a revolution led by Sheik Khalaf.'' Again, he expelled a harsh laugh. His former cool had deserted him. This was a man on the ragged edge. ''The fools! Zahir and Khalaf want to rule in arid desolate kingdoms where nothing grows. Why?''

''Oil,'' Natalie said.

''Fuel for unneeded machines for pampered, ridiculous people. It disgusts me.''

Apparently, his dog didn't agree. Wagging his tail, the dog scampered toward Natalie. When she leaned down to pet him, his owner snapped another order. ''Don't reach toward the gun.''

She remained upright. So poised and calm. Quint couldn't believe she was a corporate executive. Her bravery in the face of life-and-death danger befitted a battle-tested warrior.

''Here's what I don't understand,'' Natalie said. ''How did Zahir think he'd get away with this? Even if he funneled the money through you, we could still track it to him.''

''I don't care,'' Nick Beaumont said with a shrug. ''Zahir is a brainless playboy.''

Quint took another step closer. He clicked his belt buckle. The Derringer slipped into his hand.

"I'll bet Quint is right," Natalie said. "If you turn in Zahir, you could get out of jail free."

"I think not." He called to his dog. "Scout, come."

With a growl, the dog obeyed.

Quint took another step. He flexed his knees, preparing to leap. There would be one chance to stop Nick Beaumont. When the man reached to open the hatch, his hands would be far apart.

"And you," Nick Beaumont said to Natalie. "You come to me. Tonight, you will take a sky jump. Without a parachute."

A tremble quaked her shoulders, but she held her chin high.

Nick Beaumont continued. "Then, we will see if money and oil will save you."

"Leave her alone," Quint said.

"You're so right, cowboy. There's no need. When I open the hatch, you'll both be sucked into the night. And this is the way it was meant to be. I will escape. You, both of you, will die."

He reached for the circular handle. Twisted and opened.

Derringer in hand, Quint dove across the cargo hold. He threw the other man's hands apart. The undetonated plastique fell to the floor.

Quint buried his Derringer in the other man's gut and pulled the trigger as Nick Beaumont released the hatch.

Ice-cold air sucked through the hold with the deafening roar of a two-hundred-mile-per-hour wind. The limp body of Nick Beaumont was dragged toward the open night like a rag doll in a cyclone. A strap of his parachute caught.

As Quint grabbed Natalie, he felt his feet go out from under him. They crashed together. He heard her scream.

Holding her tight against his chest, he clawed at the ribbing on the walls, struggling to reach the lever. Loose cargo rattled around them. The bodies of Smilin' Jack and the weightlifter tumbled against the walls. They were caught inside a tornado, but Quint wouldn't give up. Above the screeching air, he heard the dog barking wildly.

"Quint, we can't make it." She clutched him. "He was right. We're going to die."

"Not on my watch."

Struggling for every inch, Quint reached the handle and twisted. The hatch began to close.

A storage trunk had come loose. As the plane tilted, the metal box careened toward them. Quint twisted to protect Natalie from the impact. The trunk whacked his shoulders and the back of his head.

Sudden darkness threatened to overwhelm him. His vision blurred. Still, he held her until the hatch was completely closed.

Gasping for breath in the sudden stillness, Quint watched the three-legged dog snuggle up to his master.

"Sorry," Quint said to the animal, probably the only living thing who would ever mourn the demise of Nick Beaumont.

"You did it," Natalie said. She peppered his face with kisses.

"Time," he reminded her.

"Three minutes left," she said.

Reaching into her pocket, she pulled out the cell phone to call Colonel Roberts. Triumphantly, she shouted into the phone, "The hijackers have been apprehended. Call off the F-14s."

She repeated twice, and as she spoke her voice seemed to grow more and more distant. Quint felt a wetness at the back of his head. He wanted to lie down flat and not move. To sleep.

Grinning, Natalie kissed him again. "We're clear to land."

It took all his effort to smile back at her. His eyelids slammed shut. He counted a million stars, and then lost consciousness.

Chapter Fourteen

Natalie knelt beside the only man she had ever truly loved and watched his eyelids close. Quint lay flat on the floor of the cold, dark cargo hold, surrounded by cluttered baggage and the bloodied bodies of the hijackers he had vanquished.

She stroked his cheek. In repose, the chiseled line of his jaw relaxed. He looked younger, almost vulnerable. "Quint? Are you all right?"

Obviously, he wasn't. He was unconscious. She needed to do something. Desperately, she searched her memory, trying to remember the first-aid treatment for a head wound, but her brain wasn't operating properly. The constant fear and stress had taken their toll, clouded her thinking. All she could see was his handsome face. All she could feel was a sudden, overwhelming horror. He might be seriously injured. He might never wake up.

"No," she said firmly. Natalie hadn't come this far only to lose the endgame.

Her hand rested on Quint's muscular chest. His respiration was strong and steady, but his eyelids remained closed. Head wounds were dangerous—that much she knew. But was his injury life-threatening?

The black-and-white Border collie sat beside her, having abandoned his former master. The dog rested his head on her knee, and she absently touched his fur.

"What should I do?" she murmured.

She was too weary to think. If only Quint would wake up, he could be the leader. She wouldn't gripe, wouldn't complain. She'd follow him to the end of the earth.

She leaned over him, needing to hear the whisper of his breath, to feel the warm assurance that he was still alive. "Quint, I love you."

He didn't respond. He lay so terribly still. When she again touched his face, she felt moisture—the dampness of her own tears falling unchecked.

"My darling." She traced his lips with her fingertip. "Don't leave me."

She couldn't imagine a life without his laughter, his drawl, his black Stetson and his ridiculous silver belt buckle. In a few short days, he'd sauntered into her world and changed every attitude she previously held dear. Her career was no longer the only driving force in her life. Though it still mattered to be the best, number one was a shallow number unless Quint stood at her side, encouraging and acknowledging her accomplishments.

"Don't die. Oh God, Quint. Don't you dare."

His heavy eyelids opened. "I don't reckon dying was part of my plan."

Relief turned her sobs to whimpers of hope. At her side, the dog harmonized with quiet yips and tail wagging. She kissed Quint once, then again.

"Ow, that hurts," he complained.

"But you're all right?" she asked anxiously.

"That whack on the head—" struggling, he sat up "—feels like a concussion."

"How do you know what a concussion feels like?"

"A man who rides horses as part of his livelihood is bound to take a couple of falls. It's not the first time I've been clunked on the head."

As his eyelids began to droop again, she gripped his arm. "Don't go to sleep again. What should I do?"

"Get somebody down here. Make sure these guys aren't going to stir up any more trouble."

"Right," she said. Her mind began to clear. "You and I should go up to the flight deck and prepare for landing."

"Sounds real simple when you say it."

For the moment, she couldn't allow herself to consider the complexities of landing a jet aircraft. "But we can do it."

"That's right, darlin'. We can do anything." With an effort, he forced himself to stand. Obviously unsteady, he leaned on her. "I don't want you to be alarmed if I drop off now and again. I'll be okay."

"You'd better be all right," she said as she helped him toward the steep stairs. "I'll be really annoyed if we crash and burn."

He laughed. Then winced. "Ow, Natalie. My head is splitting."

Together, they stumbled up the stairs with the hijacker's dog following behind them. As they came through the hatch, they confronted Maria Luisa, who stood ready to face whomever or whatever might emerge from the cargo hold. She braced a pistol in both hands, looking much like a television cop. When she saw Natalie and her wounded partner, mixed expressions of joy and worry crossed her face.

"Is he—"

"A concussion," Natalie said. "He tells me he'll be fine, but I think that's the macho talking."

"He doesn't look fine," Maria Luisa said. "He looks like crap and seems to—"

"Ladies," Quint interrupted, "let's move along."

Even when he was half-unconscious, Quint expected to be treated like the boss. Natalie smiled. She liked that tough-guy quality in her man.

"You're right," Maria Luisa said. "We should go to the flight deck right away."

"Why?" Natalie asked.

"There are a couple of flashing lights on the instrument panel. We have Colonel Roberts on another cell phone. He said we're low on fuel."

Swell. One threat followed on the heels of another. She hurried with Quint through the plane. As they moved, she gave Maria Luisa instructions about preparing the rest of the passengers for a rough landing.

At the makeshift infirmary near the flight deck, she checked in with the pilot. Though he was awake, his reactions were as slow as a drunk on a three-day bender. There was no way he could manage an emergency landing.

"We're going to land this plane," Quint said. "You and me."

She wanted to believe that was possible. "That shouldn't be a problem. I mean, you're a pilot."

"I'm an ace when it comes to piloting a baby Cessna. On this thing, I need your help."

She hammered at the safety door to the flight deck until Jerome Harris popped it open. His eyes were wild. His nose twitched.

"Thank God, you're here," he said.

Behind him, the instrument panel flashed with red warning lights.

Gregory from Marketing looked up in panic. "I don't know what to do. This isn't like the small planes I've been on."

"It's okay." Quint gestured for him to get out of the pilot's seat. "I'm back."

As Gregory staggered toward her, Natalie assured him, "You've been great. Quick thinking. Smart."

He tried to smile, but his face was frozen. He managed to blurt, "Quick thinking is a good quality for a vice president."

"Gregory, you've got the promotion." She grinned. Only a marketing man would try to sell himself in the midst of a crisis. "I have one more job for you. Take the guys from legal and go down to the rear cargo hold. Tie up the hijackers. There's one really big guy you'll want to be careful with.''

When Natalie lowered herself into the co-pilot's seat and looked through the side window, she saw an F-14 to her right. There was another fighter plane on the opposite side. She held the cell phone to her ear. "Colonel Roberts, this is Natalie. We've still got the F-14s. Is something wrong?''

"Don't worry," the colonel said. "They're acting as an escort.''

"I'd prefer friendlier companions." The fighter planes were built for one thing only—efficient warfare. "You've talked to them, haven't you? They know not to shoot us down, don't they?''

"Yes, ma'am," the colonel said. "Let me speak to Quint.''

She looked over at her cowboy, who was concentrating hard, dealing with each set of flashing lights and making necessary adjustments on the instrument panel. As he leaned forward, the wound on the back of his head was visible. His thick brown hair was matted with blood. He needed medical attention.

"Quint, your head. It looks—''

"I'm okay. What does Roberts say?''

"He wants to talk to you.''

"I've got both hands full," he said. "You have to relay the instructions.''

In the midst of all this high-tech machinery, it seemed impossible that they didn't have some device to transmit Colonel Robert's voice over the cell phone into the flight deck. She turned to Jerome and explained her need.

"We're riding on fumes," Quint said. "And there's no extra fuel in the auxiliary tanks.''

"But we should have had enough to make the round trip from Washington.''

"The hijackers must have jettisoned some of our fuel," he said. "They wanted to force us to fly low so they could make the parachute jump. Tell Roberts we need to come in for a landing. Right now.''

She relayed Quint's words to the colonel.

In an utterly calm voice, the colonel said, ''You're approximately sixteen minutes away from Chicago, cleared to land at O'Hare. In seven minutes, you'll need to prepare for landing. Do you copy?''

''I think so,'' she said.

''You can't *think* it,'' he said crisply. ''You have to know for certain.''

''Well, excuse me, but I've never flown a turbojet before. You can't seriously expect me to pretend that I'm going for a walk by the lake.'' Her voice rose to match her level of tension. It felt as if the co-pilot's seat was upholstered in pins and needles. ''I'm a tiny bit nervous.''

''Calm down, Natalie. It's better if you pretend you know what you're doing. Trick yourself into being unafraid. Roger that.''

''Roger yourself,'' she snapped. ''I've hardly even been in a cockpit.''

''Flight deck,'' he corrected. ''Trust me. If you do as I instruct, you'll be fine. Let's start by having you talk like a pilot. Roger.''

''Roger,'' she grumbled. She sighed and relayed his instructions to Quint.

''Seven minutes?'' he asked.

''Probably six by now. Why?''

When he looked at her, his gaze seemed unfocused. His breathing was shallow. ''I don't want you to worry, but I'm feeling like a cat that's been swung around by his tail.''

''Don't pass out, Quint. Please.''

''If I can't get my vision clear, you're going to have to be my eyes, Natalie. If something happens to me, here's what you do.'' He pointed to a switch near the middle of the panel. ''Flip this, and you've got the con.''

''The what?'' Hysteria was building inside her.

"The control. Control, Natalie."

It was going to take more than deep breathing exercises to make her feel that she was in control. "Maybe I should get somebody else up here."

Weakly, he smiled. "I never thought I'd see the day when Natalie Van Buren stepped aside."

"My God, Quint, this isn't a press conference. There's several tons of complex machinery here. And no room for error."

"You'll have instructions. And you've got more than that."

"Do I?" She was rattled. "What more do I have?"

"A hell of a good reason to go on living." He reached out toward her. "I love you, Natalie Van Buren. And I want you to be my bride."

Her heart went *thud*. She swallowed hard. "Was that supposed to calm me down?"

"Think of our life together. In Chicago. And on the ranch. You can teach me how to eat escargot, and I'll show you how to ride."

It sounded crazy and impossible and absolutely wonderful. More than anything, she wanted to share her life with him, to mingle their two worlds into one spectacular universe as endless as the eternal stars.

"Will you marry me, Natalie?"

"Roger that," she said. On this issue, she was confident. "I love you, cowboy. And I'll gladly be your bride."

Jerome returned to the flight deck. Quickly, he hooked up the cell through the speakerphone so they could both talk to the colonel at the same time. Though she couldn't keep her hand linked with Quint's, she felt connected to him. They were going to be married. He would be her husband. She would be his wife. His second wife. It seemed like the best job in the world.

"Actually," she said, "it's good that you were married before. You've already been broken in."

"Guess so," he said. "I know how to leave the toilet seat down and to pick up my socks off the floor."

The thought of Quint's socks on the floor gave her a rush of pleasure. Domesticity flooded her mind, and her panic began to ebb. She'd do anything to ensure the wonderful life that lay ahead. She would land this plane. They would live happily ever after.

"It's ready," Jerome said.

"Colonel," Natalie said, "we have you on speakerphone. Can you hear me?"

"I read you loud and clear. Is Quint still there?"

"Yes, sir," he said.

"In two minutes, I want you to turn off the autopilot. You're coming in toward O'Hare, south by southwest. There's a high cloud cover."

"No joke," Quint said. "I can't see through it."

Natalie peered through the windshield. Below them was a landscape of thick, fluffy clouds that appeared to be soft as a sea of pillows. When she was a child, she imagined this was what heaven looked like.

Colonel Roberts advised, "Weather on the ground is clear. Low wind shear."

Natalie turned to Jerome. "It's best if you leave us now. Close the door and tell everybody to prepare for landing."

"Can I take the dog with me?"

She nodded.

As rabbity little Jerome exited, he called, "Come along, Skippy. We need to take care of the passengers."

"His name is Scout," Natalie said.

"Not anymore. This puppy is going to have a whole new life. He needs a new name."

And Skippy was a good name for a dog that had formerly been known as Scout, the pet of a monster. It pleased her to think of Jerome giving the Border collie a good home.

"Ready?" Quint asked. He had both hands on the yoke. "I'm taking her off autopilot."

"What should I do?"

"For now, sit tight."

When he pressed a button on the yoke, the plane took a little jolt, then immediately evened out as Quint grasped the yoke.

Over the speaker, Colonel Roberts advised, "You need to capture glide slope. One dot high on the glide slope. Minimum drag speed at two hundred knots."

"Roger," Quint said.

He felt the power of the massive turbojet engines coursing through the yoke and into his body. Flying a small plane made him feel free as a hawk sailing on currents of wind. Handling this jet was like riding bareback on a rocket, but Quint was up to the task. He could handle this plane. He wouldn't need Natalie's help.

The throbbing inside his skull had eased to a dull ache, and his motor skills remained sharp. He was able to make sense of the instrument panel and comprehend instructions from Colonel Roberts.

But his head wasn't right. Leaning toward the window, he sensed a tilt to the wings, but the LCD screen showed they were stable. Quint feared his inner equilibrium was messed up from the blow to his head. His peripheral vision was fuzzy. There was no way in hell he could navigate the last phase of the landing. Natalie was going to have to guide the plane into touchdown.

He glanced over at her. His future bride. Competent. Capable of anything. At least, he wanted to believe that she could do anything. Landing a turbojet at night was asking a lot.

She relayed more instructions from the colonel.

Quint checked their speed. Two hundred and ten knots. Every landing was a matter of thrust and pitch. Balance and rudder. On instruments, their descent was a graceful slope, perfectly smooth.

They entered the cloud cover that obscured the earth below. With no visual markers, their only guideposts were

the LCD screens on the instrument panel. It was a neth-
erworld, limbo. They emerged. City lights flared below
them.

He heard Natalie gasp and reassured her, "It's pretty,
isn't it."

"Pretty scary," she said tersely. "The clouds looked a
lot softer."

"It's the real world," he said. "That's what we're coming back to. And it's a good place. A good world."

"With only a few bad people," she said. "By the way,
Colonel Roberts, would you relay a message to Vincent?"

"Tell me."

She said, "I want Zahir's butt taken into custody as soon
as possible. He's behind the hijacking."

"Roger that," the colonel said. "The Feds are already
on top of the situation. The prince is in the slammer."

Quint saw two F-14s pull even with the flight deck. He
struggled to focus on their sleek outline, and noticed a
skull and crossbones painted on the tail of one. The fighter
planes darted in front of them, riding at their nose. Simultaneously, the F-14s dipped their wings from side to
side.

"What are they doing?" Natalie asked.

"Wishing us good luck," Quint said. "It's kind of a
salute."

The rear jet engine on the fighter planes flared dramat-
ically and they zoomed away, through the clouds and out
of sight.

"Wow!" Natalie stared up, trying to follow their
swooping departure. "I'm glad those guys are on our
side."

"The world's finest," Quint agreed.

Over the speakerphone, Colonel Roberts said, "Do you
have visual on the airfield?"

"Negative," Quint responded. "We're still too far out."

He squinted through the windshield, and all the lights
became a blur. He could manage the instruments, but there

was no way he could sight in precisely enough for the actual touchdown.

Now was as good a time as any to tell Natalie. "I've got a little problem here. My vision isn't so good. I can work the instruments and get us right on top of the runway, but you're going to have to guide us down."

"Okay." She sounded breathless. "I can do this. Colonel Roberts, did you hear what he said?"

"Copy that," the colonel said.

He offered no further words of encouragement. "Okay," she said. "How do I make the plane go down?"

Over the speakerphone, Colonel Roberts groaned.

"We're on a slope," Quint said. "When I tell you, just keep it steady and steer with the yoke like you're driving a car."

The colonel added, "It's not hard to land, Natalie. Do you have visual? Can you see the airfield?"

She saw an impossibly narrow corridor of lights. "Yes, I think I see it. I mean, roger."

Her ears buzzed with the sound of the engines. Shivers raced through her body.

"Prepare for final approach," the colonel said. "Quint, you need five degrees nose up."

"Roger," he said. "I'm sorry, Natalie. I'm letting you down, but I can't see the landing strip. It's a——"

"Shut up, Quint."

Colonel Roberts said, "Two-point-five degrees nose up for flap thirty. Stabilize."

"Roger," Quint said. "Natalie, I want you to take hold of the yoke. When I tell you, steer toward the runway. Line up the center of the landing strip to run directly between your knees."

"Landing sequence," the colonel said. "Flaps to slow. Lower the landing gear."

"Roger." Quint flipped a switch, and she felt a clunk as the landing gear descended.

The earth rushed up to meet them. Suddenly, they were

close to the ground. She stared at the blue flares outlining the landing strip. There were a lot of other lights. Emergency vehicles. Police cars.

Colonel Roberts said, "Thrust reversers to idle."

"Roger," Quint responded. "I'm turning it over to Natalie. Get ready, darlin'."

He hit the switch. The turbojet was in her hands. Raw power surged through her. They were only fifteen feet from the ground. "I can't handle it. It's too much."

"You're doing fine. Aim for the center."

She wanted to be cool like everybody else, but it was impossible. Staring with all her might at the runway, Natalie steered toward the center line. Too fast. It was coming too fast. Keeping her gaze fixed to the line, she opened her mouth and screamed like a banshee.

The wheels hit ground and bounced.

"Good," Quint said. "I'm taking back the con."

White-knuckled, her fingers continued to grip the yoke. She felt the power transfer.

"Nose gear down," Colonel Roberts reminded.

"Roger," Quint said.

Several more instructions passed between them, but Natalie heard not a word. They were on the ground. The plane was stopping. They were safe at last.

She felt Quint's hand on her arm as he reached across the center console. "You did good," he said.

She transferred her death grip from the yoke to his forearm. Her eyelids blinked rapidly, trying to erase the images of rushing lights.

Once the plane had come to a stop, he helped her stand up. "We're okay, Natalie."

She collapsed against him. "Don't ever do that to me again."

"In the future," he drawled, "I reckon we ought to avoid hijackings."

She clung to him. With a gasp, she started breathing

again. It was really true. They'd landed. They were safe
at last.

Quint opened the flight deck door. The first one through
was Skippy, the hijacker's dog. He was followed by Jerome and Maria Luisa. Everybody was cheering and crying
and laughing in a big, happy blur.

But there was little time for congratulations. Natalie
found herself being rushed by the flight attendants toward
the emergency exit in the middle of the cabin. She and the
other passengers who were uninjured bounced down in-
flatable ramps to the tarmac. At the same time, emergency
personnel from ambulances charged into the plane to assist
those who were injured. Two fire trucks stood at the ready.
There were at least a dozen police cars. Plainclothes de-
tectives led by Special Agent Yoder of the FBI raced onto
the aircraft with guns drawn to take the hijackers into custody.

She looked up at Quint and grinned. "Where were all
these people when we needed them?"

His gaze—still unfocused and squinty—aimed toward a
small clump of people who stood apart from the others.
Chicago Confidential.

Together, she and Quint approached Whitney and Vincent and Andy. In the midst of congratulations, she even
smiled at Law Davis.

When they met Colonel Robbie Roberts, an eagle-eyed
older man who wore a sweater-vest and golf slacks, Quint
snapped a crisp salute. Natalie flung her arms around the
retired colonel. "Thank you," she whispered.

He whispered back, "You almost popped my eardrums
when you landed."

"Not my thing," she said. "I promise never to enter a
cockpit again."

"Flight deck," he corrected.

He kept one arm around her and placed his other hand
on Quint's shoulder, turning them toward the rest of the
Confidential crew. "Ladies and gentlemen, I overheard a

conversation between these two on the plane. I think they have an announcement.''

''Wait,'' Quint said.

Questioning, she glanced toward him. Had he changed his mind about marrying her? Now that he had both feet on the ground, perhaps he'd thought better of his proposal.

Quint separated from the group and walked toward a solitary figure. Her father. Henry Van Buren stood alone on the tarmac. The flashing lights from emergency vehicles reflected on his white hair. She watched as Quint approached him.

Natalie couldn't hold back. These were the two most important men in her life. She ran so fast that she passed Quint as she leaped into her father's arms and gave him the biggest, most enthusiastic hug since she was a little girl and believed he could make every rainy day turn out bright.

He kissed her cheek. His chest heaved with silent weeping. Tears of relief. Tears of gratitude. They would have another chance for a better relationship.

He released her from his fatherly embrace but kept hold of her hand as he spoke to Quint. ''Thank you.''

''Mr. Van Buren,'' Quint said. ''Sir, I would like to formally ask for your daughter's hand in marriage.''

''No words I have ever spoken give me more pleasure,'' Henry Van Buren said. ''Natalie and Quint, you have my blessing.''

''Mine, too,'' said an unfamiliar voice with a Texan drawl. ''And I'm going to be best man.''

Quint introduced her to Daniel Austin. As the other members of Chicago Confidential crowded around, she slipped comfortably into the arms of her groom-to-be. Her happiness was complete. The only slight disappointment was that Caroline wasn't here to share her joy. Natalie couldn't wait to e-mail her sister with the good news.

As she walked Quint toward the ambulance so the paramedics could examine his head wound, he looked down at her and grinned. "It's official."

"Yes," she said.

"I'm thinking we ought to get married on horseback."

"Not a chance," she said. "I'm wearing an original gown by Vera Wang. There will be fresh orchids. For a caterer, let's try for Wolfgang Puck."

"Fine. If he can rustle up a barbecue on the north forty."

Aghast, she stared up at him. "Are you joking?"

"Are you?"

Not really. But it didn't really matter how or where they got married. "Anything you want is fine with me. You're the best, Quint."

"I love you, Natalie."

As she kissed him lightly, a small niggling doubt crept into her mind. "For the wedding," she said, "I just have one tiny request. Lose the cowboy hat."

"I don't go nowhere without my hat."

"How about that god-awful belt buckle."

Teasing, he leaned close and nipped her ear. "If you want, I'll strip naked as a jaybird and walk down the aisle like that."

She went up on her toes and nipped him back. "Darlin', you can get naked anytime you want."

"Soon as possible," he said.

She could hardly wait.

* * * * *

And the story continues...
Next month don't miss
the next exciting installment of
CHICAGO CONFIDENTIAL:
LAYING DOWN THE LAW
by Ann Voss Peterson
Turn the page for a sneak peek!

Chapter One

The voices in Chicago Confidential's special-operations room hushed. All eyes focused on Lawson Davies.

Oh, hell. He glanced at his Rolex. Negotiating the Chicago Loop in rush-hour traffic had been a nightmare as usual, but he'd made the trek to Solutions, Inc., a front for the Chicago Confidential office, in record time. That only left one reason for the dire looks on the faces turned toward him. Something had happened. And Law could bet he wasn't going to like it. Not one damn bit.

He focused on Vincent Romeo, the head of operations at Chicago Confidential, an elite and very covert division of the Federal Department of Public Safety. "What is it, Vincent?"

Vincent stared at him, his expression unchanging. Since the day Law had become an agent of the relatively new Confidential branch in Chicago, he had rarely seen Vincent's expression change. The man was always brooding, focused and intense. And this morning he certainly wasn't looking to revise his image. "Take a seat, Law."

Law scanned the faces of the others in the high-tech room. His gaze immediately landed on the only nonagent present—Natalie Van Buren, vice president of public relations at Quantum Industries, the largest buyer and seller of oil worldwide. She sat in a chair at the briefing table. A nonagent was rarely allowed inside the special-operations room. No doubt this briefing had something to do with the Van Buren family-owned Quantum Industries.

Law couldn't help but notice the uncharacteristically dark circles under Natalie's eyes and the pinched lines of worry flanking her mouth. Natalie was tough. She'd recently weathered an explosion in her office, the murder of fellow Quantum executive Gordon Doeller, and the hijacking of Quantum's private jet. But there had to be a limit to that toughness. What more did the poor woman have to deal with?

He looked back to Vincent. "The terrorists? Did they hit another target?"

"No," Vincent answered. "And though Zahir Haji Haleem is in custody, he still isn't talking. But Javid is in place, posing as his twin, Zahir. We'll find out the rest of the terrorists' plans eventually."

Law nodded and sank into his chair at the round table behind the built-in laptop computer used for briefings, expecting the others to take their seats as well.

Vincent's wife and partner in the formation of the agency, the high-born Whitney MacNair Romeo, offered him a gentle smile. But she didn't move from her spot behind Natalie Van Buren. Quint Crawford, fellow Chicago Confidential agent, Natalie's former bodyguard and now her fiancé, towered behind Natalie. His black Stetson clutched in his hands, Quint was all business, a serious glower replacing his usual aw-shucks grin. Even Andy Dexter was subdued. The slightly loopy telecommunications and computer forensics genius hovered over some of his high-tech equipment lining the walls of the room.

"Care to fill me in?" Law asked.

Vincent gave a nod. Quint, Whitney and Andy filed out of the room, leaving only Natalie, Vincent and Law seated at the table.

Unease gripped the back of Law's neck like an icy hand. Something was going on, all right. And judging from the looks of this meeting, it had something to do with him.

The moment the door closed, Vincent leveled his black stare on Law once again. "We have a situation. And judging from your experience and what Natalie has told me, you are the best man to handle it."

Law raised his eyebrows in question. He understood the part about his "experience." He'd been an attorney for the past eleven years. First with the Cook County state attorney's office, and the past five years with the oil distributor Petrol Corporation, the biggest competitor of Quantum Industries. He knew criminal and corporate law and had plenty of experience within the oil industry.

But Vincent had lost him with the comment about something Natalie told him. Law didn't know Natalie personally. And he'd had few business dealings with her. Even when he'd headed up Petrol's lawsuit against Quantum over a patent five years ago when he'd first come on board at Petrol, he hadn't dealt with Quantum's public relations department or the vice president in charge of public relations, Natalie Van Buren.

He glanced from Vincent to Natalie and back again. "Care to elaborate?"

"It appears that Caroline Van Buren has been kidnapped by the Solar Sons eco-cult," Vincent said.

"Caroline?" Law's heart seemed to stop in his chest. When it started again, it immediately kicked into overdrive. "I'd heard she joined the cult, but kidnapped? Are you sure?"

Natalie rose from her chair. "I've had a bad feeling about this from the first. Caroline is concerned about the environment, but I just couldn't see her joining a cult. Especially not a radical one like the Solar Sons. And now I know I was right. When you see her face on the video..." Her voice failed her, but her eyes flashed with challenge, as if ready to defend the honor of her little sister.

Vincent's earlier comment about what Natalie had told him fitted into place in Law's mind. Guilt slammed into his gut, as unforgiving as a charge of contempt from a judge's lips.

Natalie knew. She knew what had happened between Caroline and him five years ago. And she knew how badly he'd handled it afterward. She knew exactly what kind of a bastard he was. And now Vincent knew, too.

Law fought the urge to look away. Instead he met first Natalie's and then Vincent's pointed stares. "You mentioned a video. Do you have evidence she was kidnapped?"

Natalie nodded. "Yes."

"Then, why don't you bring it to the police or the FBI? They're better equipped to handle this kind of case than Chicago Confidential is."

Natalie shot him a look that would have killed a lesser man. Or one with half a conscience left. "She doesn't want to leave. She's been brainwashed."

"Brainwashed? How can you tell?"

"I know my sister, Mr. Davies. Though obviously you don't. And never wanted to."

She was partly right. Except for his one night with Caroline, he didn't really know her. But it wasn't because he didn't want to. It *never* had been because he didn't want to.

Vincent held up a hand to stop the volley between them. "WGN received a videotape from Caroline this morning. They are planning to air part of it tonight." He punched a button on the remote in his other hand and the high-definition video screen stretching across the room's far wall sprang to life.

Caroline Van Buren's face filled the screen. She was looking down, as if reading over a written speech one last time before delivering it. She was thinner than Law remembered. Her shoulder-length blond hair hung listlessly to her shoulders, and circles dark as bruises underscored her eyes. But there was no mistaking her face—her long eyelashes, that petite, freckle-flecked nose, and those full, lush, extraordinary lips. A pang registered in Law's chest and shot downward to his groin.

On the screen, Caroline raised her eyes to look straight into the camera.

Law felt a chill. Caroline's eyes—her brilliant blue eyes that danced and sparkled, the eyes he still saw in his dreams—had changed. Instead of shining with life and energy, they were dull, flat, emotionless. As if every bit of passion had been drained from her and all that remained was a pretty shell.

Caroline drew a deep breath and launched into her speech. "Hello. I am Caroline Van Buren. Recently my disappearance has made the newscasts along with a lot of speculation and lies. I want to clear up the falsehoods and tell you the truth.

"It has been suggested by my sister, Natalie, that I was kidnapped, but I'm here to tell you that isn't so. I thank the Solar Sons for delivering me from my own greed and sin.

"I have always wanted to defend Mother Earth. But like so many others, I was blinded by the power and money of my family and its arm of destruction, Quantum Industries. My parents gave me the best schooling and more money than I could ever spend, but in return demanded that I turn a blind eye to their sins against the earth. Well, I can't do that anymore.

"Thanks to Hutch Greely, the leader of the Solar Sons, I have changed from the selfish, greedy person I was. I've grown. I've become conscious and can never go back to the life I led before. Nor do I want to. As a result of Hutch's teachings, my love has expanded to embrace the earth. I only wish others had the courage to join me and fight for the mother who gave us all birth.

"I would like to ask my sister, Natalie, to stop spreading lies, both about me being kidnapped and about Quantum Industries. You may call your job 'public relations,' but we all know in wartime 'public relations' really means propaganda. And make no mistake, this is war. Quantum Industries is the enemy of the earth. And now it is my enemy, as well. And as the vice president of evil propaganda, you are no longer my sister but my foe.

"All who would be sinners against the earth are now my enemies. I take up the scepter of the Solar Sons and I will fight to the death against your sinning ways."

The screen dissolved into static, and Vincent turned off the tape.

Law stared at the blank screen and raked a hand through his hair. Natalie was right. Caroline had been brainwashed. He flinched inwardly at the thought of her flat, dull eyes. He could picture each bitter word zinging straight from cult leader Hutch Greely's lips into Caroline's ear, to be reproduced on the video as if they were her own thoughts.

Law had seen brainwashing at its worst while prosecuting a religious cult leader for the deaths of some of his followers, back when Law was with the state attorney's office. And the thought of Caroline—sweet, dedicated, passionate Caroline—falling victim to the kind of humiliating and abusive techniques necessary to erase free will and replace it with utter devotion made his stomach turn.

Unable to meet Natalie's tear-filled eyes, Law focused on Vincent. "The fact that Caroline now wants to be in the cult ties our hands, unless we can come up with solid evidence that she's there against her will."

Vincent shook his head. "I don't want you to pursue this in the courts."

"What do you want me to do?"

"You're going to get her out."

There it was. The reason all eyes had been on him the moment he stepped into the office. Vincent had chosen Law to extricate Caroline from the Solar Sons. "And how do you propose I do that?"

Vincent deposited the remote on his desk, picked up a sheet of paper and thrust it at Law. "You're her husband, and you want to bring your wife home."

Law looked down at the paper. A marriage license stared back at him, complete with names, dates, witnesses and his and Caroline's signatures. For a moment he couldn't speak.

Vincent filled the silence. "Natalie wanted to go, but I won't allow it."

Natalie glanced at Vincent and blew a frustrated breath through tight lips.

Vincent continued as if he hadn't noticed. "As you can tell from the video, Eugene Greely, commonly known as Hutch Greely, has focused his efforts on turning Caroline against Natalie. Besides, we all know how dangerous the Solar Sons and Hutch Greely can be."

Law asked, "Do you really think Caroline will agree to leave with a husband she doesn't remember?"

Vincent's black eyes zeroed in for the kill. "As I understand it, there can be many effects of brainwashing, including cognitive inefficiencies and short-term memory loss."

Law frowned. Vincent had done his homework, as usual. "Along with blunting of emotion, suggestibility and indecisiveness."

"Exactly. All of which will make it easier to convince her of the marriage. Besides, I'm counting on her remembering something of the time the two of you spent together."

Another pang of guilt clenched Law's gut. Just as he'd suspected, Natalie had told Vincent about the night Law and Caroline had spent together. The night Law had unknowingly taken her virginity. The most explosively passionate night of his life.

And the last night he'd seen Caroline Van Buren.

And now he was going to use her memories of that night to manipulate her to do his will. The same way Hutch Greely was preying upon her devotion to the environment to brainwash her to do his will.

Law swallowed the bad taste in his mouth. There was no doubt about it. He really was a bastard.

Who was she really?

Where Memories Lie

GAYLE WILSON

AMANDA STEVENS

Two full-length novels of enticing, romantic suspense—by two favorite authors.

They don't remember their names or lives, but the two heroines in these two fascinating novels do know one thing: they are women of passion. Can love help bring back the memories they've lost?

Look for WHERE MEMORIES LIE in July 2002—
wherever books are sold.

HARLEQUIN®

Makes any time special®

Visit us at www.eHarlequin.com

BR2WML

If you enjoyed what you just read,
then we've got an offer you can't resist!

Take 2 bestselling
love stories FREE!

Plus get a FREE surprise gift!